Bodymore Murderland 2

Lock Down Publications and Ca$h
Presents
Bodymore Muderland 2
A Novel by *Delmont Player*

Lock Down Publications
P.O. Box 944
Stockbridge, Ga 30281
www.lockdownpublications.com

Copyright 2021 Delmont Player
Bodymore Murderland 2

First Edition June 2021
Printed in the United States of America

This is a work of fiction. Names, characters, places, and incidents either are products of the author's imagination or are used fictitiously. Any similarity to actual events or locales or persons, living or dead, is entirely coincidental.

Lock Down Publications
Like our page on Facebook: Lock Down Publications @
www.facebook.com/lockdownpublications.ldp
Cover design and layout by: **Dynasty Cover Me**
Book interior design by: **Shawn Walker**
Edited by: **Nuel Uyi**

Stay Connected with Us!

Text **LOCKDOWN** to 22828 to stay up-to-date with new
releases, sneak peaks, contests and more…
Thank you!

Submission Guideline.

Submit the first three chapters of your completed manuscript to ldpsubmissions@gmail.com, subject line: Your book's title. The manuscript must be in a .doc file and sent as an attachment. Document should be in Times New Roman, double spaced and in size 12 font. Also, provide your synopsis and full contact information. If sending multiple submissions, they must each be in a separate email.

Have a story but no way to send it electronically? You can still submit to LDP/Ca$h Presents. Send in the first three chapters, written or typed, of your completed manuscript to:

LDP: Submissions Dept
P.O. Box 944
Stockbridge, Ga 30281

DO NOT send original manuscript. Must be a duplicate.

Provide your synopsis and a cover letter containing your full contact information.

Thanks for considering LDP and Ca$h Presents.

Delmont Player

February 2015

"It's official, Dummie—the bitch Elinore throwing a project party tonight," my right-hand man, Frank 'Nizzy' Lance, spoke, walking back into the kitchen, showing me the screen of his phone. "It's all over Instagram."

"That's what it is," I replied, getting up from my bowl of Captain Crunch at the table with it on my mind before heading for my room. It appeared that the information I'd received from my man—Bozack—was on point. Now, it was time to use it to our advantage to catch up with the Murphy Homes ducks we'd been hunting since they bum-rushed my 'Street Sixteen' birthday bash at the "Shake 'N' Bake" Roller Skating Ring on Pennsylvania Avenue, two weeks prior on some Bean-man, Bag-man, BGF gorilla shit, and started beating and robbing mother fuckers. "Text Deli and give him the heads up. Tell him to stop around the strip and pick up Monk."

"Already," Nizzy replied, laying his phone down to take a few scoops of cereal, as I continued towards my room ready to drag on these project niggas.

You would've thought that because it was Valentine's Day weekend, niggas would be feeling the love. Yet, here we were— about to go purge and send the streets a much needed message that said that the 'Dummie Squad', a name earned by going against all odds. We were about to really make our presence felt and let everybody know that we weren't going for absolutely nothing. We would drop our nuts on anybody, anywhere, anytime. For any reason.

I entered my bedroom, and went straight to the closet. Opening the door, I reached up on the shelf behind all my shoe boxes, pulled down a black leather duffle bag and tossed it on the bed. I slowly unzippened the bag and removed my newest toy. An H&K-VP9 SK. I had been dying to crack a nigga with this bitch since the African arms dealers we were fucking with first delivered it to me along with two semi-automatic 10/22 Rugers and a Vektor H5 pump-action rifle right after New Year.

"Oh yeah," I mumbled to myself, analyzing the H&K. I hadn't put the chopper on a nigga since the North Avenue and Dome beef.

"Deli on his way and I'ma bout to—" Nizzy entered the room and paused when he saw me playing with the H&K's laser. "Damn, Dummie, I wanted to do me with that bitch!" Nizzy spat, watching me aim the laser at the wall.

"Nah, Dummie, I'ma go nuts on them niggas with this joint," I said. "You better work them Rugers or something, 'cause you're definitely not getting this big bitch."

"That's crazy." Nizzy shook his head, disappointed, digging into the duffle bag. It was go time.

***

"Man, let's just run up in there and start spanking niggas like they did," Lamont 'Monk' Curtis fired impatiently from the back seat of the stolen Chevy Suburban, as we sat down the street from Elinore's house on Myrtle Avenue, watching party goers come and go. "Fuck all this sneaky ass shit! Them niggas trashed my cousin!"

"Nah, Dummie, I ain't trying to bring that shit to Elinore's spot like that," I confessed, taking my eyes off the house momentarily to glance at Lamont 'Monk' Curtis. I knew it was more personal for him, but we weren't about to do nothing reckless. Not today, not this time, because I wanted to make sure all the right niggas got touched. The niggas that had stormed into my party and ruined my night by sending three of my guests to the emergency room and leaving a certified Dummie named David dead on their way out.

"If they're in there, they're gonna have to show their faces sooner or later," I said. "The party's already dying down," I added, remembering I'd given Bozack my word.

"Look, Dummie!" Nizzy fired excitedly, hitting the back of my seat. "There go some of them niggas right there."

I spotted Alien and Lil 'Deezy first, then I saw Itchy-Man,

Prince and Thugg—all spilling out of Elinore's, playing. I couldn't believe our luck. Not only were they some of the main niggas who'd pulled that bitch shit at my party, but they were some of the project's elite. So, being able to lay a few of them down together would be a blessing. Plus, it would send the exact type of message I wanted to send.

"Fuck is y'all doing?" my other right-hand man—Delvon 'Deli' Whack—questioned anxiously, tying a black custom-made 'Dummie' bandana with a huge smile on it around the bottom half of his face. "Cover y'all faces up, so we can spank these niggas!" Deli reached for the door handle.

"Hold up, Dummie." I grabbed Deli's arm. "Sit tight," I whispered, as if Prince and them could hear me. My mind was racing. I knew that both Prince's Mercedes-Benz C63 AMG 507 Edition and Alien's brand new 2015 Lexus RC F were parked on our end of the block. So, if nothing else, those two had to come our way. I was just trying to figure out what we would do if the rest of them decided to split up, because we couldn't afford to do no stuntin' with these niggas.

Every last one of them got it in. Prince and Itchy-Man had just come home for letting their guns go off. It was also no secret that Alien was a true mortician who knew his way around a body. Rumor had it that he had a small graveyard under his belt. And I personally knew from past experiences that both Lil' Deezy and Thugg were about that smoke.

"Yo, they're coming this way, Dummie," Nizzy spat, and it appeared that the 'Gangster Gods' had answered my prayers.

"Shit!" I cocked the H&K, laid it across my lap, and pulled my own black custom-made 'Dummie' bandana with the large frown on it up over my face as Itchy-Man and them made their way towards the tinted-out Suburban, oblivious to the danger that laid in wait. "Everybody, just be cool," I mumbled, slouching all the way down in my seat, trying to remain calm, thankful for all the shot-out street lights, as Itchy-Man and them stumbled right on past the truck, smoking, drinking, talking shit, and fucking with their phones.

"Once they get up near that beat-up pick-up, we're going straight at 'em," I informed, watching Lil'Deezy and Alien in the rearview mirror. "A'ight get ready, we're about to move." I could feel my palms sweating as I gripped the H&K tighter. "Get as close as you can before you start letting off." "Deli, you stay with me!" Nizzy ordered, cracking open the door slightly. After Nizzy and Deli carefully pulled up their twin yellow 'Dummie' bandanas with enormous mean-mugs on them and readied their tones, I nodded to Lamont 'Monk" Curtis and told him it was go time. I kept my eyes on Nizzy and Deli as they eased out of the truck and carefully jogged across the street. Then Lamont 'Monk" Curtis and I climbed out of the truck and followed suit.

I watched Nizzy signal to Deli to crouch down, and smiled under my mask as they slowly began to creep down the block behind Prince and 'em". There weren't too many squads like ours: Squads where everybody was trained to go.

Somebody must've been praying for Prince and 'em because we were about two—maybe three—car-lengths away from completely boxing them in when Alien looked over his shoulder and spotted me. I had the H&K tucked behind my leg, slightly laid up against my thigh. But, I guess the all-black made Alien's street instincts kick in because he went straight into survival mode.

"Watch out!" Alien yelled, waking everybody else up to the approaching danger, as he threw the bottle of Patron in his hand at me and took off running.

I weaved the bottle, and it was on. 'Monk' started dumping, and I didn't waste no time letting the H&K go.

Gwopp! Gwopp! Gwopp! Gwopp! Gwopp! Gwopp!

Thugg, Prince, Itchy-Man and Lil'Deezy all ran for cover in different directions, caught off guard as Alien went down reaching for his tone. They didn't even see Deli and Nizzy until they emerged from the darkness and tried to cut them off. By then, Lil'Deezy and Itchy-Man had gotten their tones out and started shooting back.

Before long, things went from cool to chaotic. 'Monk' moved past me to finish Alien before I could grab him, and it was too late. Prince—who by now had taken cover behind the old, beat-up pick-up truck—threw about four fire balls from his Mac-10 around the back and knocked Lamont 'Monk' Curtis off his feet, as Deli crept up and took half of Alien's head off with a few rounds from the Vektor H5 pump-action rifle and dragged Lamont 'Monk' Curtis across the street behind a van. I came up and tried to cut Itchy-Man down when it appeared that he was gonna make a move on Deli, but he saw me and opened fire. A couple slugs slammed into the car I was hiding behind, and forced me to relocate. That's when I realized that I was trapped off, because there were niggas shooting recklessly from down near Elinore's house. Shit was getting ugly.

Prince saw my dilemma and tried to come in for what I guess he thought was an easy kill, but Nizzy floored him with about seven or eight shots from both of his Rugers. I looked up and saw Thugg trying to flee in a dead run. *I got you, bitch!* I thought, as I kneeled down 'Colin Kaepernick' style and switched the H&K to its three-round-burst setting, used the laser to line Thugg up, and tore him up like a flimsy piece of metal.

"We gotta get the fuck outta here, Dummie!" Nizzy exclaimed, running over to kneel down beside where I was pent down between two parked cars that weren't providing much cover. "We ain't got no win!"

I knew he was right. We were outnumbered, and outgunned with few options. "We gotta get to Deli and 'Monk' first," I replied, clutching the H&K as the car shook from hot rocks.

"You ready!" Nizzy peeped over the hood of the car real quick and continued. "Watch Itchy-Man! He's over there behind that red Toyota."

Nizzy fell back into position. Staying low, I sat the H&K up on the hood of the car in front of me, aimed in the direction of the Toyota, and let that motherfucker crack a few times. When I saw Itchy-Man and Lil'Deezy scatter from behind the car, I told

Nizzy to come on, and took off running across the street towards the van where Deli had dragged Monk.

"Fuck!" I barked, ready to go for broke when I came around the van and saw Monk laid out with his chest busted wide open.

"Oh, I'ma 'bout to let these niggas have it."

"Hold up, Dummie." Deli grabbed my arm, as I turned towards Lil'Deezy and them, ready to empty the H&K. "We still gotta get out of here."

"You're right," I admitted, knowing I had to use my sixth sense to think and not start thinking with my emotions. Especially under the circumstances.

"Oh, shit! Dummie, you're hit too!" Nizzy exclaimed, forcing me to look.

"Where?" I questioned, checking myself for wounds.

"Not you," Nizzy corrected. "Deli."

"I know," Deli admitted, passing Nizzy his empty tone.

Damn! I had been so blinded by my thirst for revenge that I had not even taken notice that the whole left side of Deli's sweatshirt was soaking wet with blood.

"How bad is it?" Nizzy asked, concerned.

"I don't know." Deli pulled his 'Dummie' bandana down around his neck. "I haven't had time to look."

"Don't!" I commanded when Deli started pulling on his sweat shirt, as if he was about to take a look. I didn't want him going into a state of shock.

"Can you still run?" Nizzy asked, probably more out of concern for Deli's life than ours.

"I think so, yeah," Deli replied, pushing himself up to a squatting position with his right hand.

"Fuck that! Can you shoot?" I inquired, knowing that our enemies were closing in.

"You already fucking know." Deli smiled and wiggled the fingers on his good hand.

"A'ight, grab Monk's tone, and let's move!" I commanded.

"Hold up, I got you," Nizzy said, moving over to pick up Monk's tone before ripping his shirt off and tying it around

Deli's shoulder. '

"Let's do this," Deli nodded, and looked from Nizzy to me.

"A'ight." I stole a look up the block and continued. "Nizzy, when we get to the truck, you drive." I went up under Deli, and gently slung his wounded arm over my shoulder.

"Say no more, let's rock and roll."

I took one last look at Monk, clutched the H&K, and came out ready for war, immediately throwing fire-balls in all directions, handling the H&K like a Vietnam Vet, as we made our way back towards the Suburban, exchanging gunfire with multiple niggas.

"Nizzy!" I yelled, as we neared the truck and spotted Xavier, a former 'Dummie Squad' goon, ducked off near some trash cans, letting go from down the streets near Elinore's house. *Fuck nigga!* I thought, wishing I'd let Deli clip his nuts a few months ago when we'd caught him down bad, coming out of a clinic on North Avenue with his little brother after he'd denounced himself from the squad and began sounding suicidal on I.G.

However, I didn't have too much time to reminisce because Itchy-Man came rolling out from beneath a car, trying to work, but his shit jammed up on him. I spun around, so Deli could use his good arm to return fire while Nizzy ran around the truck and hopped behind the wheel. "Open the back!" I demanded, as Deli continued to air the block out. I pulled the hatch on the Suburban and helped Deli climb—or more like rolled—into the back.

"Go! Go! Go!" I yelled repeatedly, jumping into the back of the truck beside Deli, as Nizzy started the truck up.

"Duck, Dummie!" Deli warned, forcing me down, firing over my head as the back window exploded and bullets tore into the interior.

I flipped over and started going berserk with the H&K, shooting through and all into the interior and everything. My ears were humming, and I can't even tell if the nigga who'd ran down on the truck was still shooting, because I couldn't hear shit.

Nizzy had always been a driving motherfucker; so, instead

of doing the obvious, he put the Suburban in reverse and backed up all the way down to the other end of Myrtle Avenue. Then he went on up on the curve, spun that big bitch around, threw it in drive, and floored it across the grass, dirt and pavement, until we came bouncing out onto MLK Boulevard on three wheels—and, maybe for a second, two-wheels—under heavy gunfire. "Hold on!" Nizzy warned, as we went flying into traffic, dodging both vehicles and bullets, as I continued to fire wildly out the back of the Suburban with the H&K, until we evaporated into the night.

Since the 'Avenue' was less than half of a mile away, it didn't take us long to get there at all. By then, Deli was all but bleeding to death, so we rushed him—against his wishes—over to the Liberty Medical Center near Mondawmin Mall, tossed him inside the emergency room and got the hell out of there. Maryland University was out of the question, for many reasons: the main one being the botched hit on Billy Lo a few months ago.

Afterwards, Nizzy dropped me off at my mother's house, and went to torch the truck and 'Dummie' bandanas before heading home while I choked on some 'Triple Mix', and surfed Facebook for the latest Murphy Homes news and gossip. I was messed up about Monk. I felt like it was my fault that both he and his cousin—David—were dead, and the 'Triple Mix' wasn't doing much to make me feel better. On top of that, my fucking ears were killing me, and I still couldn't really hear shit. So, by the time another certified Dummie named James 'JuJu' Tanner showed up talking about another on-going situation that I had really been trying to avoid, I was all but ready to kill anything moving.

"—talking about he ain't Billy Lo. Niggas aren't ready," JuJu continued to explain what was happening on the block, as we sat outside on my front, passing a bottle of Hennessy back and forth. "Then this old nigga had the nerve to jump off with some yellow tops like he's straight up saying fuck niggas—"

I guzzled the Henny, closed my eyes, and enjoyed the burning sensation as it went down my throat. I was truly trying to keep my cool and focus on getting at these project ducks again for their most recent sin against the Squad, but Ronnie-Moe and his partner—Tony-Bey—were really starting to get out there. I was trying to respect their gangster and give them their space because the Avenue was a gold mine, and there was enough money for everybody. However, they were beginning to make me think that they didn't see it that way. So, maybe JuJu was right, maybe them old niggas really thought that the Avenue was theirs. Especially since Billy Lo and them were gone; but if that was the case, they were in for a rude awakening.

"I'ma holler at Tony-Bey as soon as we deal with this project shit," I assured.

"Man, we need to do something about this old, stiff ass nigga Ronnie-Moe now," JuJu retorted.

"I said, *I'm on it*, nigga!" I barked, eyeing JuJu. He was acting like I had picks on something. Like I wouldn't split Ronnie-Moe's wig. "Right now, I'm just focused on the niggas that just trashed Monk and shot Deli."

"Me too," JuJu confessed. "You know I'm trying to do them niggas dirty for that shit, but at the same time, this old nigga Ronnie-Moe gonna make a nigga do that to him."

"Come on, Dummie," Nizzy interrupted. His crib wasn't far from my mother's, so I had called him over when JuJu came around, and he'd joined us in next to no time. "You already know, if we have to, we'll spend them old niggas bend. Let's just finish these project squires off first."

"That's all I was saying," JuJu nodded, satisfied. "All these old niggas gonna have to evolve or dissolve, flat out."

Even though my focus was more on the project situation at the moment, I knew that what JuJu was saying was true. Niggas were gonna have to get down with the lay down, or end up with a tagged toe. "Like Nizzy said, let's handle these project ducks real quick. Then, we can step to the situation with Ronnie-Moe and Tony-Bey if need be."

JuJu had just began to curse a big-butt, flat-chested bitch who'd walked up looking for some work out, when I heard a sound that made me turn my head. Then I saw a group of army-fatigue-wearing niggas bend the corner on bikes; they headed in our direction. "What the fuck is Murdock doing? He know them dumb ass bikes gonna wake my mother up!" I said, shaking my head.

"You that know that silly nigga love them bikes, Dummie?" Nizzy said, as some of them began wheeling their bikes down the block.

"Watch out," JuJu stepped forward, nonchalantly dismissing the big-butt fiend as we all strained to get a better look at exactly who Murdock was riding with.

"That's not Murdock, Dummie," JuJu looked over his shoulder and smiled. "That's a bunch of bitches," he continued, as the first group of females wheeled down the block right on past us.

"Nah, man." I stepped forward, trying to wave the next group off. "Take that shit somewhere else!" I warned.

"Them some strong-looking bitches, Dummie, you may want to leave them alone," Nizzy joked, as the next group brought their bikes up, wheeling towards us.

"Shit, Dummie! Check this bitch out, she giving it to 'em with one hand!" JuJu shouted, very impressed by a lil' dark-skinned chick's stunt. "I wonder who taught her how to ride like—"

JuJu was about to continue when the bitch reached inside her fatigue and whipped out and started shooting, as her homegirls brought their bikes to a sudden stop in the middle of the street. I dived behind the steps as Nizzy grabbed the big-butt fiend and used her as a human shield just as the other two bikers opened fire.

"Move, Dummie!" JuJu ordered, stumbling into Nizzy, trying to get out of the line of fire and draw his tone at the same time. I didn't know what the bitches had. But it sounded like some cannons. A bullet struck my neighbor's granddaughter's 'Power Wheel,' and flipped it over before knocking a grapefruit-sized chunk of concrete off my mother's steps.

16

I cringed and reached for my tone, only to realize that I'd never strapped back up after stashing all the tones under the couch before coming outside to fuck with JuJu and Nizzy. I cursed myself for being stupid, and ran for the front door behind Nizzy. I knew better. Being outside without my tone was an amateur move that had cost a lot of good niggas their lives. It was just a good thing that Juju stayed strapped and was able to back them niggas down with his tone, long enough for us to run into the house, or we'd probably all have been dead.

"Damn!" JuJu spat, coming through the door as the bikes road off. "Who the fuck was that?"

"Fuck if I know—I thought it was Murdock," I replied, peeping out the living room window to see if the coast was clear. "Whoever it was, they definitely weren't playing."

"Yeah, they caught niggas slipping."

Nizzy was panting. "Dummie, I'll bet you any amount of money, that was them project niggas. One of them bitches had a mouth full of *slugs*"

"Okay, okay." I shook my head. I could still hear dirtbikes in the distance. "That's what it is," I continued. "Round the squad up—It's about to be open season on all them bitches!" I threatened, knowing that a lot of project niggas were about to fall for bringing that shit to my mother's door. "All bets are off. We're about to fuck the city up."

Delmont Player

Chapter 1

"Please, you've probably been a good girl your entire life." Anthony 'Billy Lo' Izzard teased Nurse Edwards, who was laughing as she continued conducting her daily routine check-up.

"Don't let the soft-spoken, God-fearing, naive personality fool you, Mr.Izzard,"

Nurse Edwards giggled like a school girl, analyzing his vital signs. "I haven't always been a goody-two-shoes now."

"Yeah, okay, let you tell it." Billy Lo cut his eyes at her and smiled. "But, it's your book, so you can write it how you want to."

"Why are you looking at me like that?" Nurse Edwards stopped to stare at him curiously.

"Nah, I told you, you just remind me so much of my fiancée," Billy Lo replied softly.

"I hope that's a good thing." Nurse Edwards blushed shyly, writing something down on Billy Lo's chart.

"Oh, it's definitely a good thing," Billy Lo assured with a huge grin. "Lakeria was smart, strong, beautiful, independent and all that. She was in a class all by herself." Billy Lo paused to look down at the name tattooed around his ring-finger. "She was an amazing woman and I was lucky to have had her."

"What happened? You'll break up or something?" Nurse Edwards stared at Billy Lo and raised her eyebrow. "Don't tell me that you broke her heart." Nurse Edwards knew from experience how hard good relationships were to find.

"Nah, she was murdered," Billy Lo replied matter-of-factly, clinching his teeth, as thoughts of Lakeria's pretty smile moments before the explosion that was meant for him flashed across his mind. It had been nearly eight months since he'd lost the only person whom meant anything to him. However, it still seemed like yesterday.

"I am sorry to hear that," Nurse Edwards said sincerely, squeezing Billy Lo's hand gently. She knew first-hand how hard of a pill the loss of a loved one was to swallow, even for God-fearing women like herself.

"You wanna know what really hurts the most?" Billy Lo finally looked back up from his hand.

"What's that?"

"The fact that I couldn't protect her," Billy Lo confessed, knowing that no matter how he looked at it, no matter whom he blamed, somewhere along the line, he'd made a mistake that ended up costing him more than he was ever willing to lose. A mistake that had costed him more pain than he knew what to do with. "That I couldn't be there when she needed me the most."

"That's not your fault."

"It sure feels like it is," Billy Lo refuted, as a sense of guilt washed over him.

"You got to give all that to God, baby. You got to trust in Him with all your heart and lean not on your own understanding." Nurse Edwards quoted one of her favorite Bible proverbs.

"I tried, I really did," Billy Lo admitted honestly. "But I guess God has other plans for me." The murders of his future wife and unborn child had left a hole in Billy Lo's heart that just couldn't be filled, and a thirst for blood that still hadn't been quenched. Billy Lo had moved against everyone whom he'd discovered—or believed was involved—in the death of his family, and rolled over top of everybody who tried to stand in his way. In fact he'd been so engrossed with revenge that he never saw or even expected the double-cross that came from Charm. Now, when it came to Herbert, it was diffferent. Billy Lo didn't expect nothing less. After all, Herbert wasn't nothing but another crooked ass, homo-cop trying to cover his own ass once it ended up on the line—which is why he wasn't surprised when Herbert told the detectives about the bus ticket. However, Charm was family. The whole team loved shorty. Especially Mumbles. So, for Charm to turn around and snake him like he had was really fucking with him. And as if going against the gain wasn't enough, Charm had the audacity to turn around and sell him up the creek to the Mob for a position of power. The same crude

20

ball ass Mob who'd been responsible for all his pain and suffering. By the time Charm had snuck into his hospital room and attempted to finish him off, Billy Lo had already put two and two together. So, he felt like the thought and need for revenge had not allowed him to die, even after Charm had put two straight into his head at point-blank range.

Billy Lo had already been laid up from the bus station shooting for a few days when Charm showed up in a half-ass decent disguise. Due to the handcuffs, leg-irons, medication, and the bullet that'd managed to nip Billy Lo's backbone and leave the whole left side of his body semi-paralyzed, all he could do when Charm raised the chrome snub-nose .38 to shoot him in the chest the first time was, lay there and watch it play out.

Billy Lo remembered staring at Charm helplessly, unable to defend himself as Charm brought the chrome snub-nose .38 up slightly higher and shot him in the head, twice. Billy Lo saw a flash of light a tenth of a second before everything went dark. He dreamed that Charm forced the business end of the .38 into his mouth with the tube and pulled the trigger. He was later informed that when the hospital personnel finally arrived back at the room, they all assumed that he was dead from the way he was laying there in a pool of his own blood, with large holes in his head, face, neck and chest. But, amazingly, he still had a pulse, so they immediately rushed him upstairs to surgery.

It had taken Billy Lo about three months before he was able to start walking again, due to the bus shooting. It took him a little over another month to be able to see out of his left eye due to the head shot. Apparently, the ammunition Charm had chosen for the hit was old and had lost most of its power. So, instead of the bullet penetrating Billy Lo's skull when Charm pulled the trigger, it only managed to flatten on impact. That was one 'slip-up' Billy Lo planned to make Charm regret. Although the head shot did happen to leave him slightly blind in one eye, he was still alive and kicking. The final shot had simply gone through Billy Lo's cheek, smashed through his teeth and exited his neck.

Everybody kept saying how lucky and blessed he was to

have survived two shootings. But, Billy Lo knew better; luck didn't have anything to do with it. It was his thirst for revenge, but he kept those plots to himself. The doctor assured Billy Lo that even with continuous therapy he would probably only gain about eighty-five percent of his seeing and walking abilities back.

Whatever the case, Billy Lo vowed that as soon as he had the chance, he was going to make sure that Charm knew that he'd made a crucial mistake by not finishing the job, because if he wasn't nothing else, he was still a hell of a chess master, even under the threat of checkmate.

"Well, no pain is without purpose, so you can't give up—that's for sure." Nurse Edwards squeezed his hand again and thought about her brother. He always said that a lot of people did the wrong thing for the right reason. "You have to bloom wherever God plants you, because he gives his toughest battles to his strongest soldiers."

"Oh, I definitely haven't given up." Billy Lo smiled. His most strategic move hadn't even been made yet. "I just learned how to put my faith in things that I've a little more control of."

Before Nurse Edwards could counter, one of the prison workers poked his head inside the room, wanting to know if she was finished, so that he could mop the floor and make it out to the yard. "Oh Lord!" Nurse Edwards looked at the pink wrist watch her daughter had given to her for her birthday, and quickly finished jotting down things on Billy Lo's chart sheet. She was thankful that the working man had interrupted them when he had.

"You can get in here now. Just let me gather the rest of my things and I'll be out of your way." Nurse Edwards replaced Billy Lo's chart at the foot of the bed, as the working man disappeared. "We're going to have to finish this conversation tomorrow, Mr. Izzard. You're not getting off that easy."

"Yes, Ma'am." Billy Lo nodded and smiled. Nurse Edwards was a special caliber of woman.

"And don't you forget what I said earlier—Doing bad things

don't always make us bad people," Nurse Edwards added, stuffing the last of her medical utensils inside her hospital-smock pocket before quickly exiting the room.

Billy Lo got lost in thought as the fine, high-spirit R.N. left. He only hoped that what she said was true, because if everything went according to plan, he was about to do some real bad things to a lot of mother fuckers—for the right reasons, of course.

"What's up, shorty?" Zimbabwe spoke, strolling back into the room, pushing the sanitation cart.

"Ain't too much, you know me," Billy Lo replied, watching his man remove the broom off the sanitation cart.

"What you in here doing?"

"Messing with Ms. Edwards."

Zimbabwe smiled and nodded, wishing he had the time and opportunity to be in close quarters with the fine, Jill Scott-looking nurse. "Oh yeah, you keep you a beauty around."

"It's not even like that," Billy Lo argued truthfully. "Ms. Edwards just cool," Billy Lo added, thinking about all the love Nurse Edwards had been showing him since he was transferred in from the hospital two months ago, after being discharged and officially booked on multiple murder charges. Nurse Edwards brought him encouraging books to read, snuck him healthier food from the staff kitchen, and allowed him to keep an MP3 player tucked away under his bed. "But anyway, what happen in court yesterday?"

"We made out." Zimbabwe smiled. "The state offered us time served. All we gotta do is eat them trumped up ass assault charges when we go back next month and we're gone." Zimbabwe began sweeping.

Billy Lo nodded as Zimbabwe began to sweep the floor. That was exactly what he needed to hear. "So Shaneeka came through, huh?"

Zimbabwe nodded. "Ain't no question. Shaneeka a soldier. She came up in there and carried that mail just like you said. Told the judge that the hammers were her deceased boyfriend's and that she had asked us—Little Dinky and I—to get rid of them for her. I still can't believe the judge bought that shit."

"I told you he would," Billy Lo said with a smile. The first part of his plan was a success. Since hitting the jail, Billy Lo had been doing everything in his power to see to it that his men would see daylight soon. After all, he'd been the reason they'd been at Shaneeka's house in the first place. He also needed them on the streets if he really wanted to show Charm how two-sided war could be, and remind the Mob why you never sent a kid to do a grown man's job. "It's all about story telling."

"Now, we can get uptown and handle that other thing you got lined up," Zimbabwe added.

Billy Lo nodded, knowing that their next move was gonna change the game. Shidddd, he was still fucked up himself that Black's girl could be so shrewd. She not only wanted to help him get his revenge, she wanted to get her own. So, who was he to deny her such a gift? Especially when she'd already been making moves to make it happen.

When Peanut had first reached out to Billy Lo about her plans, he'd definitely been skeptical. Between Charm's little stunt, the threat of a Federal 'Continuing Criminal Enterprise' indicment, and the state trying to tie him to a new case every month, he didn't know who to trust, but he decided to take a chance with Peanut. After all, Billy Lo knew she was solid and thorough—even from the way she'd carried it for Black when it was crunch time. There weren't too many women who'd sacrifice their own flesh and blood—regardless of whether he was snitching or not—for the freedom of their man. So, Billy Lo knew one thing if he didn't know nothing else. Peanut was a cold bitch.

"Oh yeah, guess who hit me up last night, talking crazy!" Billy Lo spat, as if he had just remembered something important.

"Who?" Zimbabwe questioned curiously, placing the broom back on the cart before plunging the mop in and out of the mop bucket full of water a few times to get it nice and wet.

"Africa's little sister, India."

"Keep fucking with that jail bait. Letting that little hopper play on your phone and shit." Zimbabwe laughed, dragging the wet mop across the floor.

"I don't even know how she got the nunber this time."

"Okay, watch." Zimbabwe shook his head. "That little girl gonna get jealous one day and call up here on your old ass."

"I know, Slim, but I can't help it," Billy Lo admitted. "See, Slim, you haven't had a young girl who can suck dick like a cougar yet!" Billy Lo joked, but Zimbabwe could tell that he was serious. "But listen," Billy Lo continued, "she gets to questioning me about Africa's death. Saying some detectives swung by her house, asking all kind of crazy ass questions about me as if I had something to do with that shit."

"Did you?" Zimbabwe stopped mopping to look at him seriously.

"Fuck no!" Billy Lo retorted, lying.

"Then what's the problem?"

"The way she's talking, they may be trying to pin that shit on me or something," Billy Lo replied.

"You act like you're surprised." Zimbabwe went back to mopping. "They do that shit every time they label a nigga 'public enemy number one' in the city. Start trying to link him to all kind of cold-cases so they can clear the books."

Billy Lo knew Zimbabwe wasn't lying. The Baltimore City Police Department stayed under fire for doing some unethical shit. "You aren't lying about that," Billy Lo agreed. "But still, I'm not trying to be the nigga locked up for slumping no bitch whether she deserves it or not. Nobody respects that."

"True," Zimbabwe acknowledged, knowing that certain crimes were frowned upon in the system and society, despite the fact that they may have benefitted. "But you didn't have anything to do with it anyway; so, you're good." Zimbabwe paused for a moment before asking: "Did you holler at them other folks yet?"

"Yeah, I got with her last night."

"And you're sure you wanna do this shorty? 'Cause like I said, Little Dinky and I can just go out there and handle that little kid ourselves." Zimbabwe assured, still unsure if he really wanted to bring more unnecessary people into his fold. That was how things always went wrong. Especially since there were so many weak mother fuckers slipping through the cracks nowadays. "I mean, I know you said she's a soldier and all that. But, we're gonna need somebody we can really trust to keep their mouth shut if shit go south."

"Yeah, I know," Billy Lo admitted that Zimbabwe was right. It was a whole different ball game when bodies started falling and the police started kicking in doors. Even a lot of so-called gangsters clammed up under the pressure. "Peanut good to go, though. If she wasn't, I wouldn't have even brought her to you," Billy Lo added, loving how conscious and calculated Zimbabwe always was about everything. It left little room for error. "Honestly, she's more thorough then most these niggas out here today. Plus, it's not like she's gonna be pulling licks with y'all or nothing. She's gonna turn y'all onto her brother, and that's it. After that, y'all will be dealing directly with him."

"It's your call, shorty." Zimbabwe surrendered, hoping that Peanut was everything Billy Lo was making her out to be. "Just be careful how much information you feed her about us. At least until we meet these jokers and make sure that everything's on the up and up."

"I got you, Slim," Billy Lo agreed. "She won't know nothing she don't need to know. She's gonna play her part and we're gonna play ours."

"That's all I need to hear." Zimbabwe nodded, satisfied. Billy Lo was his man, and he trusted him with his life. So, if he said shit was good, then it was good. "Now, after she introduces us to her folks, what's next?"

"Then you and Little Dinky do what it is that y'all do." Billy Lo smiled wickedly, knowing how much Zimbabwe loved to put his robbery game down. "From what I gather, Peanut's brothers are already on Charm's line. They were already scoping things out before Peanut and I even hooked up. I just think they need a certified grave-digger and a seasoned robbery expert."

26

"I'm telling you now, shorty. I'm not about to be running around baby-sitting," Zimbabwe said.

"Oh, you're going to be doing a lot more than baby-sitting." Billy Lo smiled. He couldn't wait to watch Charm crumble as he took away everything that his little ass loved and valued.

Delmont Player

Chapter 2

"As-Salaam-Alaikum, Ock" Donald 'Wakal' White entered the North Branch Correctional Institution dayroom in Cumberland, Maryland, and greeted his Muslim brother—Suf'yan—that had become somewhat of a mentor to him.

"Wa-Alaikum-Salaam," the older, light brown-skinned, physically fit brother with the huge beard replied, giving Wakal a handshake and brotherly hug, as he walked up. "What are you up to this morning?"

"Not too much." Wakal broke the embrace, looking around the dayroom. "What's good with you?"

"You know me, Ock," Suf'yan held up his *Wall Street Journal*. "About to go call my aunt and check some stocks before I go up this barbershop."

"I heard *that*." Wakal looked towards the control station. "You didn't happen to see who had the tier this morning did you?"

"I think it's Fox. At least that's who did count this morning."

Wakal nodded because Fox was cool. "Inshaallah, she can get me in the back to see my case managers."

"Why? What's up?" Suf'yan questioned more out of curiosity than concern. Guys in prison only communicated with the adminstration for a few reasons.

"That's what I'm trying to figure out now," Wakal replied, pulling out some security papers. "I got these last night."

"Oh, you're on that M-C-I transfer list now," Suf'yan said, recognizing the paperwork.

"That's what I thought," Wakal confessed, without much enthusiasm, remembering how a lot of guys without jacked-up prison jackets were being shipped over to the prison next door to make bed space due to an on-going war.

"What? You don't want to go or something, Ock?" Suf'yan looked at Wakal like he was insane. He could not imagine anyone wanting to remain in North Branch if they didn't have to. "It's way better over there, Ock. You get more recreation, they got better jobs, and they got trades and shops over there. Plus, family day." Suf'yan continued: "I know you're not trying to stay in this raggedy spot? This joint anything, Ock, there's nothing shaking over here."

Wakal knew that Suf'yan was right. All guys did in North Branch was, gossip, back-bite and go from one cramped space to another, beefing, looking for more reasons to remain divided. There were only a few conscious, strong men left, and they were far and few in between. Besides that, there weren't really any programs or something. So, most guys just ran around selling their souls and manhood for jobs and funny-looking, funny-built white women. However, Wakal wasn't about to admit that and have to explain why he wanted to stay. "It's got its benefits too," Wakal smiled, thinking about a few white female guards who loved seeing a nigga's dick.

"Name one," Suf'yan challenged.

"First, I got the brother working on my case, trying to get me back in court."

"There are jail house lawyers everywhere, Ock, and a lot of them are much better than our brother!" Suf'yan countered.

"Yeah, but how many are as cheap?"

"Yeah, well, tell your case manager to let me take your place," Suf'yan laughed because honestly, he couldn't understand Wakal's dilemma.

Wakal, formerly known on the streets as D.W., was the only surviving member of one of the deadliest team of wig-splitting, stick-up crews to have ever emerged in Baltimore City's history. In fact, his history was the reason he'd converted to Islam, changed his name, altered his appearance as much as he could, and stopped doing anything that would draw unwanted attention to himself, the community, or contradict the Sunnah. Especially since all the 'alleged' snitching talk had started to die down.

When D.W. had first taken his *Shahadah* (pledge to Allah) and hit the compound in the Penitentiary Annex after coming off of protective custody, he made it his business to lay real low, despite the fact that he had quickly realized that a lot of the so-called prison rules and laws he had grown up hearing about were either no longer in effect, simply did not exist, or were just old penitentiary myths. Most dudes didn't care if you told on someone, just so long as you hadn't told on them or someone they truly dealt with. The same thing went for murder, rape and robbery. It wasn't about 'if' you did it. It was about 'who' you did it to. D.W. didn't know if it was due to the fact that the streets just weren't as loyal to dudes behind the walls as they once were, or the fact that everybody seemed to be clicked up in one sense or another.

Whatever the case, Wakal stayed out of the way and refused to question it. And everything was going good until a couple of wild ass kids decided to toss a guard over the third tier to his death a few months back, and he ended up being one of many lifers who'd managed to stay under the radar to be shipped out into the mountains, to make room for the guys transferring in from over the 'Cut' when the governor declared a 'state of emergency' and forced the commissioner to close the 'Cut's' doors for good.

To some degree, it was almost comical that D.W. had become a Muslim, let alone a Sunni. Even if it was initially just for protection because during his heydays, he and Lil' Dray used to clown the Mob. To them, they weren't nothing more than a homophobic, Christian-hating, rat-harboring gang that used religion and the Holy Qu'ran to play a bunch of dope fiend games. However, after great study, D.W. realized that everything he had once thought or been told about Mob were wrong.

"Speaking of the devil," Suf'yan gestured towards their tier with his head. "There go your girl Fox right there."

Wakal looked over and saw the Katja Kassin lookalike walking back on to the tier, flipping through the log-book. Wakal smiled as Fox took a seat behind her desk. "Let me go see if I can get her to get on top of this transfer shit for me," he said before walking off.

Fox was a bad, exotic, snow-bunny with short, strawberry-red hair and mad ass. She had a hint of freckles around her nose, and a pair of sexy lips that she kept glossed up to let a nigga know that she could probably suck the skin off a dick.

"Excuse me, Miss Fox," Wakal strolled up, inhaling her berry-vanilla fragrance, and had to pause for a moment. It was something about white women that just did it for him. "Do—do—do you know if anybody from case management came in yet?"

"You know what, White? I think I saw Miss Simpson this morning," Fox replied, referring to another cute, little Rhonda Rousey-looking white girl, who Wakal would've loved to go a few rounds with to see if he could make her tap out.

"Can you see if she'll see me? It's an emergency."

"You're going to have to do something for me first," Fox warned.

"What?" Wakal hesitated. "I'm not doing no telling."

"Everybody knows you're a man, White," Fox stroked Wakal's ego and disarmed him with her crystal-blue eyes and warm smile, just like she'd been taught by the administration. "I just want to know what gang you're in."

"Gang?" Wakal repeated with a surprise laugh. "Do I look like a waiter to you?"

"A waiter?" Fox asked, confused.

"Yeah, like I take orders."

"That was good—I haven't heard that one before," Fox admitted. "But, if you're not a gang member. I mean, waiter, why do you have M-O-B on your arms?"

"Oh, this?" Wakal looked down and rubbed his forearm as if he'd forgotten all about the tattoo. "It was a Tupac thing, 'money over bitches'."

"You're in prison now, so you may want to change that," Fox suggested, rolling her eyes.

"I already have." Wakal smiled.

"So, what does it mean?" Fox questioned, truly curious.

"Money orders basically," Wakal said, and Fox fell out laughing.

"You is something else, White," Fox said, getting to her feet, still laughing as Wakal spotted the multiple-colored tongue-rings running up the middle of her tongue. "I got you, though. Just let me make my rounds first and then I'll go and check and see if Ms. Simpson is here."

"Thanks." Wakal stepped back as Fox closed the log-book and came around the desk. "I appreciate that."

"I am not making no promises she'll see you though. But I'll let her know it's an emergency." Fox walked off, leaving Wakal spellbound from the intoxicating smell of her fragrance. *Damn! All that ass!* Wakal thought, licking his lips unconsciously before re-adjusting his now hardening dick, as he watched Fox strut down the tier—throwing her hips like she'd gotten dick down real good that morning. *I bet money that pussy as good as Friday Ju'mah service.*

Wakal smiled to himself, shaking his head. She got to be fucking black dudes. Can't no white boy make that bitch strut like that! He had heard that she used to work down the Baltimore City Supermax too. Yeah, she knows what that Mandingo hitting for. Wakal smiled. Even after all the trouble them fucking white girls had caused Wakal, he still had a mean sweet tooth for them nasty, no-holds barred bitches, even behind bars. It was just something about them that drove him insane. The way they looked. The way they carried themselves like they were God's gift to man. He remembered how they felt. But more than anything, it was the way they were down for whatever when it came to sex that continued to drive him crazy.

Delmont Player

Chapter 3

"Hold up! Let me slow down for a minute and bring all the readers who aren't hip to me up to speed. On February 5th. 1999, I came into the world feet first. Pure and uncontaminated, destined to be a gangster, even if it killed me. My father was a nigga I didn't remember and had never forgiven. As far as I was concerned, only a real fuck-nigga would leave his nineteen-year-old wife and newborn to go die for a country that did not give a damn about him or his family.

So, the only thing we had in common was our names, Calvin N. Johnson. My mother was a hustler's dream and a woman's worst nightmare. Which is why every well-known hustler and certified gangster in the city wanted a taste of Nicole 'Peaches' Johnson, a 5'5, peanut-butter-brown goddess with the face and frame of a video model. It was nothing to see money getters like Warren Davis at our door. Shiddd! Even corporate good boys wanted a piece of my mother, but that was before she met and fell in love with the father of my sister—Tiffany.

Tiffany's dad was an East Baltimore heavy hitter by the name of Duran 'Money' Cola, who had a stronghold on everything from Harford Road to Lafayette Projects during the Anthony Jones reign. He was another helluva gangster who had a lot of serious niggas feeling like bitches.

For a while, things were good. My mother enrolled back in college, and Money Cola became somewhat of a father to me. Teaching me everything there was to know about all the golden rules and sacred street codes. Then the unthinkable happened. Money Cola was murdered while saving my mother's life during a sketchy home invasion, leaving nothing behind except his legend. Without Money Cola around to fend for us, life became hard.

I had never seen my mother so broken up and stressed out. She quit school, refused to work, and basically just started running the streets, partying with a bunch of no-good bitches—women who went through life looking for a handout, waiting for some man to do for them what they can in fact do for themselves. It was as if witnessing Money Cola's death had taken her spirit.

At first, I didn't believe the rumors. No matter how much they seemed to make sense. I mean, I just couldn't imagine my mother getting high. She was too intelligent, too thorough, too hard, and too damn slick to get down like that. So, I figured that all the last-minute school clothes, late bills, and various times coming and going all hours of the day and night were just her way of getting back on her feet. Until the day I came home from school and found all our things sitting out in the street.

From that moment on, everything changed. We were forced to move in with my aunt Joyce, who had five mouths of her own to feed. It was only little that she could offer. It wasn't long before I was running the streets behind my aunt's eldest son, Slate, doing whatever I had to do to ensure that we were never hungry. I looked up to Slate. I mean, the nigga was the epitome of a true young gangster. And he had a crew of young Dummies following him to prove it.

In early 2013 my cousin—Slate—and I were arrested along with Monk and David for allegedly stabbing this wild bitch-mad ass nigga named Shawn Stanfield to death for violating one of his sisters. And even though everybody kept their mouths shut, Slate was still committed because of his juvy record.

After Slate was shipped off to training school, everybody started calling me 'Charm' because of my ability to weasel my way out of anything, including the long-arm of the law without breaking any rules. So, by the time Mumbles became my mentor and put me on, I was running wild with the Dummie Squad and all but taking care of my little sister and I by myself. So, motherfuckers couldn't tell me nothing unless they were putting food in my stomach, clothes on my back, a roof over my head, or money in my pocket. And it didn't matter who they were. As far as I was concerned I was grown. I didn't need or want nobody's sympathy, and I definitely wasn't asking for no fucking handouts.

Mumbles was different though. He reminded me so much of Money Cola. He didn't try to tell me what to do or play me like I was a kid. Instead he led by example. He wasn't like the friend who did or accepted anything to receive your approval. Nah, Mumbles was the mentor who challenged you, even when you were bucking, because he wanted you to succeed. Mumbles had me with him so much that everybody began to think that I was his biological little brother. I had never met a certified street goon like Mumbles. Not only did he mold me and put change in my pocket. But, he schooled me on how to deal with multiple niggas while only remaining loyal to my own. And since I'd never been one of those dudes who were quicker to take oaths than to honor them, I paid close attention to every lesson because I took my job serious.

That is why, when the Mob reached out and offered me the keys to my former mentor's kingdom, I did what any true prince would've done without a moment's hesitation. I stepped up to claim my throne I mean, by then, Mumbles was dead, I'd lost my little sister, and I was finally beginning to overstand what Slate meant about loyalty only being admirable in a follower. For a leader, he said: "It shows weakness." By the time I accepted the deal to crack Billy Lo in order to reign supreme, he was all but finished anyway. D.W. and Diamond were both telling, dry-snitching, or whatever you wanted to call it in one sense or another, and I was basically the last man standing.

I know a lot of you motherfuckers judged me. Called me a snake, said I was cruddy, but I don't give a fuck! Yeah, I chose sides and joined forces with the same niggas who were directly responsible for the demise of my mentor. And yeah, I didn't hesitate to pull the trigger on Billy Lo. So what! Rather intentionally or unintentionally, that nigga was responsible for the death of my little sister.

Furthermore, when it's time to come up, there are only two things that I won't do to reach the top. That's, tell on a nigga or fuck one. Everything else goes. Plus, I honestly didn't think Mumbles would be mad at me for seizing the opportunity. After all, he'd did the same exact shit to Diamond when it came down to it. To be honest, that is why I couldn't allow noone else to tell my story. This is why I refused to let another motherfucker tell my story. I can't have bitches lying, or niggas twisting the truth, trying to take credit for shit that they didn't have absolutely nothing to do with. If my story had to be or needed to be told, I had to be the one to tell it because I can't trust my family, friends or foes to tell the story uncensored without exaggeration or downplaying the whole shit. This isn't one of those other cable TV shows all you motherfuckers love so much. My life is the shit a lot of those shows are based off.

In a nutshell, I came up as a rowdy little snotty-nose nigga, hugging the block, and all I ever wanted to be was a gangster. I had everything that catapaulted me to this level. The right teachers and circumstances that forced me to man up. So, there's nothing fake or flawed about me. Now, I want you to sit back, relax, and learn the ropes of the game from me. Because I'ma bout to teach you what it's like to come up off a hit for your mentor's enemies and get turned onto the biggest Muslim distributor in the city.

Chapter 4

"You should get that bitch Mary Jo Livingston that Black use to use all the time," I suggested, remembering how she'd successfully defended Leon a few times as Billy Lo and I continued to discuss his case. I just couldn't believe that the new District Attorney bitch, Carilyn Cosby, had decided to seek the death penalty. "When Black first hired her, she told me that after the case was over, I would love or hate her, but promised to do everything in her power to beat the charges."

"Yeah, I'm hip. Black said she wasn't no slouch. But I retained Susan Kerin when I was on the run. Shorty a pit-bull in a skirt. Plus, she's gonna represent me if the Feds decide to indict."

I shook my head, more out of amazement than pity. The Feds were playing a dirty game. "How the hell they gonna indict you with some motherfuckers they know that y'all were beefing with? That's just crazy."

"Don't start me to lying—It's probably just another one of their little tactics to get niggas to start rolling on each other," Billy Lo explained.

"Yeah, well, hopefully it doesn't work," I said, ready to drop the issue. If there was one thing that I hated more than phony bitches, it was weak, bitch-made niggas.

"Hopefully." Billy Lo didn't sound as optimistic.

"By the way, what's up with your boys? Did they make out?"

"Yeah, everything's good," Billy Lo assured.

"They still leery?" I asked.

"A little, but don't take it personal. They're old school."

"I get it," I admitted honestly. I could respect where they were coming from. I mean, it was a treacherous game with little honor nowadays. "I'm not too fond of motherfuckers I don't know either," I said, never one to bite my tongue regardless of the benefits or consequences.

"I hear that." Billy Lo laughed in my ear. "But everything

cool though. All everybody got to do is stick to the script."

If I didn't know nothing else about Billy Lo, I knew that he was about his work, and I knew that his word was bond because when he first came home from prison a few years back, he did exactly what he said he would do and brought Black home. And that was something that I could bet my money on.

"A'ight, Peanut, let me end this call before they come back through for count."

"Oh, okay, I'll text you the address for your boys in a few days."

"Bet. Walk slow, think fast and be safe out there."

"Yeah, you do the same." I ended the call and got up off the couch to stare at myself in the large mirror that covered the entire wall of my living room. If things lined up like they were supposed to, niggas would regret killing my daughter's father. Especially since they'd been dumb enough to leave me breathing as if I was some weak bitch who couldn't pose just as much—if not more of a—threat than Leon. But that was okay, because I was about to teach niggas that when you fucked with my family, I am as dangerous as they come. People need to understand what niggas had taken from me when they killed Leon. They don't understand just how much I loved his black ass because if they had, they would've realized that as long as I was breathing, nobody who'd participated in—or benefited from—his death would be safe. Ever!

Not with the lengths that I was willing to go to or the sacrifices that I was willing to make to get revenge. But they were definitely about to learn the hard way.

The sound of my phone snapped me out of my daze. I looked at the screen and saw Cat's face. She was just the person I needed to get with as regarding my plans for the remaining motherfuckers who had something to do with my boo's demise.

"Praise the Lord!" I began on the phone, disguising my voice.

"Peanut?" Cat sounded unsure if she dialed the right number.

"As-salaam-alaikum!"

"Peanut, bitch, if you don't stop playing. You know I know your damn voice by now!" Cat fired into my ear.

"What's up, hooker? I was about to call your ass."

"Girl, bye!" Cat sucked her teeth.

"I'm serious," I retorted honestly. "I got something to talk to you about."

"Yeah, well, since I called your ass first, you've to wait until I say what I have to say first!" Cat declared, and began going in on some bitches she'd already put hands on, whom she swore were still on Instagram, indirectly coming for her. It was crazy how tight the deaths of the men we loved had made us. Cat and I had even hung out a time or two on double dates with Leon and Mumbles, but we weren't really that close then. However, I knew that Cat was thorough ever since she cornered two bitches and robbed them of their limited addition Gucci bags and earrings.

"Girl, fuck them shade throwing bitches. Everybody know you got hands," I said. "Anyway, Cat, I'm talking about getting to this bag!"

"Getting to what bag?"

"Oh, now I got your attention, huh?"

I laughed, knowing that Cat had always been about her man and her money. Mumbles used to say she was his best friend and money's worst nightmare. "You sure do. Now, what's all this talk about the bag?"

"I can't with you," I said, shaking my head. "Can you still get in contact with them wild ass Mexicans Black and Mumbles used to deal with?"

"Yeah, but I'll have to make some calls."

"Good, I need a number on them asap."

"Nah, bitch, why? What are you up to now?" Does this have something to do with Charm again?" Cat sounded concerned. "Because I done told you to leave that shit alone. I mean, I know what you said he did, but he still like a little brother to Michael and I don't think he would want no harm to come to him."

"This ain't got nothing to do Charm—One of Black's cousins just came home and I'm trying to help him get on his feet," I lied. Leon had taught me to never let the left hand know what the right hand was up to. Especially when the left hand wasn't in agreement with what the right hand wanted to do. It was how he had remained successful for so long when it came to keeping himself and I safe. And it would the reason I'd be successful.

"And he gave me a finder's fee."

"How much?"

"Damn yo, don't I always break bread?" I questioned.

"Bitch, how much?" Cat demanded.

"Three bands," I confessed, sounding reluctant.

"Cash app me half and I'll have the information for you before the night is out."

Greedy hooker, I thought to myself.

Chapter 5

"Hey, Pooh bear." Detective Bruce 'Bunchy' Baker entered the office of his partner and sometimes lover, and closed the door.

"Hey, babe." Detective Lashaun Gibson was sitting at her desk, going over everything they had on the Izzard case. She wanted to make sure all the pieces fit together, and tied up any loose ends.

"Penny for your thoughts," Detective Baker said softly, walking around Gibson's desk to kiss her on the top of her head before massaging her shoulders.

Detective Gibson took a deep breath, closed her eyes and leaned back as Baker massaged her tensed shoulders gently with his strong hands. Detective Gibson wanted so much to prove that Izzard had somehow been involved with Yusef Brinkley's death so they could have another crack at him and really seal his fate. "Just going over Izzard's file again, making sure that we've crossed all of our t's and dotted all of our i's. I want everything laid out nicely for Cosby; that way, she can serve his ass up to the jury for death without the fucking Appeal Court tossing the conviction."

"Don't worry, baby—This one is open and shut," Detective Baker replied confidently, thinking about all the evidence they'd mounted on the Catholic church shooting. The two eyewitnesses and the murder weapon. They even had managed to lift latent prints, obtain DNA samples and recover the actual disguise used during the shooting from the motel room where Izzard had been hiding out in. "There is no way in hell Izzard walking away on this one."

"I guess you're right," Gibson exhaled. "It's just that I know that the FBI are holding out on us," Gibson confessed. "Think about it. It's been over five months since the would-be baby-face killers attempted to murder Izzard and they're still acting like they know nothing."

Detective Baker wasn't surprised, but he wasn't stupid either. The FBI were definitely holding back. But, as far as he

was concerned, their job was done. They'd caught Izzard before

her barely hidden phat pussy.

"Shhh—" Baker mumbled, kissing and sucking on her face, neck and shoulder, until he found his way around to her lips. "Just let me give you what you need, baby.

"Bunchy," Detective Gibson moaned as Baker spun her recliner around and stood in front of her. Detective Baker carefully took both of Gibson's legs and carefully placed them over the arms of her recliner. Then he knelt down to watch her pretty pussy slowly open up like a flower after he pushed her purple boy-shorts to one side, and pulled her forward until she was on the edge of the recliner.

"Yeah, this how I like my food. Hot, wet and ready."

"Sssss," Detective Gibson inhaled deeply and arched her back the moment Detective Baker's tongue made contact with her clitoris. "Ohhhh, my God, baby, you know that's my spot right there! Keep doing that right there!"

Detective Baker smiled inside and kept eating Gibson's pussy, as she grabbed his head, held on to the recliner, slapped the desk and came all over his face. Detective Baker knew his pussy eating skills always did it for her because she had taught him well.

"Bunchy! Oh, shit—Bunchy! You're gonna make me—you gonna make me—Fuck!" Gibson's toes were cracking and curling each and every way as she watched Detective Baker's tongue slowly darted in and out of her pussy. "Oh, my God, Bunchy, I just came again," Detective Gibson gasped for air as she strongly rolled her hips, dug her nails into Detective Baker's scalp and tried to run all at the same time. "Yes, baby, yes. Get it! Eat that pussy!"

Detective Baker took his time, gently, yet aggressively eating Gibson's pussy until she came a second time. He was biting and nibbling on the cheeks of her baby-soft ass and thighs, like he was trying to eat her alive.

"Damn! I love the taste of your pussy," Detective Baker confessed, licking up the cum that ran down in between her ass cheeks as she shook and moaned. When it was Detective Baker's turn to get his, Detective Gibson stood up on shaky legs and wiggled out of her boy-shorts, as Baker quickly got undressed. Then, she spat in the palm of her hand and slowly ran her hand up and down his rock-hard dick. "What do you be feeding this thing?" Detective Gibson teased.

"Beef." Detective Baker declared, reaching around to squeeze Gibson's ass cheeks. Then he slowly turned her around and pushed her face down over the desk before kicking her legs apart so that he could hit it just the way he liked. Detective Baker slowly spread Gibson's ass cheeks apart and shook his head, as she looked back at him over her shoulder. It never ceased to amaze him how pretty, pink and wet her pussy always was. Besides the sexy little light stretch mark streaks on her cheeks, there was nothing more beautiful. Detective Baker took the head of his dick and carefully rubbed it in between the soft, wet folds of Gibson's pussy lips before firmly gripping her hips and sliding in, balls deep.

"Gosh!" Detective Gibson quivered, arched her back and went up on her toes as Detective Baker's thickness stretched her tight little pussy open. "Mmmmh, I always love it when you first put it in."

"I know, baby," Detective Baker whispered, holding her in place so she couldn't run before taking long, steady, deep strokes as she continued to moan and mumble things he could not understand. After a few minutes, Detective Gibson said something about them getting in trouble again. So, Baker began to pick up speed.

"Shit! Shit!" Gibson yelled, slapping the desk, throwing her ass back wildly, forgetting all about where they were for a moment. "Get it! Get that pussy!"

Detective Baker felt Gibson's over-heated pussy clutching and squeezing his dick, working a magic of its own, and knew it was time to get his. Watching her ass run back and forth in little waves made his nuts began to tighten up. "Here it comes, baby!" Detective Baker grunted through clenched teeth as he nutted deep in Gibson's soft pussy. Then he fell forward, collapsing across her back, spent and satiated.

"I swear, Pooh bear, you got the best pussy in the world," Detective Baker managed to say, softly kissing the nape of Gibson's neck.

"I know," Detective Gibson blushed. "Now, get your heavy ass off me!"

Delmont Player

Chapter 6

"What time do you want me to pick you up?" I asked Ebony, as we pulled up in front of the Coppin State University Community College.

"Around six-thirty," Ebony replied, leaning over to kiss me. "We got a play coming up in a few weeks, so class is probably going to run late."

"A'ight, just text me." I squeezed Ebony's thigh and gave her another quick kiss.

"I sure will," she agreed, opening the door. I watched as Ebony climbed out of the car with her books in hand and used her hips to bump the passenger door close. "Bye, babe." Ebony waved before making her way towards the building in a pair of low-riding, hip-hugging, skin-tight jeans, and all I could do was shake my head.

I couldn't wait to get up in that good pussy again. Ebony was a cross between Taraji P. Henson, fine and Fantasia-thick. And from the moment I first laid eyes on her coming out of 'New Identity's Barbershop and Beauty Salon a few months ago, it was a wrap. I was on her line like a stalker. What really captured my attention about Ebony was her raw beauty, sexy eyes and gangster braids. I immediately went inside asking questions to find out exactly who Ebony was. Once I got the scoop I moved in for the kill.

At first, Ebony tried to stunt on a young nigga, rejecting all my advances and shit. But, like a true Aquarius, I was headstrong. So, it only made me more determined to win her over. For the next few weeks, I made it my business to not only show up at all her hair and nail appointments, but to foot the bill also. This act of mine kind of got her attention. I mean, that wasn't no light feat because Ebony wasn't no basic bitch. Shorty was all exotic and sophisticated. So, in the end she had to respect that and give the young boy some of her time. And you already know that a young nigga took cold advantage of it. Yeah, got up in that butter-soft pussy and showed her what the young boy could do. And the rest is as she posted on Facebook: *'in a relationship'*.

I hit the horn as Ebony entered the university, made a quick illegal U-turn and headed for the hood.

Shit had really been hectic since Monk got murked. After the funeral, we just started giving Murphy Homes the blues. Spending them niggas bend left and right, knocking heads off. Since the beef had heated up, Deli, Lil'Deezy and Thugg—who would never freely stand on two feet again—had all been snatched out of the hospital and taken into custody. Then, Itchy-Man was trapped off and arrested outside of his aunt's house. Now, Prince was wanted and detectives were coming through the Avenue, asking questions about Nizzy and I. So, we were laying low. However, shop was still open for business because the plug still had to be paid.

I finally caught up with that nigga Xavier too. Caught his dumb ass bull-shitting one night on my way down South Baltimore to drop another Dummie off, and gave him the business. I hit that nigga with the entire clip of my heater. But, there was still some cleaning up to do because although Alien was dead and Itchy-Man was over in the city jail, Prince was out for blood and we wouldn't be waving the white flag any time soon.

I had just parked my Acura Legend and got out on Division Street when a Dummie named Calton 'G-baby' Gales came rushing around the corner with another soldier. "What's up, Dummie?" I questioned, looking from G-baby to Drako as they both began going off.

"Hold up," I cut them off. "Slow down, both of y'all can't talk at the same time!" I cautioned. "Right now, G- baby, tell me what happened."

G-baby took a deep breath and began. "The hoe ass nigga Ronnie-Moe and his man Tony-Bey pulls me up around on Division earlier tripping. Talking about niggas got to go. We can't hustle on Gold Street no more 'cause we been making shit hot."

"What?" I exclaimed in disbelief.

"That's not the end of it though," Drako warned, interjecting before G-baby could continue. "Tell him what that bitch ass nigga did."

"Oh yeah, so, as I'm standing at his truck telling him that's not happening, he grabs the hood of my jacket and pulls my head inside the truck. Then this bitch rolls the window on my neck right here—" G- baby paused to show me the long line indentation going across his neck and continued. "And drives around the block a few times." G-baby confessed, embarrassed.

"None of y'all wasn't strapped?" I questioned.

"Nah," Drako said. "The 'Green-Team' been out this bitch all morning jumping out on niggas."

I looked at G-baby and knew that his ego was bruised, but I didn't really know what to say. I was standing there, still trying to process everything. "Where the Fuck Nizzy and them at?" I questioned, looking around for Nizzy's truck.

"I don't know." G-baby hunched his shoulders. "But, I'ma bout to go grab the 'K' 'cause JuJu still around there talking to them niggas."

Drako was about to say something when JuJu came running around the corner, giving off the Dummie Squad's call for war, with Ronnie-Moe right on his heels. "Whoa, Ronnie-Moe!" I fired, blocking Ronnie-Moe's path. "Fuck is you doing?" I quizzed, pushing him back. I wasn't about to let nobody harm one of my niggas. Especially not a Dummie.

"Go grab that, G-baby!" JuJu ordered as Ronnie-Moe's partner Tony-Bey came flying around the corner.

"Hold up, Dummie, chill," I pleaded, trying to figure out exactly what the fuck was going on.

"Nah, Dummie, fuck that chill shit!" JuJu retorted. "This nigga just pulled a tone out on me."

"Huh?" I looked down at Ronnie-Moe's hand, dumbfounded. I hadn't even noticed the .357 at first. "Is you crazy, Ronnie-Moe?" I questioned seriously. "You pull a tone on my homie?"

"Ain't no more rap Dummie," JuJu spat, turning to G-baby again. "Dummie, go grab the 'K'."

"What, little nigga?" Ronnie-Moe challenged, coming forward.

"Chill, Ronnie-Moe yo," I warned, grabbing his wrist as G-baby took off down the street. "That shit not even for us," I added. I had known Ronnie-Moe and Tony-Bey since they were copping work from my sister's father. They had practically watched me grow up.

"What the fuck that suppose to mean?" Ronnie-Moe seemed to turn his attention towards me now. "What's not for us?" Ronnie-Moe questioned aggressively.

"Don't make me treat your little bitch ass out here, Charm!" Ronnie-Moe threatened. "And get the fuck off of my arm, nigga!" Ronnie-Moe snapped, snatching his wrist free.

"You got that, Ronnie." I submitted. Now wasn't the time to get off into no gangster shit. I was the only one strapped.

"I know I got that, bitch!" Ronnie-Moe fired.

"I heard that," I smirked arrogantly. Wasn't no sense in talking reckless in a no-win situation. Ronnie-Moe had the drop on me. "I don't want no smoke, homie."

"Y'all little niggas done around here," Ronnie-Moe said. "Shop closed!"

"Fuck outta here, niggas ain't going nowhere!" JuJu bucked when he saw G-baby jogging back down the block toward us in an oversized coat. "So, what's next?"

"Fall back, Dummie!" I commanded, trying to calm JuJu down. It was now too many witnesses present to be gambling with niggas' freedom. "So, that's what it is Bey?" I looked at Tony-Bey.

"Come on, Charm, you know y'all little niggas got shit extra hot around here with all that foolishness," Tony-Bey replied. "But, out of respect For Money Cola and your mother, I'm willing to let you live. However, the rest of them little niggas gotta go, flat out!"

"Don't take it personal, Charm," Ronnie-Moe laughed as

Juju huffed and puffed. "It's strictly business."

"You really got the game fucked up, if you think you really gonna run niggas off Gold Street," JuJu said, smiling as G-baby came up.

"Yeah, that's definitely not happening," Drake seconded confidently.

"Like I said," Tony-Bey spoke as if he wasn't paying Drake and JuJu any attention, "on the strength of Money Cola and Peaches, you can come in with us. It's all good. But the rest of your little team got to go."

I stood there transfixed. Frozen like a hare caught in the gaze of a snake. Closing shop or going against my squad was definitely out of the question. Honestly, I couldn't believe that Ronnie-Moe or Tony-Bey would even try me like that. I mean, I knew what JuJu had been saying, but I'd spared them both when the Mob had turned me on to and offered to rid the area of any competition. "Y'all niggas tripping," I shook my head in disappointment. "We ain't closing shop."

"You don't have a choice," Tony-Bey threatened, stepping forward. "You're either rolling with us or you're getting rolled over."

"That's funny," I said, unable to bite my tongue any longer. Even under the circumstances. "Because if you think—"

My head jerked back so fast that it took me a good second to realize that Tony-Bey had just put his hands on me. "Nigga!" I shouted, about to reach for my tone when I saw the front of a police cruiser out of the side of my eye. "Oh bitch, you a dead man!" I promised, as the officer came over the loud-speaker barking orders for us to clear the corner.

"That was your warning, Charm," Tony-Bey said, as Ronnie-Moe quickly slid the tone into his pocket while they backed off. "Take it or leave it, 'cause I won't give you another one."

"Fuck y'all old niggas!" JuJu exclaimed, looking from the police cruiser to G-baby as if he too considered his next move. "That's what's up."

I shook my head, forced to retreat at the moment. "Message received, but you're definitely going to answer for it," I assured Tony-Bey before he and Ronnie-Moe disappeared around the corner. I couldn't afford to go off. Especially at the moment; the police were already looking for me.

My pride was crushed. Disrespect was a major no-no in the streets, and Tony-Bey had just violated to the highest degree. I honestly couldn't get over the fact that this nigga had slapped me like I was a bitch. I had to make him wear that.

Once we got inside the traphouse, I called for an emergency 'Dummie' meeting and rapped to Drako about Nizzy until all the official 'Dummie Squad' members began to arrive. A lot of people were under the impression that there were more of us than there actually were. But, if truth be told, there were actually more Dummie Squad soldiers and wannabes than anything. Because just anyone couldn't be a 'Dummie'. First, a nigga had to be cut from a certain cloth. Then, he had to be hand-picked and agreed upon by every last official and active member, no exceptions.

"Listen, the reason why I called this meeting is because we're about to turn it up and a few changes are gonna have to be made. So, from now on, all three shifts will have an official Dummie standing watch at all times." I emphasized my point by looking at Nizzy before continuing to the main purpose of the meeting. "The first thing we need to do is make sure we're always available."

"Fuck is you looking at me for, nigga?" Nizzy played stupid but everybody knew that all he and Lor'Homie wanted to do was, chase bitches all day.

"Yeah, okay, you can play dumb all you want," I looked from him to Lor'Homie and shook my head. That tender dick shit must run in their family. "Anyway, for anybody who isn't familiar with what took place today, JuJu and G-baby had some static with Tony-Bey and Ronnie-Moe behind Gold Street. And Ronnie-Moe ended up putting his hands on me. So, I want everybody—"

"Yeah, I heard them old niggas been asking for it," an official East Baltimore Dummie Squad member named Jason Murdock fired after I laid out the new Dummie blueprint. "So, let me just go around there and give it to 'em real quick?"

I knew Murdock was the type of young nigga to wade into a pack of wolves for the squad. His motto was, *'he would rather be judged by twelve than carried by six'*. But, the shit with Ronnie-Moe and Tony-Bey was a little different. The streets were talking, so everybody basically knew about it now. Which meant we had to think strategically, if we wanted to lay these old niggas down and get away with it.

"Not this time, Dunmie," I said, after a short pause. "We got to study on this one. We got to overstand exactly what and who we may have to go against once we crack these niggas. Plus, we can't afford to lose no more Dummies. Deli already locked up."

"You hear this nigga?" Damon Lor'Homie Holmes joked. "We got to be strategic," Lor'Homie said. "Last week it was, *'we got to use our minds, not our eyes,'*" Lor'Homie continued, making everybody laugh. "Fuck you been reading, nigga? Let's just spend the bend and wear them old ass niggas out."

"Chill out, Cuzzo," Nizzy tapped Lor'Homie on his arm because he knew that I wasn't in a playing mood.

"I got to admit, I'm with Murdock and Lor'Homie on this one," Odie O Hill spoke up. "Everybody knows it takes blood to bring order."

"D's right, Dummie," Ryan 'Shaggy' McClain seconded, always ready to put in work under any circumstances.

"Yeah, all that sounds slick, but everybody out there heard what happened," JuJu said.

"Well, it ain't what you know, it's what you can prove." As always, Daniel 'Young Danny' Carter had to add his two cents.

"True, but we need to make sure our money still flowing." I looked to B for support. At nineteen, he was the oldest Dummie in the squad and everybody looked up to and respected him in one way or another—especially since he and my cousin Slate had actually started the 'Dummie' thing.

"That's what it is then," O said in agreement.

I nodded in appreciation. You see, another thing people didn't know was that there was no actual leader amongst us. Niggas were equal, and everyone had to earn their keep. The only reason I had the most say-so for real was because my cousin—Slate—was the founder. Besides that, I had the plug. Finally, apart from Murdock and Lor'Homie, I had put in the most work.

"A'ight, now check it, Shaggy, I want you to hold G-baby down out here tonight!" I declared.

"What about Tony-Bey and Ronnie-Moe?" Shaggy questioned.

"Fuck them niggas! Their little threats don't scare me. It's business as usual," I replied. Them old niggas were going to have to make a believer out of me because I wasn't easily shaken. "If they come back, y'all already know what it is."

"Say no more." Shaggy nodded.

"Cuzzo," Nizzy spoke up. "I want you to back Shaggy and G-baby up tonight just in case them old niggas decide to get stupid."

"You already," Lor'Homie agreed without hesitation. It was no secret that his trigger-happy ass was always ready to impress his cousin.

"Murdock, I'ma need you to come over here and hold the morning shop down for now because nobody really knows you," I said.

"You know I got that community service shit up," Murdock argued.

"Damn, I forgot about that," I admitted, looking around the room. "Well, we're gonna need somebody to cover the morning for now. At least until we handle this shit."

"I can hold it down on Mondays, Thursday and Fridays," Murdock volunteered. "But on the days they got swimming lesson, I can't do shit. They be all over a nigga to clean the pool."

"Hold up, Charm," G-baby spoke up. "I thought Drako had

the morning shift?"

"Not for the time being. I told you I want all official Dummies overseeing things."

I watched G-baby's face twist up like he'd just eaten a sourball. I knew Drako was his lil' apprentice. "What? I said something wrong, Dummie?"

"Nah, all is well." G-baby shook his head and fell back.

"Good, let Drako tag along with you tonight." I looked at Shaggy. "What about you, Dummie? You got a problem moving to the night shift for now?"

"Nah," Shaggy replied quickly.

"A'ight, Nizzy and I will rotate evening shift," I said. "And JuJu, you and Lor'Homie can handle the morning."

"You already know that I'm down for whatever," JuJu replied as Lor'Homie nodded.

"That's what I like to hear—Let's get up outta here before Ms.Candy get back—Y'all know how she get when it's too many Dummies in her shit," I said, and everyone immediately started moving. "Sit tight, Young Danny!" I ordered. "I want you to take a ride with me and Nizzy. We just got a delicate matter we need to attend to."

"Cool," Young Danny replied, sitting back down. It was time for him to earn his Dummie stripes.

Nizzy, Young Danny and I all sat outside, down the street from what turned out to be Prince's son mother's place in Sandtown, ready to carry out the Dummie Squad's form of 'poetic justice'. "You ready to earn your wings?" I questioned, breaking the silence.

"Yeah." Young Danny nodded.

"Don't play with that nigga, Dummie," Nizzy warned, ready to test Young Danny's heart. "Get right up on him and let him have it. All head shots too." The plan was for Young Danny to spank Prince because he had that baby face and wouldn't appear to be a threat because they didn't know him, of course.

***

So, by sending Young Danny, we had the upper hand. Shiddd, wasn't nothing fair about war; regardless of how you got your man, they still called it murder in the court of law.

"Don't be just nodding like shit cool," I fired, knowing first-hand that Prince could be more dangerous than the average gangster. "You better make sure you air that nigga ass out!"

"I will. Dummie, watch!" Young Danny assured calmly.

"A'ight then, handle your business," Nizzy encouraged.

"And snap a few pics of that nigga for the gram," I joked, as Young Danny got out of the car with the bag of cold ass McDonald's food and made his way down the street to sit on the steps near Prince's Mercedes-Benz C63 AMG 507 Edition. "You think he ready, Dummie?" I asked Nizzy.

"He better be because Prince definitely is."

Nizzy wasn't lying about that. I just hoped Young Danny didn't end up getting himself killed bullshitting.

It took about an hour for Prince to show his face. He came out of his son's mother's house, talking on the phone and stopped to observe the block for a good minute. So we knew that he was on point. However, he never really paid the young boy sitting on the steps eating much attention.

"Here we go," I mumbled, sitting up in my seat to get a better view of the action as Prince came down the steps and headed for his Benz.

"Fuck is he doing, Dummie?" Nizzy stole a quick look at me. "Why ain't he moving?" Nizzy questioned out loud. "This lil' nigga about to freeze up, Dummie."

"Come on, Young Danny—Represent, Dummie—Don't choke up on me, soldier," I said to myself, watching Prince approach his car as Nizzy continued to doubt Young Danny's heart.

I was just about to agree with Nizzy when the McDonald's bag in Young Danny's hand exploded. "Oh shit!" I jumped, caught off guard a little bit, as the impact of the first Kimber-

Warrior .5 round knocked Prince up against the side of his Benz. Young Danny quickly closed the distance and stepped over top of Prince.

"Damn! Young Danny a natural!" Nizzy said excitedly as Young Danny slowly stood over top of Prince and hit him in the head two more times. "Oh, yeah, young boy a savage!" Nizzy smiled as Young Danny pulled out his phone and began snapping photos.

"Oh shit!" I said, hitting Nizzy's leg as Young Danny's camera phone light flashed. "Go get this lil' nigga before we all end up in prison."

Nizzy started the car and drove down the streets. "Man, get your crazy ass in this car!" I ordered, looking at Prince's body stretched out in the streets when the car came to a jerking stop. His whole face was damn near gone.

Young Danny jumped in, and Nizzy mashed the gas, burning rubber. I knew that we were about to be the topic of every barbershop and beauty salon in Baltimore City for the move we'd just put down, because Prince was a major nigga in West Baltimore,

"What the fuck was you doing?" I questioned, looking over my shoulder, as we put some distance between us and the crime scene.

"You said snap some pics for the gram," Young Danny replied like he was as cool as a fan, and I could not do nothing but smile. For him to be the youngest Dummie in the squad, he carried himself like a vet.

"Give me that damn phone!" I demanded so I could break it up and melt the chip. When we pulled up on the block and found out what all the yellow crime-scene tape was about, our victory high was blown. Turns out that while we were out duck-hunting, Tony-Bey and Ronnie had decided to follow up on their threats. To add insult to injury, when we walked down the streets to where all the action had taken place, these old niggas had the nerve to be standing on the other side of the street grinning at us.

"Fuck nigga!" I mouthed to Ronnie-Moe, mad as ever,

knowing that it was time to strike back before my niggas begin to lose respect for me.

"Be cool, Dummie," Nizzy whispered to me as I continued to look across the street with rage in my eyes.

"You were supposed to be holding shit down!" I blamed Lor'Homie for Drako's death and Shaggy's trip to the emergency room.

"I was," he argued. "That shit just happened so fast."

G-Baby began, "He's not lying, Dummie. I didn't even realize it was Ronnie-Moe until he opened fire. I thought he was a fiend. He was in the line and everything."

"How the fuck Shaggy get hit?" Nizzy questioned.

"Standing down there with Drako bullshitting," Lor'Homie confessed.

"Fuck!" was all I could muster, disturbed as I stood there watching the police stuff another homie inside a body bag. "I should've never slept on them old niggas."

"That shit on all of us, Dummie," Nizzy put his hand on my shoulder.

I nodded, but honestly, I was hurt. Had I just let JuJu get at Ronnie-Moe from the jump, Drako would still be here. That was the second time I had made the same mistake. I wouldn't make it a third.

"A'ight, look, y'all niggas get up out of here before people start pointing fingers," Nizzy paused and then continued. "But, I want everyone at JuJu's house first thing in the morning."

"That's what's up." Lor'Homie nodded. "We're out."

"Catch you niggas in the morning," G-Baby said, giving Young Danny and I some love before following Lor'Homie.

"It's time to make an example out of these old niggas," Nizzy spoke calmly, staring across the street at Ronnie-Moe and Tony-Bey. All I did was, nod because no more needed to be said.

Chapter 7

"What did you expect to get out of a woman who all you fed were drugs, alcohol and sex?" Suf'yan questioned Wakal, as they made their way back to the housing unit with the other brothers coming from Jum'ah. "You didn't build anything of substance or install anything in her worth keeping."

"I was with that bitch five years, Ock!" Wakal fired, looking at Suf'yan. "What else am I suppose to do?"

"Look at you." Suf'yan shook his head. "There you go again disrespecting the sister." He never understood how a Muslim, or any conscious brother for that matter, could call his own woman a bitch and profess to be a man.

"Five years isn't nothing, Ock? I got workout shoes older than that."

Suf'yan laughed.

"You think you're special? You think you're the only brother in prison experiencing woman problems? Having a little rough patch?"

"Rough patch?" Wakal repeated. "My bitch gone!"

"I see why," Suf'yan said. "But at least you ain't got to deal with all that relationship bullshit. Some of these sisters on the phone just lying for no reason. Promising visits, sending pictures and money that never arrives. What's crazy to me though is some of these fools still dream and pray about going home to them. I wish the hell I would. Can't nothing honest be built on a lie."

Suf'yan paused. He didn't even know why he was even talking to Wakal about women.

He didn't even have a good eighteen months in yet and he was already going through the prison-honeymoon drama phase.

"So, I'm just supposed to forget about all the shit I did for her?" Wakal questioned.

Suf'yan looked at Wakal. He didn't want to crush his spirits, but he knew that as a Muslim, he had to speak the truth regardless of the circumstances. "Yeah, Ock, all that materialistic stuff doesn't mean anything. You didn't give her the things that counted."

"What about love?"

"What about it? Love's not everything, Ock. How many of us claim to love Allah only to turn around and act like the devil?"

"Yeah, but still," Wakal paused to gather his thoughts, "love has to mean something in a relationship."

"It does. It just takes more than love to have a good relationship, Ock. That's what a lot of people, especially women dealing with men in prison don't understand. You need respect, communication, commitment, honor, definitely faith and some more stuff."

Wakal just shook his head because he knew that Suf'yan would never understand how much Tiara had hurt him. How she had snaked him out even after he'd given her everything. "That's why I can't wait to win this appeal so I can—"

"Inshaallah," Suf'yan said, cutting Wakal off.

"You're right," Wakal said, knowing that things only happened by the permission of Allah. "Inshaallah. May Allah have mercy on me and I win my appeal. I'ma make everybody that ever wronged me feel it."

"You're something else, Ock," Suf'yan ran his hand over his beard and looked at Wakal. He didn't know if he was taking heed to the things he'd just said or not. But, he knew that if he was fortunate enough to make it back to the streets and he hadn't, he would end up like all the rest—back in a box or worst. "What's up with your move though?"

"Oh yeah, I forgot to tell you. My case manager said I'll probably be gone some time next month."

"Alhamdulillah," Suf'yan smiled but Wakal wasn't so sure that being moved over W.C.I.was a blessing.

"Don't forget to get word over there for me, Ock."

"I already took care of that," Suf'yan assured honestly. "I sent word to the Imam when you first put me down with your situation."

"Please make sure he got it, Ock," Wakal said. He had already given Suf'yan the spill about a possible on-going street beef with a kafir named Fat Tom, who'd tried to stab him over the jail behind a robbery and shooting. "I'm not trying to get caught down bad again!" Wakal warned, remembering how close Fat Tom had gotten to fucking him over the last time they'd crossed paths.

"I'm all over it, Ock," Suf'yan vowed, as they came up to the housing unit. He wasn't about to let one of his brothers get caught slipping, coming into a prison butt naked. That was how most dudes ended up late. "Honor's not only an ancient warrior's code, Ock. Don't let the crooked smile and humbleness fool you. I'ma make sure you got an *equalizer* (knife) as soon as you touch the compound."

"I heard *that*," Wakal said, satisfied. "The knife would make a sweet equalizer," he added in a whisper, smiling. One of the things that hadn't changed in prison or been a myth was a man's word. It was still bond. Wakal and Suf'yan greeted a couple of brothers and headed on inside the building.

***

"Damn girl!" Billy Lo fired, slowly stroking his greased up dick as he watched Shaneeka suck on a large black dildo on his cellphone screen. "Deep throat it for me," Billy Lo encouraged, reminiscing about how Shaneeka used to crawl up beside him, lay across his leg with her soft, pretty, hard-nippled breast resting on his hip as she ran her hands back and forth across his six-pack and sucked his dick nice and slow.

Shaneeka moved her head in small circles, as she rolled her tongue around the tip of the dildo, reminding Billy Lo of how she used to take him to the head-clinic when he was home. Then, she looked straight into the screen of the cellphone, mumbled something and deep-throated. "Like that, daddy?" she teased as the wet dildo slipped from her mouth.

"Yeah, baby, just like that," Billy Lo encouraged, stroking

his dick faster. He loved the way Sheneeka's little nostrils flared up and her eyes got watery as she deep-throated. Shaneeka smiled, took a deep breath, wiped her teary eyes and slowly began to stuff the 11-inch dildo down her throat again.

"I swear to fucking god!" Billy Lo exclaimed as his toes began to curl. On the real, he could wife Shaneeka off the head game alone. "You about to make a nigga bust!" Billy Lo squeezed his dick harder and tried to jerk extremely slow. That way, he could enjoy every second of the session.

"Fuck me, daddy," Shaneeka begged as she stroked the saliva-coated dildo and stared at him. "In my mouth!" she demanded, opening her mouth wide enough for the camera to see down her throat.

"Stick your tongue out, baby." Billy Lo grunted, as his nut shot across the cellphone screen, as if he was really nutting inside her mouth. "Good girl," Billy Lo said.

It was a blessing being housed in the infirmary alone. Billy Lo could still hear the slurping and sucking sounds Shaneeka'a mouth made, as he continued to watch her shove the dildo in and out of her mouth while he squeezed the last droplets of nut out of his dick. "You're too sexy to be that nasty," Billy Lo taunted as spit escaped the corners of Shaneeka's overstuffed mouth like cum when she tried to take the dildo a little too deep and gagged. "That's what you get for showing off."

"You love it though," Shaneeka teased, coming up for air. She knew from experience that nothing drove a man more crazy than a pretty woman who could give good slow-neck.

"You know I do." Billy Lo wiped the screen off with a cloth. "How you got a nigga all sleepy and shit!" Billy Lo felt like he'd just had real sex. That new face-time shit was the truth. It was almost like Shaneeka was in front of him. The image was so fucking real that he could literally see her pussy juices when she played with herself.

Shaneeka giggled, wiping her face off with the sheets. "You don't make no sense."

"That's your little freak ass," Billy Lo said.

"Who made me like that?" Shaneeka questioned with a serious look. "Exactly," she added when Billy Lo remained silent.

"On another note—" Billy Lo laughed because he knew she was telling the truth. He'd turned her little ass out. "Did you talk to Susan yet?"

"Susan?" Shaneeka gave a questioning look.

"Yeah, Susan Kerin—my lawyer."

"Oh, so y'all on the first name basis now?" Shaneeka rolled her eyes. "Let me find out."

"What? Shaneeka, stop playing with me." Billy Lo stared at her. There was nothing less attractive than an insecure woman. "Did you call my lawyer like I asked you to or not?"

"Oh, I called and her secretary said she was in a meeting. So, I'ma call back today when I come in from work."

"Make sure you tell her to come see me," Billy Lo ordered, knowing how hard it was to sneak a call in during the 7 a.m. to 3 p.m. shift.

"Okay, sleepy head," Shaneeka joked when Billy Lo yawned. "You just go ahead and get you some rest, old man and I'll talk to you tonight."

"Yeah," Billy Lo smiled. "Don't make me call up to your job and get that pussy. You remember how I had your ass walkin' around with no draws on the last time I made that motherfucker tender."

"Anthony, bye! I got to get ready for work."

"Yeah, that's what I thought," Billy Lo spat, satisfied. "I'll get with you later, baby."

"You better!"

"Billy Lo waited for the cell to disconnect, then decided to give India a call.

Strolling down his call log until he found the name, he hit the call button and waited for her to pick up.

"Hey, baby," India answered joyfully.

"Hey to you, sexy." Billy Lo smiled.

***

"You should've just asked him to text you," Murdock said, referring to Nizzy. "I don't trust talking on them phones nowadays. Text messages could land you in court. That shit like evidence you can't get rid of or something." Young Danny educated Murdock and me.

"Yeah, well, whatever," I said. Young Danny, Murdock and I were all posted up on Division Street. Right up the block from where Ronnie-Moe liked to lay up from time to time with the young bitch that he had strung-out off the dope-dick, waiting on Nizzy's call. At the moment, he and Lor'Homie were across town in Tony-Bey's bushes, literally. It was time to show these old niggas that times had changed and the streets were ours, rough and tough.

Nizzy and I had come up with the perfect plan. We all knew that Tony-Bey was the brains behind the operation and understood that wisdom was much stronger than aggression. So, we decided that Tony-Bey needed to go first. Then, we could turn Ronnie-Moe's hot-headed honor into a blinding, valuable weakness. Because we all knew that his loyalty and courage would make him react without thinking once he got wind of Tony-Bey's death.

"Oohh Dummie," I answered the instant my cellphone rang and listened carefully as Nizzy explained the situation. "That's what it is, we'll meet y'all back at JuJu's." I ended the call as Young Danny and Murdock looked on. "A'ight, they trashed Tony-Bey, so be on point. Because as soon as this bitch Ronnie-Moe show his face, we're doing him dirty."

We sat there for about twenty minutes before Ronnie-Moe came flying out of the house half- dressed, tussling with his young bitch. "Here he comes now. Tighten his ass up!" I ordered, as both Young Danny and Murdock took out their tones and started moving. "Don't let that nigga get in the truck!"

Ronnie-Moe must have really been full of blind rage because he didn't even sense the approaching danger until it was about to cost him his life. Murdock and Young Danny ran right up to Ronnie-Moe and remorselessly let him have it. The young bitch screamed and took off running. When I realized that I was going to have to assist Murdock and Young Danny because Ronnie-Moe wasn't just going to lay down easily, I rode down the street and jumped off my bike quickly. By the time I got to Ronnie-Moe, he'd dropped Murdock and somehow managed to jam his thick ass finger behind Young Danny's trigger to stop him from being able to fire his tone.

I ran up behind Ronnie-Moe and shot him twice in the back. Someway, somehow, he was able to elbow me in the face with enough force to rattle my teeth. The only thing that kept me on my feet was the fear of death.

"I'ma kill you little bitches!" Ronnie-Moe threatened with a wicked smile, closing his hand around Young Danny's neck, squeezing. "Yeah," Ronnie-Moe sniffed, lifting Young Danny up off his feet by the throat as all the color began to drain from his face.

"Let him go, bitch!" I struck Ronnie-Moe on the back of his head with the tone a split second before blood and brain matter went everywhere. Across my face, in my mouth, in my ear, and all over my clothes, as Ronnie-Moe and Young Danny fell. It took me a moment to realize that Murdock had just crushed Ronnie-Moe with a monstrous head shot.

Once I shook off the initial shock and got up, I helped Murdock roll Ronnie-Moe's slumped body off top of Young Danny. Then, I jumped back on my bike and got the fuck out of dodge, as Murdock and Young Danny took off running. I could not believe that that old nigga Ronnie-Moe had stood up underneath a hail of bullets like that—plus the two Sturm Ruger .357 rounds I had hit him with from the stainless-steel, 'Dirty Harry' style revolver. Especially after my man assured me that one shot could stop a bear. That nigga had to have that shit in his system.

I beat Murdock and Young Danny to JuJu's aunt house. But, once they got there and we all got cleaned up, we sat down to talk and wait for Nizzy and Lor'Homie. It was time to switch the hustle up. Especially after what we'd just went through with Ronnie-Moe and Tony-Bey.

"Oh, Nizzy's meeting with the connect in a few days," I said, bringing my niggas up to speed on our next line of action.

"Man, niggas don't know nothing about no *girl*—the coke, I mean," Young Danny confessed as I explained the coming changes.

"Don't worry about it, Ms. Candy go both ways." I informed, knowing Ms. Candy dabbled in both coke and heroin.

"You and Ms. Candy boy I tell you," JuJu interjected with a goofy ass smile.

Ignoring Juju's dumb ass with a wave, I continued to lay out our next line of action. "Nizzy's meeting with the connect in a few days to—"

"I just don't understand why we got to separate," Murdock admitted after I explained part of the plan.

"We're not," I assured him. "We're just branching out into groups, so we don't have to have all our eggs in one basket."

"The plan is to avoid what we just went through," I explained, looking at Murdock, wondering what words I could use to make him understand that once niggas sensed our mounting power, they'd join forces either consciously or unconsciously to bring us down. "The reason a lot of this just happen is because we're only really eating off one plate and everybody knows it. So, when shit jumps off we got to be out here, feel me?"

"You already know these fuck niggas gonna hate on the squad," Murdock argued. "That's what bitch niggas do, Dummie."

"True," I replied honestly, knowing that Murdock was right. Niggas were going be bitch niggas regardless. "But, we can't keep taking losses. Now imagine if we had been spread out. Then we would have easily closed shop with no problem at all and took care of business."

"I'm starting to like the sound of this," Young Danny spoke

up.

Just then, Nizzy and Lor'Homie came through the door.

"Especially since everybody gonna end up having their own shops," I continued. "Plus, I want to fall back on fucking with Ms. Candy's spot too much."

"I bet you do." JuJu laughed, grabbing the back of my head, playing.

"Stop playing, Dummie!" I hit JuJu with a body shot that curled him up before I continued. "Nah, but seriously, we know that success breeds envy, so we're going to need somewhere to lay our eggs."

"I told you I got some niggas out in Catonsville who about that paper," Nizzy said.

"Ohhh, I don't know about that, Dummie," I shook my head, really unsure. "The only thing I ever heard about Catonsville was that they be laying niggas down out there."

"That's why you got to fuck with someone from out there," Nizzy assured.

"We'll see," I said.

"I'm still lost," Murdock admitted with a confused look on his face.

"About what? The Catonsville dudes?" I questioned curiously.

"Nah, the whole branching out thing."

"Trust me, Dummie. The way we're going to put this shit together, nobody's even going to be able to tell the difference." I assured with a smile. "All we got to do is work out a few kinks and figure out who's gonna control what. I bet the sky won't even be a limit and everybody will still be eating."

Delmont Player

Chapter 8

Adnan Shyydie watched from the back room security monitors as Nizzy waltzed into 'Al-Fatihah' Oil and Incense Shop in Baby Mecca, like he owned the place, followed by Tariq Grandison and Rashid Salih. Since riots were erupting all across the city behind the recent killing of an unarmed, black teenager by a couple of western district cops, and people were looting businesses, Adnan had taken extra precautions. Adnan, like Tariq and Rashid Salih, had come in contact with Charm and Nizzy through an Italian business associate after the untimely demise of Don Delamonte and the major federal indictment of the Playorente Family.

Adnan's Italian friend had reached out to him from behind federal prison walls with an offer he could not refuse. To be more exact, if he agreed to supply Charm, he would be given the LEN French Connection and Golden Traingle pipeline, and his rodent problem would be taken care of. Adnan did not have to think twice. He knew that most hustlers thought the LEN pipeline was a myth. But honestly, next to the Buram, Laos, Thailand routes, the LEN controlled the purest heroin entering the United States.

"I like this kafir," Adnan gestured towards the monitors, talking to Yah-Yah—one of the newest members of his security detail—a dark-skinned, bald-headed, nappy salt-and-pepper bearded, Jamaican brother whose murder game was without question. Adnan had taken him along when he killed a brother named Samad Knight to keep him from testifying in front of the federal grand jury. The two had kidnapped Samad and taken him out to Yah-Yah's great-grandfather's farm and fed him to a pig-pen full of wild hogs. "He's young, but he's not dumb. So, he's gonna have a bright future in the streets."

Yah-Yah looked at the big headed, popping-eyed, straight-haired, bearded Pakastani Imam, and nodded. He too had taken a liking to Nizzy. Especailly after he and one of his little sidekicks had driven all the way out to North Philly and knocked off

Tariq's son to spare him the embarrassment of seeing him cooperate with the government in an on-going investigation into a major narcotics distribution ring.

There was a light tap on the office door a second before Tariq, Nizzy and Rashid Salih walked in.

"As-salaam-alaikum," Adnan came around the desk and extended his hand. "How you doing?"

"Cooling," Nizzy replied, giving Adnan a firm handshake. "I ain't got no complaints." '

"Good. It's always a pleasure to know that all your people are happy." Adnan stepped back and sat down on the edge of his desk. "So, tell me what this urgent meeting is all about." Adnan clasped his hands together and placed them on his lap, and waited for Nizzy to locate a seat and get comfortable. He hadn't seen or spoken directly to him or Charm since they had agreed to clean up the Philadelphia situation with Tariq's son, to make up for the botched hospital hit.

"Well, first, we want to expand our territory into East and South Baltimore. Charm's lil' sister's uncle found us a couple nice spots." Nizzy paused. "We also want to tap into the cocaine and maybe even pharmaceutical market because we're looking at some locations out in Maryland that may be wide open."

Adnan smiled. "I always did love expansion. New territory means more real estate, which equals more money. The thing is, you keep saying 'we'. But, you haven't explained to me yet how I can benefit from all this."

Nizzy looked Adnan straight in the eyes and laid out, in details, the plans he and Charm had.

"So, what exactly is it that you need from me?" Adnan questioned, after a long moment of silence once Nizzy finished laying out the money-making blueprint.

"Besides your blessing," Nizzy replied, "we're gonna need a heavier heroin shipment and a steady cocaine connect."

Adnan smiled again. He really did like Nizzy and respect his hustler's ambition. "Are you sure this is what you want? I mean, I want to be sure that you both have thought this through.

Because the eyes has a way of lying to the brain and tricking the stomach. And before you know it, you got more on your plate than you can actually eat."

"I'm good," Nizzy assured. "I would never take more than I can eat because I've never been greedy."

"Well, in that case y'all have my full support." Adnan got up off the desk and extended his hand again. He had a Muslim brother out in Iran that had some of the best coke on the face of the earth.

"We appreciate it." Nizzy stood up and shook Adnan's hand to seal the deal.

"I always take care of my friends." Adnan looked at Tariq. "Ock, make sure you set them up with Big Al and E-Don. Because if they plan to set up a major shop anywhere in East Baltimore, they'll have to clear it with them or be ready to clash with them."

"Big Al and E who?" Nizzy inquired with a grin. Adnan must not have understood who he was dealing with. The Dummie Squad were more ruthless than ISIS.

"Don't worry about it—I'll take care of it," Tariq assured Nizzy. He admired both Charm and Nizzy's heart. But, Big Al and E-Don were on another level. They had most of the East Baltimore drug turf in a cobra's clutch, and neither one of them had any problem going to the extreme to keep it that way.

***

Wakal sat in one of holding cells, mad as hell. After being humiliated—strip-searched and basically sexually violated—by several red-neck correctional officers, who seemed to have an infatuation for the sight of a black man's dick when he first arrived, he had went on to play all type of homosexual 'Simone Says' games. "Open your mouth, lift your sack, separate your package, lock your legs, bend over at the waist, spread your cheeks, hold still—" Wakal had his ears and eyes open from the moment he arrived at the Western Correctional Institution and entered the holding cell.

Wakal got more anxious every time someone he knew or recognized looked inside the small holding cell and acknowledged him on their way to or from property. Because he knew from experience that reputations were like ID-numbers in prison. They followed you everywhere you went, be it for the good or the bad. Sometimes they were all you had.

"Man, they say this joint wide open compared to the North Branch," a short, chubby, light brown- skinned, clean-shaved, fat-faced dude with a fresh pair of Jordan's on spoke up, as they waited to be processed with everybody else.

"Yeah, I heard," Wakal admitted for the sake of conversation, snapping out of his daze.

The fat-headed dude continued. "My rap buddy—Juice—and my man, Nutty-Bar, sleep over in housing unit three. So, that's where I'm trying to go at. I haven't seen them niggas since we were all over the jail in ninety-seven together."

"I'm just hoping these crackers let me hit the compound," another big, red, pot-belly dude with freckles said, as he continued to pace the holding cell, making everybody nervous. "Last time I was over here, these bitches they tried to play games with my wife, and I ended up breaking one of them whores jaw!"

Wakal only heard half of whatever it was that dudes were talking about. Honestly, his mind was somewhere else. He was silently praying that word of his arrival had already reached the Imam, and not Big Paul. So, he could care less about a bunch of dudes sitting around in the holding cell trading old penitentiary war-stories, missing their cousins and rap buddies.

"Okay, guys, listen up!" an extremely tall, rat-face looking C.O. finally poked his head into the holding cell. "When I call your name, step outside and line up on that wall there—" He pointed. "Artist! Derrick Bell! Arron Holly-El, John Satterfield! And ummmmm—White! Let's go! Move your asses!"

"Man, you better watch who the fuck you talking to," the big dude with the freckles warned, walking out of the holding cell.

"Ain't no question," seconded the Moor brother with the

black and gold crown on.

Wakal followed the other dudes out of the holding cell, and lined up on the wall as instructed. Then he watched the C.O lock the holding cell door, as another C.O. approached to double check our identities. "Artist, Bell, Holly-El, Satterfield—"

"Yeah," Wakal nodded, stepping forward at the sound of his name.

"Follow me." The C.O. led Wakal down the hallway to one of the small offices where everybody was getting processed. "Have a seat." He pointed to a chair near the door, as they entered the small room.

"So, how are you this morning, White?" the captain asked, making his way around the desk to take his seat.

"I'm okay," Wakal replied.

"Good," he said, flipping open a large brown folder. "Well, allow me to introduce myself. My name is Captain Softball. I am the head of intel. And as I am sure you are aware we have been having a lot of gang problems over here as of late. So, I just need to ask you a few questions, okay?"

"That's cool." Wakal nodded. After the usual questions concerning Wakal's sentence and charge, Wakal was asked if he had any known enemies at the institution and or if he was gang-affiliated. Once Wakal finished answering all the captain's questions in the negative, he was informed that he would be placed in housing unit #5 on 'temporary housing' until a bed in the general population became available. Then, he was directed to the property room.

Wakal was as nervous as an ex-con with a car full of loaded guns during a traffic stop, when he walked out of the captain's office and headed towards the property room. The property room bullpen wasn't crowded. Most of the dudes who'd come in with Wakal early were still being interviewed, but that didn't stop him from putting his back against the wall, keeping a close eye on the door after handing his ID to the property officer behind the counter. He'd seen the officer pass his ID off to one of the working men, and figured that he had a better chance of fending off something that he could see coming.

When Wakal was called to get his property, he stepped up to the counter and accepted his ID back. "As-salaam-alaikum," the dark-skinned property worker with the slick glasses greeted. "I see you made it."

"Huh?" Wakal looked around, playing dumb. "You talking to me."

"Yeah, Wakal, right?" He smiled, adjusting his glasses.

"Yeah," Wakal admitted cautiously. He overstood that just because a brother salaamed you and shared the same faith didn't always make him a friend.

"I've been waiting for them to call you all morning," he said. "You know Suf'yan, don't you?"

"Oh, my bad, Ock," Wakal let out a nervous laugh and relaxed. Suf'yan hadn't told him that the Imam worked in the property room. "Walaikum salaam. I didn't know who you were at first." Wakal stuck his hand across the counter. "You don't look nothing like Suf'yan described."

"Oh, nah, Ock, I'm not Ameen," the brother quickly corrected with a sincere laugh and slight smile. "My name is Jihad. Some people call me G-Money, though. I'm on security. Ameen gave me your name and told me to be on the look out for you."

"Oh, a'ight," Wakal replied, finally understanding. "How can I hook up with the Imam? 'Cause they got me going to something called temporary housing."

"Don't even trip," Jihad reached behind the counter and passed Wakal an extra towel and wash cloth. "You're only going to be down there a couple days at the most. We're gonna get you pulled down housing unit two with us first thing smoking."

"So, ummm like, ahhh," Wakal was trying to find his words. "Temporary housing is, like, what? Can anybody come down there? Do we get yard?"

"You're good, Ock," Jihad assured. "Ameen already told us what's up. And I pulled straight up on Wise Truth."

"Wise Truth?" Wakal repeated curiously.

"Yeah, Thomas Cook, Fat Tom, or whatever you use to call him," Jihad said. "He goes by Wise Truth now. I think he's in the Nation of Islam. Anyway, I rapped to him about y'all situation and that's dead."

"Just like that?" Wakal looked at Jihad. He'd cranked on Fat Tom behind robbing and pistol-whipping his cousin around Hollins and Pulaski.

"Yeah, Ock, dudes don't be on that city jail and street stuff in here. Niggas trying to get home to their families. All that street shit not about nothing. The streets don't love nobody but the streets."

"Thanks." Wakal was honestly thankful that that was one less situation he had to worry about. Now, he had to figure out what he would do about Big Paul because now, he was right in his back yard. Wakal and Jihad chopped it up while the other property worker got his property together, and he began to feel better. Suf'yan had come through. Wakal sat all his property down inside the moving cart, so the boxes with his government name scribbled across them in large, black letters weren't visible, and laid his mattress over the top.

"Don't forget to holler at the brother Kaamil when you get on the tier—He's the tier wezeer down there," Jihad said, handing Wakal his bedroll. "I think he's in cell nine. You can't miss him though. Stocky, brown skin brother around five-ten with a raspy voice and unconnected baby beard. He got something real nice for you just in case, you feel me?"

"Good looking out, Ock," Wakal replied wholeheartedly. There wasn't anything worse in prison than walking into a dangerous situation blind and butt-naked.

"Ain't nothing to it—We look out for our own," Jihad guaranteed. "Inshaallah, we can get you moved in the morning. If not, I'll just see you in the big yard."

"Bet," Wakal tossed the bedroll into the cart and pushed it towards the exit. "As-salaam-alaikum, Ock."

"Walaikum salaam," Jihad replied, stacking the next men's papers and boxes up on the counter top for processing as Wakal went out the door. "Holly-El!"

Wakal hit the compound and pushed his cart down to temporary housing without incident. There were colorful flowers and fresh cut grass similar to that of a college campus. At one point he did witness what appeared to be a press-up in progress. At least a nigga was getting his pockets ran, but decided not to stop and draw a tip. One of the first laws of survival he'd learned in prison was, to mind your goddamn business. So, that's exactly what he decided to do.

"What's your name, bud?" a big, six foot four, sweet-smelling, two-hundred-and-something pound guard asked, before spitting some chewing-tobacco into the cup in his hand, looking at the tier roster when Wakal got to the building.

"Donald White," Wakal replied.

"White—White—" the guard mumbled repeatedly out loud to himself, running his eyes down the roster. "Gotcha!" He looked up. "Okay, bud, you're going down there just past the washer and dryer to cell twenty-three." He pointed as if there weren't huge white numbers painted on the doors. "Everybody's out in the yard right now. But, you can get a shower if you like."

"Yeah, I gotta get my shower grip out though," Wakal explained, very familiar with the 'bud' acronym. His uncle had told him all about the 'black uneducated dog' years ago.

"So where are you coming from? Down the road? I use to work at Roxbury back—" He began asking a thousand questions, following Wakal down the tier. "Open cell twenty-three," he radioed and continued talking about nothing. Wakal wanted to tell him to shut the fuck up. Instead, he stroked his ego and played along. Because Suf'yan had told him when he first arrived at North Branch that it was better to treat the male guards how they smell, and the female guards how they looked and he'd be okay.

Wakal pushed the cart right up to the door and looked inside the cell. Instantly, he could tell that nobody had occupied the space for a good while because there was dust and trash everywhere. "Come on, man," Wakal looked at the C.O.

"Looks like you got your hands full, bud," the guard said, peeping into the dirty cell. "You're going to have to scrub-a-dub-dub."

"Can I get something to clean up with?" Wakal asked.

"I'll see if I can have one of the workers bring down a bar of soap when they come in from the yard." He spat some more chewing-tobacco into his cup. "That's the best I can do. Bell cleaning's on Sunday though."

'*What the fuck am I suppose to do with a bar of soap?*' Wakal thought, staring at him. "I'm good, thanks." Wakal pushed the cart into the cell and stepped inside. "I'll just wait till Sunday."

"Suit yourself." He signaled for the control center to secure the cell door before wiping off the thick, brown chewing-tobacco juice that leaked out of his mouth and rolled down his chin. "Give me a holler if you still want that shower or whenever you're done with the cart bud," he added, wiping his hand off on his work pants as the cell door closed.

After the door slid closed, Wakal just stood there for a second, shaking his head, looking around the filthy cell. Then, he threw his mattress up on the top bunk, busted one of the boxes open, grabbed some soap power, asked Allah for some patience, and went to work.

Chapter 9

Things seemed to be going exactly as planned. First, Adnan increased our delivery. Then, he came through with probably the sweetest cocaine connect on the East Coast. Not only was the cocaine doing numbers, but the prices were so right that we couldn't do nothing but flood the city. We were moving weight, slinging pills, hitting niggas on consignment, and setting up shop all over West Baltimore with our famous yellow tops. JuJu and Lor'Homie had all day shop up Whitelock. Lor'Homie had North Avenue & Pulaski jumping. Young Danny and Murdock basically took over the East Baltimore projects that my sister's uncle had turned us on to—after E-Don and Big Al gave Adnan the green light of course. Shaggy, who by now was out of the hospital on crutches, was jamming around on North & Warwick. G-baby, however, decided to hold Gold Street down all by himself, despite the police heat and possible project retaliation. The only problem up until today was the fact that Deli was still over the jail waiting on a trial date because Thugg's bitch ass was now telling on any and everybody he knew for a fact had something to do with the Wild-West project shootout. Including his own brother Itchy-Man. I was so glad I'd never pulled my scarf down. I rubbed some cold water on my face to calm my nerves. I had to get my 'G' in check. The text message I'd just received had me ready to go off. First, Shaggy's Warwick trap was hit, and now some silly ass niggas had just robbed G-baby and shot one of his runners around on Gold Street.

'*Calm down, Dummie,*' I told myself, staring at my reflection. I didn't know if it was due to the fact that the crime rate had increased drastically since the riots, police weren't responding to calls quick enough, or simply because niggas were feeling stupid. Whatever the case, it seemed like a gangster's work was never done. Not today. I thought of sending my phone straight to voice mail as the next call came through. I'll deal with this shit later. Today, I just wanted to be left alone to enjoy Ebony's company. She'd invited me up to the college to see her play, and I planned on enjoying it. I filled my cupped hands with cold water one more time and ran them over my face again, then exited the bathroom in route back to the auditorium. Intermission was just about over, and I didn't want to miss the rest of my baby performance.

I took my seat about five minutes before Ebony came back out onto the stage dressed as a young, black, modern female panther named 'Afeni' in a play called 'BLM#21'. It was a story about black love and the strength of black women during the mass incarceration and genocide of black men in Amerikkka. I wasn't feeling the fake ass, wannabe 'Mutula'—or whatever his name was—kissing and touching all on my baby. Beyond that, I truly enjoyed the show. It was very educational and taught me a lot of things I didn't know about Baltimore's connection to the black power movement. I went outside and waited while Ebony went and got changed. I heard people talking about how good Ebony was, and I had to admit she was. That much couldn't be denied. At the end of the show there was even a standing ovation.

"Charm." I heard a familiar voice and looked up to see Cat—Mumbles' old girl—walking towards me.

"Oh shit yo, what's up?" I embraced Cat with a warm, brotherly hug.

"I thought that was your lil' ass," Cat confessed, breaking the embrace. "You got all big and shit."

"I know," I smiled. "So, how you been doing though?"

"I'm good. Working and going to school."

"What? You go to Coppin?" I asked, surprised.

"Nah, my college days are over," Cat laughed. "I go to business school downtown. I was just up here checking out my cousin's 'Black Loves Matters 21' play."

"Yeah, me too," I said. "My girl was playing Afeni."

"Your girl?" Cat repeated, and I couldn't tell if she was more surprised by the fact that I actually had a girl, or that I was really growing up.

"Yeah, my girlfriend," I smiled again. "What? I said

something wrong?"

"Maybe," Cat replied.

"Come on now, sis. You know them good girls love bad guys."

"Boy, I can't with you." Cat shook her head. "Anyway, I gotta run. Give me your phone so I can put my number in it." She reached for my phone. "Make sure you call me because we definitely need to talk."

"I heard that," I said, as Cat walked off mumbling something about 'girlfriend my ass!' I was watching Cat climb into a tinted out, creme-colored, 929 Mazda, when Ebony appeared out of nowhere with an arm full of roses, stuffed animals and chocolate.

"You okay, baby?"

"Yeah," I replied, leaning up off the car to give her a kiss. "I was just zoned out thinking about Mumbles," I admitted. I would give anything to go back to when my lil' sister and Mumbles were alive.

"You ready to go?"

"Ain't no question." I walked around and opened the passenger seat door for her. "You did good too."

"Thanks, I was trying to impress you anyway." Ebony gave me that look.

"Impress me how?"

"By letting you know that I know how to play my part." Ebony kissed me again.

"It worked." I smiled.

I gently closed her door and walked back around to the driver's side. As I unlocked the door, Cat drove by, hitting the horn. I nodded, opened the car door and slid behind the wheel. "Who was that?" Ebony questioned, as soon as I pulled the driver's side door closed.

"You jealous?" I joked.

"Don't play!" Ebony warned with seriousness in her voice. "Who was that?"

"That was my man old girl."

"Oh," Ebony said, satisfied. "So what now?"

"I don't know—You tell me." I said, down for whatever. "It's your night. You wanna go out to eat or something?"

"I was thinking we could go to my house, watch a movie on Netflix and chill," Ebony teased, reaching over to run her soft hand up the inside of my leg to fuck with my mind. She knew I was dying to get up in that pussy again.

"Yo, don't even play like that," I warned.

"Play like what? You don't wanna Netflix and chill?" Ebony squeezed my dick. "Better yet, what if we just skipped the movie and straight fucked?"

"Oh, you ain't got to say no more!" I exclaimed, unable to start the car quick enough. I prayed that Ebony wasn't playing because I hadn't been putting in all this lovey-dovey, date-night overtime for nothing. The last time we were together, she just let me eat her pussy for an hour straight and then kicked me out with a hard dick.

The moment we were locked inside of Ebony's house, it was on. Ebony told 'Alexa' to play her 'play-list' and India Arie's 'Brown Skin' began playing throughout the house. Ebony pushed my back up against the front door and started tonguing me down, as my hands went straight to her phat ass. I loved the feel of that thick mother fucker. I shook it to test the weight. *'Yeah, that's all beef,'* I thought, squeezing Ebony's cheeks together and pulling them apart.

"Damn, you phat as shit," I mumbled in between kissing and sucking on Ebony's lip. I felt the pressure on my shoulders, as Ebony forced me down to my knees, mumbling something about, 'betting me that I wasn't able to eat her pussy better than I'd the last time'. I smiled, pushed her skirt up, snatched her thong off, told her to 'bet', and went to work. She didn't know who she was fucking with. When it came to pussy-eating, I had graduated at the top of my class with honors. Ebony threw her leg over my shoulder, cupped the back of my head gently and looked down at me.

"Go ahead, get that money." Ebony rolled her hip in my face, but all I did was look up and smile. "You better eat it good too."

I pressed my face into Ebony's pussy and inhaled deeply. There was nothing in the world like the smell, look and feel of a woman's pussy—especially when it was good. I softly kissed Ebony on the inside of her thighs, and slowly licked my way up to her pretty pussy. I took my time and proceeded to passionately feast on Ebony's pussy.

"Hmmmm!" Ebony panted and shivered, as I carefully parted her pussy lips and deliberately attacked her clit. Ebony's was extremely juicy, like a fresh orange that had just fallen from a Florida tree. However, it was the intoxicating, delicious sweet taste that honestly made me want to eat her alive. I sucked, kissed, licked, nibbled and tried to devour Ebony's pussy, tenderly teasing her clit. I did this trick where it seemed like I was repeatedly trying to tie her clit into a knot and swallow it whole, and it drove Ebony nuts. However, all she could do was, clutch my head, dig her heel into my back, beg me not to stop, shiver and cum. But, I was far from finished. Now, it was time to turn her out.

"What are you doing?" Ebony questioned, out of breath, when I suddenly stopped eating her pussy. "Ain't nobody tell you to stop."

My mother had told me over and over again how much women loved having their pussies eaten from behind. "I want to show you something," I replied, prying myself from Ebony's grip before spinning her around to face the door so I could really get at that pussy. "Put your hands up on the door and lean forward for me," I instructed, reaching over to grab one of the chocolate drops out of Ebony's candy box.

"You about to eat it like this?" Ebony questioned, looking back over her shoulder, all sexy.

"Just put your hands flat on the door and arch your back like I told you!" I slapped Ebony on her ass. "Yeah, just like that," I admitted, as she complied. "Now, don't move!" I ordered, letting my eyes wander along the gentle slope of her back.

Ebony had that soft chocolate skin that looked like it had

been baked in the hot sun all day. Unable to wait one more second, I carefully placed my hands up under the cups of Ebony's ass cheeks, and pushed up until that phat mother fucker began to crack open for me. I slowly inserted the chocolate drop into her soft, wet pussy and ran my tongue up and down the crack of Ebony's ass. Ebony was so phat that I had to literally hold her ass cheeks apart and turn my head sideways to get to her clit from the back. I teased her clit and slowly licked her from her clit all the way up to her asshole. I repeated this until her pussy got so hot that the chocolate began to melt and leak out.

"Sssshit!" Ebony barked, pushing her ass back into my face. "Boy, you eat pussy like a grown man! Put your tongue in my ass!"

I paused for a second to pull back and get one more good look at Ebony's lovely, little chocolate covered pussy before turning my attention to her asshole. It was slightly open, but tight, so I thought, 'fuck it', licked around her asshole again, made my tongue into a firm point, and stick the tip of that motherfucker right on up in there.

"Deeper!" Ebony directed, leaning completely up against the door before reaching back to hold her ass cheeks wide open. "That's it—sssss—ohhhhh—" Ebony twisted her hips, went up on her toes, and continued to force-feed me. "You—you—gonna—make—make—me—cu—cu—cum—again."

I kept working my magic until she started to shake and cum again.

"Clean your plate, baby," Ebony said. She panted, shook, and kept grinding her ass and pussy back and forth across my tongue. "Clean your plate." Once I had that pussy squeaky clean, we both got completely naked and made our way towards the bedroom. Ebony had those dick-sucking lips, and I was hoping like shit she was finally about to show me if she knew what to do with them. When we got to the bedroom, Ebony went inside the nightstand and tossed me a condom. Then, she crawled across the bed and started playing with herself. If she was trying to drive me crazy, it was definitely working.

"You ready, baby?" Ebony teased her clit, slowly rubbed her finger up and down her pretty pussy lips, penetrated herself a few times, and sucked the juices off her finger. Then, she leaned back, spread her legs open and cocked them all the way back. "Come get this pussy!" Ebony ordered as I slid the condom on. Now, I was starting to believe what my mother always said about women. When it came to bedroom sports, they were in a class all by themselves. I stood at the foot of the bed and stroked my dick a few times before dragging Ebony to the edge of the bed and slowly sliding my dick into her tight pussy. I had to take a deep breath when the heat and wetness of her pussy hit me through the condom.

"Damn!" I fired, shaking my head. It should've been illegal for a bitch's pussy to be that good. "What the fuck! Your insides made of lava?" Ebony's pussy was dangerously hot. I took my time because honestly, I had never felt anything this good in my entire life. It was better than the last time, and I wanted to make love to that pussy.

"Don't get up in there and start playing. I'm trying to fuck!" Ebony exclaimed. I swear to God, her pussy muscles did some shit I couldn't explain.

"I got you." She didn't have to tell me twice. I locked her legs around my arms, planted my feet up on the bed, and started pounding away. That pussy was deep too, but I could still feel Ebony's pussy muscles working like they had a mind of their own, as I slid in and out of that hot pussy.

"Unn-hn, get up!" Ebony demanded, pushing on my chest. "Watch out. You're not getting deep enough like this."

I backed up so she could roll over onto her stomach and get up on her hands and knees before falling face first into a pillow, and reaching back to spread her ass cheeks wide open again. "If you can't hit it right like this, then we might as well call it a night. 'Cause, I'm trying get fucked good and deep. I'm talking about I want you to touch the bottom, like you're trying to break something."

"I got you." I edged back up to the plate between Ebony's legs.

"You said that a minute ago," Ebony reminded, staring at me questionably, as I rubbed my dick just around the rim of her soft, mushy looking insides to get it wet.

"I got you," I assured, slapping Ebony on her ass and entering her at the same time. It was time to lay some serious pipe.

"That's right! Punish this pussy!" Ebony shouted, pushing all the pillows off the bed so that she could lay face down with her ass up. "Ohhhh—that's it! Beat that pussy up! Get it, baby! Make it go deeper for me, daddy!"

Ebony continued to throw her jiggling ass back at me and talk shit. I grabbed Ebony's hips, and continued slamming into her, as her big ole ass was wobbled all over the place. I was going balls-deep, trying to hurt something.

"Yeah—that's it!" Ebony shuddered and groaned through clenched teeth. "There you go, baby! Make it talk, daddy!" Ebony's mouth fell open, as she panted over and over again. "Ahhhh, baby, if you keep hitting it like that, I'ma let you have it anyway you want it tonight!"

I didn't respond. I just grabbed Ebony by her hair, pulled her head up, and continued to tear that pussy up. It was going to be a long night because I was definitely trying to get some of that slow neck and phat ole ass before the night was over. "I'ma hold you to that too!" I assured, slapping Ebony across her ass as I began to fuck her harder.

***

"Allahu Akbar—Allahu Akbar—Ash hadu alla ilaha illallah—Ashhadu anna Mohammadar rasulullah—" Wakal got to his feet and lined up in the fourth ranks between two brothers after listening to the Muezzin call the Iqamah. It felt great to be amongst the brotherhood. But, he still couldn't get his mind off of the old-looking, gray-haired brother fondly known as Big

Paul. From the way Diamond used to talk about him, Wakal had almost expected to see a giant. However, when Kaamil—who had turned out to be none other then Lil' Dray's cousin, Sleepy, from North & Chester—had actually pointed Big Paul out to him in the big yard, and informed him that he'd taken his shahadah and now went by Shabazz, all Wakal saw was the end to another one of Diamond's legendary penitentiary myths.

It had only taken Wakal a few days to figure out that WCI was just like North Branch, and the Annex. full of a bunch of followers, get-withs, and crush-dummies dying to make a name for themselves. Add to that, the lazy ass, racist guards, drugs and cheap value for human life, and you had a recipe for disaster. That is exactly why Wakal kept the butcher's knife, or equalizer—as Suf'yan liked to call it—on him at all times.

After prayer, Wakal made his way out of the make-shift mosque, along with everybody else, and waited for Ameen and Jihad—as he'd been instructed that afternoon when they'd left the housing unit together. Wakal posted up across the hallway from the exit, and watched as brothers stood around talking about everything from Ameen's khutbah to a few things that was sure to earn them a spot in the hell-fire, if they weren't careful.

"Jihad!" Wakal called out the moment he saw Jihad, Kaamil and Ameen spilling out of the mosque that doubled as a gym, where they'd just attended Ju'mah service. "Over here!"

"Assalaam alaikum, Ock!" Jihad greeted, walking over to Wakal first, followed closely behind by Kaamil and Ameen.

"Walaikum assalaam," Wakal replied.

"Where Shabazz go?" Ameen questioned, looking around.

"He already left out with a couple brothers," Wakal said. He still wondered how the old mobster had managed to find Islam and become Muslim.

"Yeah, I told him to wait for us up by the school, because I didn't want everybody in our business when we all got together," Kaamil said. "Brothers already running around whispering."

"Ameen and I told Kaamil about the situation with between you and Shabazz," Jihad said when he saw the confused look on

Wakal's face.

"Oh," was all Wakal said, although he'd already put Kaamil down with the whole lick.

"Yeah, we had to," Ameen seconded. "He's the head of security."

"You ain't got to worry about that though, Ock," Kaamil said, confidently playing along. "That's dead," he added. "Shabazz already know what time it is up here. This not the 'Cut'."

Wakal just nodded and followed Kaamil down the hallway. He had already told him how a lot of the brothers in the community felt a certain type of way about the stunt Shabazz had pulled in the 'Cut' with Diamond. And as if having Diamond stabbed to death wasn't bad enough, the fact that Shabazz—who had also allowed two kafirs (non-believers)—was a kafir at the time it was carried out had only made it worse.

"It doesn't make a difference!" Ameen stressed, as Wakal explained how the whole beef started between he and Shabazz again, as they continued towards the school.

"Shabazz ain't doing nothing to no brother about no old street foolishness that he shouldn't have been involved in the first place."

"Yeah, the Imam's right—That's your past life—Your blood is sacred now and that's it," Kaamil agreed.

"Yeah, that's how I feel," Wakal said, thinking about everybody that he'd lost during their feud. The family, the friends, everything. "Shabazz ain't the only one that took a loss."

"Like I said, that stuff is over—We're all brothers in here." Ameen rubbed his beard, as they turned the corner, and saw Shabazz leaning up against the school building wall talking with two younger brothers. "Plus, we got enough to worry about, dealing with these white folks and gangs up here already. So, if Shabazz got a problem with that then he's gonna have to deal with me."

Wakal hadn't known Ameen very long, but he liked him already. The husky, baldhead, big-bearded, pigeon-toed

Washingtonian was always down to make the ultimate sacrifice when it came to the community. Now, Wakal understood why he was the Imam. Everything Suf'yan had said about him was true. And Wakal didn't know too many brothers who'd lost their passion for the game, yet managed to hang on to their morals and principles as a man.

"Assalaamu alaikum," Ameen greeted Shabazz and the two brothers standing with him, before shaking hands.

"Walaikum assalaam," Shabazz and them replied in unison.

"Listen, let us holler at Shabazz real quick," Jihad said, gesturing for the younger brothers to step off.

"Nah, I want them to hear *this*, Ock!" Shabazz declared. Not only did he want Latif and Shaheed to hear what was being said so that he had a witness. But, he also lived by the motto 'safety first', and Shaheed was strapped, so he definitely wanted him close by just in case Kaamil and Jihad got on some dumb shit. He knew exactly how they felt about him behind Diamond's punk ass.

"Maybe next time, Ock," Ameen said. "They ain't got nothing to do with this.

"Shaheed does!" Shabazz retorted.

"What Shaheed got to do with you and Wakal?" Jihad challenged, agitated.

"His cousin got killed," Shabazz said.

Ameen didn't feel like going back and forth with Shabazz, so he just nodded and asked Latif to excuse them even though he knew that Wakal was really already locked up when the bodies started dropping.

"Go ahead, Ock," Shabazz nodded when Latif looked to him as if he wasn't going to leave unless he said so. "I'm good. Just slow walk."

"Yeah, go ahead Ock," Jihad repeated sarcastically, as Latif looked at Wakal and twisted his face up before walking off.

"You got this, Ock?" Kaamil questioned, staring at Jihad. "'Cause I'ma go holler at this kid real quick and see what's on his mind."

"Go ahead—I got this," Jihad assured, shaking his head. He too had been offended by Latif's little stunt. "Now that the little side show is over, we can deal with what's really important," Ameen said, looking at everybody. "Because whatever happened out there in them streets before both of you brothers got on Deen is over. You got to let that go, Shabazz."

"Yeah, I know—That's what I was just talking to Shaheed and Latif about," Shabazz lied. "I was out of order for even being involved in that stuff from the jump. I told Diamond from the start that we—"

Wakal stood there and listened carefully to Shabazz as he went on and on about the situation until it was his turn. Then, he pretty much said the same thing. He didn't want no trouble. At the end of the day, they were brothers now, and—according to the teachings of Islam—their blood was sacred. So, not only did they have to give each other their Islamic rights, but they had to protect one another if some shit went down—especially if it had something to do with some kafirs.

"So it's dead?" Ameen questioned, praying that it was, because honestly, the mayhem that Wakal and Shabazz had caused as a non-believer and hypocrite could never be revenged.

"Yeah, it's dead," Wakal and Shahazz said in unison, shaking hands, giving Jihad and Ameen their word as both man and Mob.

And just like that, it was over. Everybody parted ways with no hard feelings.

Chapter 10

I pulled up in front of my mother's house, hit the horn, and waited for my mother and Keystone to come outside, so that we could go over to the bail bondman's office and bond Nizzy and Murdock out. They'd both gotten jammed up in a house raid last night with nine ounces of coke, a couple of handguns, three bullet-proof vests, two scales, a police-scanner, a strainer, and all kind of other drug paraphernalia and cutting equipment. Young Danny had already been picked up by his mother from the Baby Bookings, and I was trying to spring Nizzy and Murdock before they saw the commissioner and ended up with ransoms for bails. I was tripping because now, all of a sudden, the bitch ass police wanted to do their jobs. Them bitches weren't anywhere to be found when the squad were getting robbed and shot at. They hadn't even been fucking with niggas. Especially since the riots. They would ride through without stopping, go the other way when shots rung out, leave bodies lying in the streets for hours, and refuse to take certain reports. But now, they decided to raid one of our trap-houses.

"Hey, baby," my mother spoke, climbing into the passenger seat before leaning over to kiss me on the cheek as Keystone hopped in the back.

"Hey, Ma?" I put the car in gear and pulled off. "What's going on?"

"Nothing," my mother replied. "Slate called the house looking for you yesterday, but I told him that you have been staying over your little girlfriend's spot lately." She laughed.

Damn! I had missed my cousin's call again. So much had been going on. Between the robberies, expanding the business, the shit with Ronnie-Moe and Tony-Bey, and Deli's legal fees. Things were crazy. Then, you had Lor'Homie's dumb ass, driving around butt-naked, high off the pills with the Kalashnikov laid across his lap, and now this raid shit.

"I'ma stop pass Aunt Joyce house today," I assured, knowing that I had to swing that way anyway when I went to pick up Nizzy's girl after we left the bail bondman's office downtown. "You got everything you need, Keystone?" I questioned, coming up on the stop sign at the end of my mother's street.

"Yeah." He nodded, holding up a stack of papers. "But this is a one time deal, Charm. I mean, you know I'll do whatever I can to help you out. But, I'm not going to be co-signing for all of your friends also."

"He's right, baby," my mother agreed.

"I respect that," I said honestly, nodding to Keystone in the rearview mirror. Keystone was a straight up good dude. He wasn't Money Cola, but he loved my mother dearly, and that was all that mattered. He had held her down through addiction and the loss of my little sister, never turning his back on her. So, for that alone, I fucked with Keystone.

First, we mapped out how shit would go. My mother would post Nizzy and Murdock's seventy-five thousand dollar bonds with the deed to the house I had finally paid off, and Keystone would co-sign, being that he had the little small cab company on North Avenue. Then, my mother and Keystone started talking about marriage and having more children. After posting Nizzy and Murdock's bails, I gave my mother and Keystone my blessing, dropped them back off at the house, and headed for my aunt's crib.

***

When I finally left my aunt's house and got around to Nizzy's spot to pick up Butta, I saw a bunch of beggars on the front and immediately pulled over to park before stuffing my tone in my jeans pocket and jumping out. As I approached the house, I eyed Butta standing in the doorway in a little, mini, hip-hugging jeans skirt, a skin-tight top, and a pair of Gucci flip-flops.

"Yo," I paused to calm myself down, "what the fuck is this?" I continued looking from Butta to all the off-brand ass niggas standing around. "My nigga ain't even been gone a hot twenty-four hours and you already out here showing your ass," I added.

"Boy, don't start with me, okay!" Butta came down the steps to give me a hug as I continued to ice-grill niggas. "Ain't nobody even doing nothing."

"Yeah, okay," I replied, breaking the embrace.

Butta stepped back and placed her hand up on her little hip like she was posing for an Instagram photo. Then, she started popping her chewing-gum just like the hoodrat she was. I still couldn't understand why Nizzy trusted this bitch so much. Everybody knew that her and her girls weren't shit but a bunch of snakes. The bitches were all a part of the infamous '38 Posse'—a group of fine ass, gangster bitches who'd made a name for themselves beating bitches down and setting niggas up in the mid 90's.

"Yeah, okay, what?" Butta teased with a smile. Her pussy had to be laced with heroin because the whole squad knew she had Nizzy addicted from day one.

"That's all you see, motherfucker?" I looked over to see Ty'shea—Butta's crazy ass, car-keying, tire-slicing twin sister—rolling her eyes at me.

"Oh, my bad, what's up, Ty'shea?" I eyed her little red-head, pigeon-toed ass, as she approached me in some seriously sheer, white leggings that clearly showed off her purple panties with the black lace trimming, and my brain went straight to my dick. "I didn't even see you," I lied and gave her a hug.

"Whatever!" she said, squeezing me tight.

"I'm serious," I lied again, as she broke the embrace.

Ignoring me, Ty'shea stepped back and crossed her arms. "Why you got them bum ass bitches on your Facebook page coming for me, trolling my social media?" '

"What? I don't even have a Facebook account," I said, throwing my hands up in surrender. It was a shame that Ty'shea was too gangster for me because what she had between her legs was fire. She had that snap-back that was hotter than a torch when a nigga got up in it. Now I knew exactly why she had gotten that little fire-shooting-water holes 'Fireman' tattooed on the inside of her thigh. "That shit for old people now!"

"Anyway," Ty'shea rolled her eyes and popped her neck, "don't make me fuck one of them little dusty bitches up, Charm!" she threatened like we were an item or something. But I just shook my head because I wasn't trying to get my whip keyed up again.

Why do all the dizziest bitches always have the best pussy? I thought, looking at her. What really had me tripping though was the fact that Ty'shea was standing there putting up a front as if she did not love pussy just as much as I did. I couldn't count how many times we'd propped some lil' bad bitch up on some pillows in a hotel room, laid our heads on opposite sides her thighs and ate her into a coma. Not to mention, the amount of times I'd paid her and another one of her '38 Posse' homegirls a few bands to let me watch them turn a bitch out.

"How you know it's not one of your lil' thots you done turned out?" I questioned.

"Because all my bitches stay in their place!" she retorted.

"Yeah, I heard that." I looked at Butta, ready to go. "Are you ready or what?"

"Yeah, just let me go grab the spare key," Butta replied, dashing into the house.

I took one last look at the crowd of clowns on my nigga's front, told Ty'shea that I would holler at her later, and headed for my car.

"You better call me too, nigga!" I heard Ty'shea yell before I slipped back inside the car to wait for Butta. I couldn't help but to lick my lips and leer at Butta as she bounced from the house five minutes later and slide into the car. All the honey-bees she had running up and all around the inside of her pretty thigh seemed to be moving, as she melted into the butter-soft, leather seat and sat back. It was so hard to tell the identical twins apart. The only way I could always tell Butta and Ty'shea apart was by the red and blond hair they rocked, and the tattoos on the inside of their thighs.

"Yo, you need to pull that lil' ass skirt down!" I ordered, aggressively sticking the key in the ignition, starting the car up, and looking back over at her. "Seriously!" I added, reaching over to adjust the skirt myself. "Pull that shit down, yo!"

"Boy, stop!" Butta slapped my hand and opened her legs further than necessary to sit her pocketbook between them. "Ain't nobody in here but you," she continued, reaching inside her pocketbook. "What? Are you scared?" Butta gave me a devilish look. "You're my brother."

"Brother, huh?" I peeped in the rearview mirror and pulled off. Butta loved to test the waters. But she knew like I did that she was off limits. Even though I could smell the whore in her leaking from every pore, I had too much honor, and too much respect for my nigga to ever cross him out. Especially for a no-good bitch. I didn't care how much pussy she was throwing my way. "Keep on playing."

"What am I playing about?" Butta played dumb like she didn't know what the fuck I was talking about before blowing a bubble in my face.

"Yeah, right," I didn't have time to play mind games with Butta's simple-minded ass today. My mind was on the fifteen bands and the Glock .40 stuffed up under the driver's seat of Nizzy's truck that was still parked over East Baltimore. "You got Nizzy's spare, right?"

"Yeah, boy, dang!" Butta held up the key. "Why you gotta be so damn serious all the times?"

"Cos a nigga don't have time to be playing!" I retorted. "You got your driver's license on you?"

"Mmmh-hmmm." Butta sighed. "Anything else?"

"Nah, that's it for now."

"So what exactly is it that you need me to do?"

"Drive my car back to the house while I push Nizzy's truck." I looked at her like she was retarded. This bitch had to have a bomb between her legs because she was as dumb as a door-knob. "What else?"

"Oh, I ain't know. I thought you wanted me to do something else." She smiled.

"Nah, we're just going to pick up Dummie's truck and bring it back," I assured. There was no need to tell her about the money and tone. "And yo, can you please stop popping that dumb ass gum in my ear?"

"Yes, daddy!" Butta giggled and started fucking with the radio, as I slowed down for a red light. "My sister told me how you like to be called *daddy*," she added before leaning over to blow another bubble in my face. When the bubble final popped, she used her finger and tongue to slowly twirl the gum up until she was able to stuff it back into her mouth.

"Your sister crazy," I said honestly.

"Yeah, well, whose fault is that?" she questioned, looking at me. "You the one got all your lil' thots playing with her on social media, throwing shade," she continued when I refused to reply to her bullshit.

"Are you finished?" I questioned, as the coming light turned green. "Cos I got other shit on my mind."

"Yes, daddy, I'm finished!" Butta teased.

I just shook my head and turned the volume up on the radio. Butta was lucky that I wasn't Nizzy because I would have had that pussy in check.

***

"So, you're telling me that this hoe ass nigga Thugg is out on bail?" Nizzy questioned again, as he and Murdock stood outside in front of Central Bookings on Madison Street, trying to get a cab after being released on bond.

"Yup," Murdock nodded. "That's what Lil' Santa Clause told me. He said Thugg was on the tier before he bailed out two weeks ago. He thinks he's on home monitor at his grandmother's house now."

"What? Lil' Santa Clause? With the fucked up hand?" Nizzy questioned, referring to a wild lil' homie from around the way who'd lost his hand playing with a Drano bomb in JuJu's aunt's basement.

"Yeah," Murdock replied.

"You sure, Dummie?" Nizzy stared at Murdock, unconvinced.

"Yeah, I'm sure. Lil' Santa Clause was going off on that nigga. Talking about how he telling on his own brother and all that. You know that's his cousin."

"Well, if he feel like that about that mutt, why the fuck he didn't put him down when he was still on the tier?" Nizzy questioned.

"Fuck if I know!" Murdock said. "He did take that sucker's tennis and shit."

"Niggas kill me with that shit!" Nizzy spat. "They'll talk about a nigga being fucked up all behind his back, then be in the nigga's face and don't do nothing."

"You know how niggas be, Dummie. They'll say whatever sounds slick at the moment, depending on who's around. Niggas be chameleons and get-withs, 'cause as soon as certain dudes gone or not around, their true colors come out."

"Isn't that nigga Lil'Deezy on the hopper tier with Deli?" Nizzy stretched his arm out and used his hand to hail the yellow cab he saw coming down Madison Street towards them.

"Yeah, I think so. I mean, he gotta be."

"Damn!" Nizzy spat when he noticed the head of a female customer in the back seat putting on mark-up. "Well, he need to get Itchy-Man to give us his grandmother's address."

"You think that nigga going to do that?" Murdock looked at Nizzy like he was seriously insane. "That's his brother, Dummie."

"So?" Nizzy retorted. "That didn't stop his punk ass from putting his name all in that shit!" Nizzy thought for a second. "Plus, if you think about it, once niggas crack Thugg, Itchy-Man will be coming home too."

Murdock considered Nizzy's words. As far as they knew, Thugg was the only one telling. So Nizzy's plan may not be such a bad idea after all. Because one thing being over the bookings had taught Murdock: Freedom was a common interest of every niggas sitting over the jail. "That might just work, Dummie," Murdock smiled. He didn't wish jail on nobody. Not even his worst enemy. Niggas he knew wouldn't hesitate to split his wig. Problems he knew he would have to solve. "But, you know we're gonna still have to spank them niggas when they touch down, 'cause they're not going to let that shit with Prince go."

"You already," Nizzy replied, knowing that it would be a death wish to allow Itchy-Man or Lil'Deezy to continue breathing once they hit the streets. "I ain't crazy. The end justifies the means. They make out, Deli makes out. After that, you already know what it is."

"If Itchy-Man's with it, how the fuck do we go about getting at Thugg on home-monitor?" Murdock questioned, truly curious.

"We're gonna have to set a nice 'rat-trap'," Nizzy answered. "Honestly, I thought about paying his bitch ass off. But then I thought, like, what the fuck can you honestly offer a nigga who would snitch on his own brother?"

"Lead-poisoning," Murdock smiled.

"Exactly," Nizzy agreed, keeping his eyes open for another cab. "Seriously though, niggas gotta come up with something, Dummie."

"Already." Murdock looked off into the clouds as if he was lost in thought for a moment. "Yo," Murdock snapped his fingers and looked at Nizzy. "What about Fish sister, Tiphani?"

"How many times I gotta tell you Tiphani is not Fish sister?" Nizzy shook his head. "That's his cousin's wife. Her last name is Glover."

"Sister, cousin's wife, whatever," Murdock honestly didn't give a fuck. He knew that Tiphani's sexy ass was gangster, and at the moment, that was all that mattered. "You know who the fuck I'm talking about."

"Yeah, well, what about her?"

"Don't she work over the jail?" Murdock questioned.

"As far as I know, why?"

"She can use her uniform to lure Thugg to the door for us," Murdock said.

"Nah, Dummie," Nizzy shook his head. There wasn't no way in the world that he was involving a female in his business. He didn't give a fuck how thorough she was. "That's too risky."

"Well, get her ass to give us one of them uniforms and badges so we can act like we're the home-monitor peoples ourselves then."

Nizzy looked at Murdock with a wicked grin. "That just might work, Dummie," Nizzy admitted, rubbing his hands together. "The only thing is, I'm not trying to involve Tiphani. So, we're going to have to get the equipment online ourselves."

"Yo, do the C.O.'s and the home-detection people dress alike?"

"I don't think so," Nizzy said. "But you know like I do that when niggas in the hood see a uniform and badge, they go blind." Nizzy laughed as an empty cab pulled up to the curve in front of them.

"True." Murdock opened the back door of the cab. "All them badges and uniforms blend together after a while."

"That's what it is then," Nizzy confirmed, as Murdock ducked inside the cab and slid across the back seat. "All we got to do now is get Deli to holler at Lil'Deezy," Nizzy said, watching his head, as he got into the cab and pulled the door close.

Murdock nodded in agreement and laid his head back on the seat. There was no more to be discussed. Deli was scheduled to start trial in a few months, and if they didn't wipe Thugg's bitch down by then, it was over.

"Where to, my friend?" The Indian cab-driver's accent was crystal clear, as he eyed Nizzy through the rearview mirror.

"Drop me off at my mother's house," Murdock said.

"I'll swing past Old York and Cator first," Nizzy dug his hand into his pocket for some money. "The west," Nizzy answered the driver. "Then I'ma get you to run me back over," he added.

Delmont Player

Chapter 11

"Did you holler at Doug and Hoark yet?" Big Paul 'Shabazz' Bulovan asked, as he continued to walk the big yard with Shaheed and Latif, scheming.

"Yeah," Shaheed nodded. "They're gonna meet you up the library tonight so y'all can talk."

"I just don't understand why we need some white boys to do our dirty work, Ock," Latif said. "Especially when we can just do it ourselves." Shabazz just smiled at Latif because he knew that he was ready to earn his bones. He also knew that if he gave the order, neither Latif nor Shaheed would hesitate to get their knives wet. Especially if the call was on Wakal. Now just wasn't the time. Not when he knew that the whole community was watching. However, that would not stop him from greasing the right palm. That way, at the right time, the battery could be put into the right motherfucker's back. This was exactly why Shabazz had reached out to Doug and Hoark. Two white boys who always kept a handful of henchmen at their disposal and were into solving the type of problem he was having.

"Nah, just be cool for now, Ock, and let me put this move together," Shabazz suggested, looking across the yard to where Ameen, Kaamil, Jihad and Wakal were working out. "We're going to use the white boys to make the hit look good."

Shabazz wasn't thinking about none of that peace shit Ameen and them were kicking. And Wakal was a fool if he thought otherwise. He, like Diamond, had violated and transgressed against him and those he loved. And like Diamond, he had to answer for it. The crazy part though was that, for some reason, Jihad and them had forgotten just how shrewd he could be. But, before it was all over with, he planned on reminding them.

"What about Ameen?" Shaheed questioned, more out of curiosity than concern.

"Ameen's too busy worrying about being loved," Shabazz replied, knowing that where there was no law, there could be no order. "But no man can rule without fear or wealth."

Shabazz had been clocking Wakal since the day he arrived. Actually, he'd known that Wakal was coming, because he'd paid one of the property workers to keep an eye out for his name months ago, after learning through the inmate Maryland locator that he was being housed over next door at the North Branch Correctional Institution. He'd even tried to have Wakal hit next door, but couldn't find anybody to step up to the plate. To Shabazz, it didn't matter that Wakal had changed his life. He could care less that Wakal had hidden out on protective custody for a minute. He didn't care that all his homeboys were dead. And it damn sure didn't matter that he was a Muslim. Because, there were just some sins that he just could never pardon.

"I don't get it," Shaheed confessed. "How are you going to pull that off?"

"Yeah," Latif seconded. "How the hell you going to get the white boys to take the fall?"

"Wakal got a rape beef on a white girl down South Baltimore," Shabazz informed. "So, when the white boys hit him, I'ma have them make it about the white girl," Shabazz explained. "That way, the community can't do nothing."

"I like that," Latif admitted, shaking his head as Shaheed smiled. Now, they understood why Shabazz always stayed in tight with all the shot-callers on the compound. It was a trick that he said he had been putting down since the old penitentiary. A trick that allowed him to use money, man-power, and sometimes drugs to silence rumors, squash beefs and eliminate competition, all while keeping his hands clean and remaining untouchable. That was one of the main things that Shabazz said he loved about fear and money. Money moved mountains, opened doors, closed investigations and gave a man power. And fear just made motherfuckers bow down. Shabazz had told them how money had actually been the only thing that was able to save him a few years prior, when he'd been forced to stab a guy to death in front of two prison guards. That and a little bit of fear, of course.

"I figured you would," Shabazz smiled. There was no reason

to flirt with death when none of them were trying to know what it was like to die. "But you haven't seen nothing yet."

***

"Ummm, excuse me. Are you Mr. Izzard?"

Billy Lo looked up to see a fine, little white girl with dark shoulder-length hair and a nice, slim figure standing in the doorway, holding a folder across her chest. "Yeah, why? What's up?"

"My name is Laura Booth. And I have been appointed by the court to do an evaluation since the state has decided to seek the death penalty in your case." She spoke nervously, slowly stepping into the room. "I am here to see if you are actually competent enough to stand trial."

Laughing, Billy Lo spat, "Look here, Laura Booth, or whatever your name is. That pretty shit don't work on me. I don't give a fuck who appointed you. I ain't got no rap!" Billy Lo dismissed her, looking back towards the television. Susan had already told him to expect the court-ordered head shrink.

"I only want to ask you a few questions—I promise," she said softly.

Billy Lo stared at her again, as her lips curved into another tender smile. This time, he took a moment to really size her up, taking her in from head to toe. She kind of reminded him of the prosecutor bitch—Angela—from the cable TV series—'Power'—he'd become hooked on. She had the same mouth and stature.

"A'ight," Billy Lo agreed, deciding to entertain her for a moment. "But, I can't promise that I'll answer all of your questions," he added, wondering if being sexy was a criteria for all psychologists.

"That's fine," she assured with a smile, opening her folder. "I just want us to get to know each other this time."

"This time, huh!" Billy Lo laughed.

"Yes, this will be the first of several sessions," she replied with confidence.

Billy Lo continued to laugh because if she thought that he was that weak for a pretty smile, then she was wasting her time. "We'll see."

***

A nigga could never get no rest because a Dummie's work never seemed to be done. I had just gotten finished 'baby boying' or—as I liked to say—bedroom-bullying Ebony, and was waiting for breakfast in bed, until the incoming call from my sister's uncle had me jumping out of bed, grabbing my tone, rushing over into East Baltimore. I had thought that the little static with the 'Hot Boys' had been ironed out. But I guess not, because—for whatever reason—Young Danny and Murdock had just gotten to rumbling with a few of them niggas and were now holed-up at Ronald's crib.

'It's always them project niggas!' I thought, as I drove over the North Avenue bridge into East Baltimore. When I got to Ronald's spot, I sat inside the car for a moment and looked around. Anger was spreading through my body like wildfire. These lil' hot boy niggas were doing too much. But I knew that now wasn't the time to get emotional. First of all, I didn't know their side of the story. And secondly, anger was a liability that could hinder a nigga from thinking clearly. I took a few deep breaths and exited the car.

"What's up, fam?" I spoke, as Ronald opened the apartment door and stepped to the side to let me enter.

"You need to talk to these little niggas." Ronald gestured towards the kitchen before peeping out into the hallway. "Especially that little motherfucker Murdock," he added, locking the door.

I didn't even respond. I just headed for the kitchen. Young Danny and Murdock were both standing around with dumb ass looks on their faces, trying to read me. "Y'all niggas, man." I shook my head before directing my attention to Murdock since he was the oldest. "Always on the dumb shit!"

"You don't even know what happened, nigga!" Murdock argued, but I wasn't trying to hear it. I knew how Murdock got down: 'Swing first, ask questions last'.

"What happened then?" I questioned sarcastically, basically already knowing the answer.

"One of them 'Hot Boys' got to acting crazy at the carry-out and you already know I'm not about to let nobody disrespect me, Dummie—I don't care how deep they are!" Murdock exclaimed. "So, I went in the niggas mouth and we got to rec-ing with them niggas."

"He's not lying, Dummie," Young Danny supported, when he saw the way that I was looking at Murdock. "The niggas was talking reckless. Like we were fuck niggas or something. If Murdock hadn't stole that nigga, I'd have."

"That's what we got a squad for!" I raised my voice, knowing that things could've been handled a whole lot better. "One of us could've easily come over here and cleaned these niggas up!" I reminded them of why we had things set up the way we did. The mind had to always be mightier than the sword.

"Honestly, I didn't think that shit would escalate like that," Murdock said. "But if you would've heard the shit coming out of this squire's mouth—I had to go in his mouth, Dummie."

"Yeah, I was tripping—Especially since you said the dude Big Al and his man sat down with them niggas," Young Danny added, as if to defend their actions. "I thought everything was good."

'Damn!' I thought to myself. Here we go again. I knew situations like this had a way of getting out of control. This was just like the shit with Ronnie-Moe and Tony-Bey. The only difference was the 'Hot Boys' had a team of young, certified goons. "Uncle Ronald, how much you know about these hot boys?"

"To be straight up with you, nephew, I don't even know where half of them little kids came from," Ronald admitted. "After Tiger and them fell for all that Lafayette shit, everybody started calling themselves *Hot Boys*. The only one of them kids I really know is my partner's son—Mike-Mike."

"Mike-Mike," Murdock echoed. "That's not the nigga with the missing fingers?"

"Yeah," Ronald confirmed. "He lost his shit in a knife fight. Why? Was he with that shit?"

"Hell yeah, that nigga was with it!" Young Danny exclaimed. "He the one that swing on Murdock after he dropped the other nigga."

"What the other kid look like?" Ronald inquired.

"Short, brown-skinned, saddle-head nigga with a full beard and a mouth full of slugs," Young Danny replied. "He had 'L.A.' tattooed on his hand too."

"Yeah, that's Mike-Mike's right-hand man—Little B," Ronald informed, shaking his head. "Him and shorty thick as thieves. Both of them play with them pistols too."

"Man, you talking like a nigga won't spend them niggas' bend," Murdock threatened. "Fuck them bitch ass niggas!"

"Them niggas can't be getting no money," Young Danny said. "Not doing no dumb shit like that."

I stood there in deep thought for a second. I knew that there was no such thing as a bad crew. There were only bad leaders. "Before we start wearing niggas out—first, let's get some more history on them."

"I think Tiger is on the yard with my man Ache'Yeyo in Kentucky," Ronald spoke, as if thinking out loud. "If so, I'ma see what I can find out. Because I'm telling you—besides Mike-Mike, aren't too many of them kids originals!"

"Cool," I said, trying to think of a way to avoid bloodshed and keep getting money. At least for now. "I'ma holler at Big Al and E-Don again too," I added. "Try to find out why these niggas geeking all of a sudden."

"In the meantime, what the fuck are we supposed to do?" Murdock asked, concerned.

"Try to give them a little cushion until I can get with Big Al and E-Don, or Uncle Ronald holler at his man in the Feds," I replied, hoping that wisdom would prevail. "There's no sense in starting a blood bath if we don't have to," I encouraged. "But, if them niggas come back around here acting stupid, wear their asses out, and we'll let the chips fall where they may."

Delmont Player

Chapter 12

"This shit is not going to work, Dummie," Nizzy warned from the driver's seat, laughing. "You look stupid as fuck," he added, eyeing the oversized corrections officer uniform O had on.

"You better hope it does!" O retorted. Since they couldn't trust nobody outside the squad to play dress up, O was up. "Because, as soon as the home-detection sucker bounce, I'm going to work."

Nizzy, Lor'Homie, and O were sitting outside of Itchy-Man's grandmother's house in the 900 block of Bennett Place, waiting for the home-detection officer to leave. It had taken quite a bit of negotiating, but Itchy-Man had finally decided to hand Thugg over. After Deli assured him that no harm would come to his grandmother.

"He's coming out now," Nizzy said, as the home-detection officer exited Itchy-Man's grandmother house. "I bet you can't pull this shit off!" Nizzy challenged, as they watched the home-detection chump climb back into his car.

"Shidddd," O replied, jumping at the invitation. "What you want to put on it?"

"Bet a stack, Dummie!" Nizzy demanded.

"Bet." O agreed, as the home-detection officer's car drove by.

"I'm talking about you got to get grandma to actually open the door and let you in, nigga," Nizzy explained so that there was no confusion. "It don't count if you got to force your way in."

"Man, I got this, Dummie." O nodded understandably.

Once the home-detective officer turned off the block, O told Lor'Homie and Nizzy to come on, got out of the car, and quickly made his way towards the house. "Make sure y'all stay out of sight," O mumbled over his shoulder, as they approached the steps. "Watch my work, Dummie." O paused to pick up a pinch of dirt out of one of the flower-pots lining the edges of Itchy-Man's grandmother's steps. Nizzy and Lor'Homie watched as O went up the steps and knocked on the Itchy-Man's grandmother's door, after smearing dirt over the peephole. He wasn't worried about Thugg's snitching ass answering the door. Itchy-Man had already informed them that he was still using wheels for legs.

"Yes?" a soft voice finally came from the other side of the door. "Who is it?"

"It's ummm, me again, Missis Stewart," O stole a look at Nizzy, disguised his voice and tried to find his words as he saw him tap Lor'Homie and smile. "Home-detection. I—ahhh—I forgot to—mhhh—check Tyree's box." O paused again to look at Nizzy and hunched his shoulders. "We have been having range problems lately."

For what seemed like an eternity, Itchy-Man's grandmother didn't respond, and O was just beginning to think that he'd have to kick the door in, but he heard the unmistakable sound of the locks being opened as Itchy-Man's grandmother began to speak again. "Well, I am glad you came back because Lord knows that boy don't need no more to worr—"

The moment Ms. Stewart cracked the door, O slammed the full weight of his body into the door like a line-backer, and sent her flying to the floor as he rushed inside, pulling up his Dummie scarf, closely followed by Nizzy and Lor'Homie.

"Find Thugg!" O ordered, grabbing Ms. Stewart by her ankles as she tried to crawl across the floor. "I get her."

"Lord, have mercy!" Ms. Stewart shouted, kicking O in the chest.

Lor'Homie ran through the house and caught Thugg on his phone—trying to roll out the back door—and kicked him completely out of the wheelchair before snatching the telephone cord out of the wall and wrapping it around Thugg's neck. "He's in here, Dummie!" Lor'Homie alerted the other niggas, picking up Thugg's shattered cell phone to make sure his call hadn't gone through. "Oh, you haven't learned your lesson yet, huh, bitch?" Lor'Homie pressed *delete* to remove the 9-1-1 digits off of Thugg's cracked cell phone screen. "Now, what you got up in here, bitch? Huh?" Lor'Homie turned his attention back to

Thugg.

"What the fuck are doing, Cuz!" Nizzy spat, after running back down the stairs and rushing into the kitchen to find Lor'Homie on the kitchen floor choking Thugg out from behind with a telephone cord. "Ain't nobody got time for that shit! Nigga, move!"

Nizzy pushed Lor'Homie out of the way and started feeding Thugg lead-poison. Thugg tried to shield himself by throwing his hand up, but it did no good. The first shot went straight through Thugg's palm and crushed into his forehead. Then, Nizzy stepped over top of Thugg and emptied the rest of his clip into his head and body, as he rolled over and balled up.

"Damn, Cuzzo!" Lor'Homie said. "I think that punk had some bread up in here."

"Man, just come on!" Nizzy demanded, leaving Thugg face down on the kitchen floor near the door in a pool of his own blood, with the telephone cord still wrapped around his neck.

When Nizzy and Lor'Homie came back into the living room, O was bobbing and weaving, ducking combination after combination as Itchy-Man's grandmother swung her Bible with one hand and tried to tase him with the other. "Man, drop that old bitch and let's go!" Nizzy snapped as O continued to struggle with Itchy-Man's grandmother. "We got to go!"

"Man, crack that old bitch!" Lor'Homie spat.

O shook his head and clipped her. He wasn't about to bust no old ass lady who had absolutely nothing to do with why they were there. First of all, he believed in karma. Second, they'd given Itchy-Man their word, and he wanted to show him that there could still be honor amongst men, even in the heat of battle. "Flip that couch over and drag it over here!" O commanded, as he straddled her body and continued to hold on to her wrist, looking at Lor'Homie.

"I hope you all burn in hell!" Ms. Stewart yelled. "The Lord is my shepherd—"

Lor'Homie walked over to O and kneeled down. "Sorry, grandma." Lor'Homie struck her on the side of the head with the butt of his tone, and knocked her out cold, as she continued to fuss and struggle.

"Yo!" O shouted, grabbing Lor'Homie's arm so he couldn't strike her again. "Why the fuck you do that?"

"Cos you looked like you were having a hard time, and we gotta go!" Lor'Homie replied, picking up Itchy-Man's grandmother's taser. "I'm keeping this."

"Man, if you two dummies don't come on—" Nizzy threatened, heading for the door. "We got to get the fuck out of here."

Nizzy, Lor'Homie and O made their way outside to the car without drawing too much attention. Before climbing in and pulling off. What had at first seemed like hours had in fact only taken five minutes from the moment Itchy-Man's grandmother opened the door.

"Did y'all see grandma?" O asked, breaking the silence. "She was more gangster than Thugg up in that bitch," he added, making everybody laugh as they sat in traffic a few blocks away.

"Hell yeah," Lor'Homie seconded, removing his gloves. "She was giving you trouble with them slow ass hooks and jabs."

"Why the fuck you hit her like that, Dummie?" O questioned still kind of angry.

"To stop her old ass from tasing you," Lor'Homie reminded him.

"What about Thugg?" O questioned, ready to change the subject to keep from going back and forth with Lor'Homie. "Did you handle him?"

"Cuzzo did," Lor'Homie gestured towards Nizzy, and kept stuffing his gloves inside the bag between his feet on the floor. "I was trying to see if that bitch had something up in the house."

"You're always trying to turn an obstacle into an opportunity, Cuzzo," Nizzy said, checking the rearview mirror for cops.

"Shiddd, you already know how I get down, Cuzzo!" Lor'Homie said, leaning forward to stick his face between the seats. "If there's money to be had, I want it."

Again, O decided to keep his two-cents to himself because he didn't feel like arguing with Lor'Homie about the consequences of being greedy.

"So what now?" O began to unbutton the fake home-detection uniform.

"First, we're going to finish putting everything in the bag so we can burn it," Nizzy said, using his teeth to bite the tip of one of his gloved fingers and pull the glove off of his hand while he to continued to use the other hand to steer the car. "Then, I'm dropping you niggas off, ditching this whip and sliding over to my lil' murder mommy house to get cleaned up." Nizzy dropped the first glove into his lap with the tone and Dummie scarf, and began working on the next one.

"Keep fucking with them crazy Mexican bitches." O shook his head. "They're going to fuck around a put a spell on your dumb ass, watch."

***

"What's good, Dummie?" I asked, getting up off of my mother's steps to give Nizzy some love. "Fuck got you up so early?"

"I had to get my shit tighten up," Nizzy replied, using his hand like a brush.

"Boy, you and your lil' Boosie fades." I laughed, as he continued to run his hand over his freshly cut fade and dust traces of hair off his face and shoulders. "Who did that?" I wondered, noticing that his hair-cut was tighter than usual. "Your shape-up sharp as shit."

"Tall Jermaine." '

"Tall Jermaine?" I questioned, to be sure because I'd never known that nigga to cut hair. "The one who plucked Deli?"

"Yeah," Nizzy laughed. "Yo was mad as shit about that last slice of pizza."

"You ain't never lied." I laughed at the memory of all of us being out on the strip drunk one night, when Deli snatched Tall

Jermaine's food—playing—and they ended up getting into it. "But, I kept telling Deli to stop that dumb ass 'snatch pop' shit!"

"Dummie went off out that bitch. He tried to cut Tall Jermaine with a broken bottle and everything. He just could not accept the fact that he couldn't whip Tall Jermaine."

"I remember," I said, checking my watch. "How did that thing with Thugg go?"

"You already fucking know." Nizzy smiled. "We went in, conducted that business and got out. Fuck happened to you though? I thought you were coming through to fuck with niggas?"

"Yeah, I was, but I ended up having to go with my aunt to see Slate," I replied honesty. "When I got back, I hit you but you never hit me back."

"Yeah, I was over my lil' bitty house. But everything went smooth. Of course, you know Cuz gotta turn everything into a come up," Nizzy explained, shaking his head. "So, he and O weren't seeing eye to eye, but we got the job done."

"I heard that."

"What's up with Dummie, though? How he holding up?" Nizzy switched the topic, and I knew he was talking about Slate.

"Shit, cooling. Still talking about all that old shit we use to get into."

"Hell no! I know Dummmie not stuck in the past?" Nizzy questioned, smiling.

"That nigga still asking about Dyesha."

"What?" Nizzy looked at me to see if I was serious. "Dyesha lil' chocolate ass was dumb bad though," he admitted. "You tell him about the Fed shit?"

"Nah, I didn't have a chance to," I confessed, remembering the day the feds raided the 'Red Beetle' like it was yesterday. "I was too busy telling him about how we're doing us out here. He think shit a joke though. I did tell him about the shit with Monk and David."

Nizzy and I sat there on my mother's front, tripping about how much shit had changed since Slate basically took the fall for

Shawn's punk ass body. "Yo, remember the video I showed you of us butchering that nigga?"

"How could I forget? I've never seen a nigga beg, scream and cry that much in my life. It was blood every fucking where." When we finally got around to talking about the robberies, Nizzy said that he believed that two wild gun-slingers by the names of Mousey and Hambone were behind them. However, I wasn't so sure that either one of them would come at us like that. I mean, I knew that they were both off the chain and about that smoke. And I was down with how they'd used a couple '38 Posse' bitches to set up a fake 'coming home party' for a major nigga out of the city and robbed everybody who'd showed up, but we had a good rapport and they also knew that we were fucking over anybody who crossed us.

"I don't care how good y'all rapport is. Them the only niggas around here making those kind of house calls, Dummie. Think about it." Nizzy tapped his temple to emphasize his point. I thought for a second. He did have a point. Wasn't nobody around the hood getting it in like Hambone and Mousey.

"You definitely right about that. But, like I told Lor'Homie, I don't wanna fuck around and sanction a move on the wrong niggas."

"Who the fuck else can it be, Dummie?" Nizzy challenged.

"I don't know, Dummie," I replied, sincerely drawing a blank. "But, niggas need to find out quick because we can't keep taking no losses."

Before Nizzy could come back with a reply, I saw police cars blitzing the block from both ends, and knew what time it was. "You strapped, Dummie?" I questioned quickly, as the police closed in.

"Nah, my shit in the truck," Nizzy mumbled, as the police came to a complete stop in front of my mother's house. Now it was time to see who they were there for.

"Calvin Johnson! Don't move!" the first officer out of the car ordered, approaching quickly, and that was all I heard.

I took off running into my mother's house as the cop gave

chase. I cut through the living room, hit the kitchen, and dipped out the back door. I dashed down the alley, hopped the fence of one of my mother's neighbors, and hid inside of an old dog-house in their junky ass backyard. My heart started pounding like shit when I heard the police walkie-talkies and voices close by. I got shook. I don't think I breathed until I knew I had them bitches beat, when the sound of broken glass and trash being kicked around began to fade. I heard the ghetto bird fly overhead a few times, but I knew that I was good. Then, I heard somebody saying something about the dog-house, and was immediately surrounded by cops.

"We know you're in the dog-house, Johnson!" one of the officers yelled. "So, you might as well come out."

I quickly eased the tone from my dip and thought about doing some gangster shit. However, I quickly realized that only a fool would gamble against my odds. So, I just wiped the tone off as best I could, stuffed it inside a chewed-up teddy-bear, and buried it in the dirt.

"Stick your fucking hands out now!" another cop demanded.

"Come on, Johnson, don't get shot being stupid." I recognized the female officer's voice from when she first jumped out and ordered me not to run. "Just come on out," she pleaded.

I did as I was told because I was trying to live to see another day. And I knew that these trigger-happy, armed-thugs were dying to bust a cap in another nigga. "Now crawl out slowly!" I heard another one order.

"Damn!" I muttered under my breath, mad as fuck when I crawled halfway out and saw the 'Green-Team'—The city's new gang-task force. I knew what was up. All them bitches did all day was, ride around in army-fatigue, jumping out on known gang members and head hitters, snatching niggas on warrants.

Once I crawled into view, they were all over me. Meshing my face all into the dirt, with the famous 'Baltimore Knee-Drop' to the back of the neck. I also felt a few punches and kicks, and heard my mother yelling at the cops about recording everything and suing the police department, as I was being handcuffed and read my rights.

"Make sure he didn't throw nothing in my yard, officer!" I heard the owner of the house in the background. When I finally got to my feet and saw the fat, stuck-up, ugly-face bitch, who lived down the street from my mother, all I could do was mean-mug her.

"You have the right to an attorney. If you can not afford an attorney, one will—" The officer went on and on, but my attention was on the cops still searching big girl's backyard. And when they flipped the dog-house over and dug up the K5, I felt an invisible rope cutting into my neck because I knew that I'd probably just hung myself.

As I was being forced into the back of the police-wagon, I heard the officer talking to my mother, saying that I was being taken downtown for questioning.

"As soon as you're formerly charged, call me, baby!" my mother yelled, still holding her cellphone up, recording as the cops carefully helped me step up into the back of the police-wagon. "And don't talk to nobody!" she added.

I smiled as one of cops slammed the wagon's door in my face. Even after all the shit I was doing in the streets, my mom still thought that I was a baby.

"Watch what happens if motherfuckers try that 'rough ride' shit with my son!" was the last threat I heard my mother make as the police-wagon pulled off. I knew that she was making reference to the well-known violent, fast-moving, unrestrained, police wagon ride to the station that had sent the city into an uproar. But I didn't think that they wanted to go down that road again—especially not with my niggas. If they thought that motherfuckers had tore the city up about 'Freddie Grey', they weren't ready to see what my squad would do behind me.

***

When I arrived downtown, the gloves came off and the

games began. But I was hipped to them all. I had been dealing with the cops for years, and the 'Green Team' were no different. So I quickly realized from the start that somebody had to have put them on me about Xavier's murder. Because, I'd taken extra precaution when it was time to rock him to sleep.

"What he looking at? First degree murder? Life? Life plus?" The Green Team chump looked at one of the detectives.

"Maybe worst," the detective replied, smiling at me when my expression changed. "Especially, if the ballistics on that forty-five caliber come back matching any of those Murphy Homes shootings."

"Man, y'all didn't get that off me!" I exclaimed. "That shit can be anybody's."

"That's not how the report is going to read." The Green Team chump laughed.

"This is the time to help yourself, Mr. Johnson," the detective interjected again. "And I don't do this for everyone. Especially, when I know I have them dead to right. But, I think you're a good kid. So, I am willing to throw you a lifeline on the Brooks murder. But, only if you give me who pulled the trigger in the Don Pulley shooting."

He dropped Prince's name and leaned back in his chair, as if to gloat. He must've misread the change in my game face, or maybe he thought he'd found a hole in my armor. But he was wrong. First of all, Nicole Johnson didn't raise no rats. And secondly, Money Cola had taught me a long time ago that the fish who opened his mouth always ended up on the hot-plate. So, I just stared at him because I knew my responsibility to the G-code and didn't need to think twice about how I had to carry it. I had been schooled by two of the best. And the one thing that they both agreed on was that, if or when the police ever got you cornered, you never said nothing or signed shit.

"Look, man, I told y'all that I don't know nothing."

"You know what? I was wrong for even asking you to give up one of your home boys. Because that would be snitching and I can already tell that you're not cut from that cloth." The detective commended like he was trying to stroke my ego. "But, in my experience, the cheetah always knows where the hyena is. So how about this—Since, it's not snitching if you give up information on your rival, why don't you just tell us who shot your homie, Lamont Curtis? How does that sound?"

"Sounds good to me," the Green Team chump said. "We get what we want. He gets to go home. Everybody wins."

'Yeah, until they lose,' I thought. He was so funny that I couldn't stop myself from laughing. Who the fuck had told that lie or used that excuse to bitch up? Snitching was, snitching. It didn't matter who you were snitching on. "You funny," I couldn't help saying. "When do I get to call a lawyer?"

"You know once we call that lawyer, I can't help you!" the detective warned. "So, are you sure that's what you want to do? I mean, think about it. You already see that we know everything."

"Yeah," the Green Team chump seconded. "We know all about the birthday party shooting at the skating ring. We know all about your little toy soldiers. All about the retaliation murders, and we know all about how you mixed the shells up in your clip to make it appear like there were multiple shooters on the Brooks case instead of just using the highly lethal, fragmenting 'Dum-Dum' rounds, like your crew usually does whenever the shooting is personal." He said this confidently. "The only thing that we don't know is, if you're smart enough to have an honest conversation or stupid enough to request an attorney," he added.

The smile that appeared on his face told me that he smelled more than blood. This cock-sucker smelled victory, but I smelled victory too. Because, in his haste to scare me into talking, he had made a vital mistake and basically signed a nigga's death warrant. Because whether he knew it or not, there were only two motherfuckers who knew that many details about Xavier's murder, and I was one of them.

"I want a lawyer," I requested because honestly, what the fuck was I going to talk to the police about? Definitely not my business, let alone somebody else's. When I had a problem with a nigga, I went and squeezed it out.

Chapter 13

"So, you're going to let me get all these for twenty dollars in commissary?" Wakal repeated, placing his hand on a stack of magazines to be sure that they were on the same page because he didn't want there to be no misunderstanding later on.

"Yeah," his cell buddy affirmed. "Like I told you, as soon as we come up, I'ma shut this place right back down about my brothers."

The jail had been locked down since a couple of Bloods walked into the church during service and started stabbing niggas for real about a week ago. Wakal had been coming from an attorney's visit when C.O.'s came running from everywhere. Wakal was still mad about being forced to lie on the ground in his only fresh clothes. A few minutes later, he saw the nurses rushing wounded inmates across the compound on stretchers. One dude was shaking like he'd just caught the Holy Ghost. Since then, it had been a whole lot of kite-passing, death-selling, and calls for war up and down the tier. So the stage was set. The Bloods, who out numbered the 'Ghristians'—Gangster Christains—three to one on the tier, had to answer for their sins against the church.

"So, I get all these for twenty?" Wakal held up the stack of 'Buttman' magazines.

"Yeah, homie," Wakal's cell buddy smiled. He knew that he was cutting Wakal a sweet deal. Buttmans alone could go for $7 dollars easy. "Now, are you sure you don't want none of these Black tails or B-V-I's?" he asked, gesturing to the black girl books still sitting on his bed.

"Nah, I'm good on that." Wakal began flipping through the Buttman with his baby—Belladona—on the cover. "How you want the twenty? Food, stamps, cosmetics?"

"Stamps and cosmetics," His celly replied, watching Wakal twist and turn the magazine, as if he could get a better view of the variety of naked pornstars getting fucked every which way. "But, I'll take that coffee if you got it though."

"Damn! Check this snow bunny out," Wakal said, flashing his cell buddy a picture of a pretty, petite white girl with a long, jet-black, wet and wavy ponytail. The girl was in hot-pink fishnet and matching high heels. "She bad!" Wakal admired, biting his bottom lip.

"Oh yeah, that's my baby Andy San Dimas right there," he announced. "She reminds me of the bitch—Coke—I told you I wanted to fuck. Remember? The one that always be power-walking with the military boots on."

"I remember," Wakal said, instantly picturing the fine, little, slim C.O. with the colorful religious shit tattooed behind her right ear. She kind of reminded him of an older version of Ariana Grande. "That's the one I said always trying to act like she's cold and empty, but is probably just as hot and full when you get her behind closed doors."

"Right, right," his cell buddy nodded. "Yeah, that's her. I'm on that white girl! One of the guards told me that her head was top shelf when I was on lock-up back in two-thousand thirteen."

"It probably is," Wakal paused to imagine. "I bet that pussy fire too," he added. "You see how she walk?"

"Fuck, yeah!" his cell buddy admitted. "Any white girl who struts around with a walk that nasty better have some good pussy."

***

"What's up, Cuzzo?" Lor'Homie questioned, climbing into the passenger's seat of Nizzy's chalk grey truck, as soon as he pulled up in front of his house.

"Cooling." Nizzy pulled back off quickly. He didn't want his aunt or Lor'Homie's nosey ass sisters to see him and call his mother.

"You heard anything about Dummie yet?" As always, Lor'Homie started messing with his cousin's CD's collection.

"Nah," Nizzy slowed down at the corner and took a quick left. "But Peaches did talk to the lawyer yesterday."

"I hope that ain't get grabbed with that four-fifth."

"Yeah, me too," Nizzy seconded. "That's the joint I did ole boy with."

"I'm hip," Lor'Homie said, finding what he was looking for. "I been told Dummie to get rid of that joint."

"Yeah, but you know how hard-headed Charm is."

"Yeah, well, hard heads make easy cases," Lor'Homie said, forcing Nizzy to look over at him for a moment, as he hit the eject button on the disc-changer. He knew that his cousin was a lot sharper than he usually acted or got credit for.

"So, what the lawyer say?"

"Nothing really," Nizzy admitted. "I mean, other than the fact that Dummie got a gun charge and no bail.

"So, she don't know if Dummie got a body or not?"

"Nah, not that I know of," Nizzy replied, finally realizing what Lor'Homie was doing. "Nah, Cuz! Leave that Lil' Scoota in there."

"Hold up, Cuzzo!" Ignoring Nizzy, Lor'Homie carefully took the CD out of the disc-changer. "I just want to hear that new 'All I Got' joint again real quick." He slid the Lil' Scoota CD back into the CD holder, and sat it in his lap. Nizzy nodded and continued to focus on the road. Nizzy and Lor'Homie drove around collecting money from various niggas they were fronting work throughout the city. It was almost time to see Adnan and re-up. The hustle didn't stop because Charm got knocked. After all, they still had to take care of business.

Nizzy drove over to JuJu's aunt's house to talk to him about the little power struggle he and Shaggy were having. Jealousy amongst the squad was a big 'no-no'.

"Why you coming at me, Dummie?" JuJu questioned, throwing his hands up in frustration. "I'm not the one with the problem."

"I ain't just coming at you," Nizzy assured, as they stood in the front room of JuJu's aunt's house. "I talked to Shag ass first."

"Yeah, well, that nigga must've given you some bad information. Because I'm telling you, Dummie, he the one tripping. Ask G-baby and O, that nigga done put his big hat on."

"Look, like I told Shag, both of you niggas need to sit down and work that shit out. Because we can't get nothing done with y'all at each other's throats."

"Yeah, I heard that," JuJu replied like he was tired of talking about it. "You're right though. I'ma get with that nigga."

"I'm serious, Dummie. Ain't nothing slick about a house divided against itself."

"I said you were right," JuJu repeated. "It's just crazy how Dummie acting like a sucker."

"What's power three?" Nizzy asked, picking up on JuJu's little attitude and body-langauge.

"Oh?" JuJu responded, not really hearing the question.

"I said, what's power number three, Dummie?"

"Love your brother like you love yourself, because in the end all you have is your brother." JuJu recited accurately.

"What about power number seven?"

"Jealousy, hate and envy are weaknesses that destroy unity." JuJu smiled.

"And why is that, Dummie?" Nizzy stared at him the same way he'd stared at Shaggy.

"Because they can easily be exploited by an enemy."

"Exactly, make sure you remember that," Nizzy said, moving towards the front door. "Although there are several of us, we're one body. So when one part of the body suffers, we all suffer. Everybody can't be the head. Somebody has to be the eyes. Somebody has to be the heart. You understand what I'm saying?"

"Yeah," JuJu nodded. "Everybody basically got a part to play."

"Good," Nizzy smiled, satisfied. "Look, Dummie, I got to get up outta here. Cuz and I are about to go drop this money off."

"A'ight, nigga." JuJu followed him to the door. "Dummie love."

"Dummie honor," Nizzy replied, embracing him before opening the door to make his way outside.

"What's up, Dummie?" Lor'Homie yelled from the passenger's seat window of the truck.

"You already know. That Dummie life!" JuJu yelled back, using his right hand to throw up the Dummie symbol, as Nizzy made his way down the steps and around the truck.

Lor'Homie waited until after Nizzy got into the truck, hit the horn, and they'd pulled off before he started asking questions. "So, what he say about that shit with Shag?"

"The same thing Shag said—It's not him. Well, they should be good. Both of 'em promised to get together. All I want them niggas to do is, remember that all of us are equals."

"Ayo, let's swing past Crystal and Pepper's spot real quick since we're right here," Lor'Homie suggested the instant they hit Dru Hill Avenue, as if the idea had just popped into his head.

"Nah, Cuz," Nizzy replied. He wasn't about to go out of his way to fuck with Crystal and Pepper today. Especially not while they had all their re-up money in the truck. "We're going to holler at Adnan about Charm and this work. All that other stuff can wait."

"So, we're not going back to the house?"

"Nah, JuJu just gave me a few bands," Nizzy confessed, turning the volume on the CD down. "Plus, after we leave Adnan's, I'm trying to see if we can catch up with Hambone and Mousey."

"I thought we were chilling on that?" Lor'Homie questioned, confused. The last time they'd talked, his cousin couldn't prove that Hambone and Mousey actually had anything to do with the robberies, and Charm wasn't with it.

"Nah, Charm was chilling," Nizzy retorted on some dumb shit. "But Charm's not here. So, we're going to handle this shit my way."

"That's what's up." Lor'Homie replied, not caring one way or the other. If it involved money, work or family, he was in. "But, after all that, we're definitely stopping over Crystal and Pepper's spot."

"Pussy whipped ass nigga!" Nizzy shook his head, laughing,

knowing that pussy would be the death of his cousin one day. But what could he say? He knew first-hand what it was like to have a bitch feeding you good and fucking you crazy. It worked every time. "Pepper must got a monster between those legs."

"Ain't no question," Lor'Homie confessed, licking his lips as if he could taste it. "I'm telling you, Cuzzo," he paused to shake his head almost as if he couldn't believe it himself, "Pepper's pussy that! And her head a bomb."

"Oh, I believe you," Nizzy assured, knowing how good Pepper's sister's pussy and head was. "Crystal lil' pretty ass got that snug too—And she deep-throats like she got a sinkhole in her mouth," Nizzy confessed, still shivering from the memory. "I be having to duck her ass out."

"I bet you haven't made her squirt yet, nigga!" Lor'Homie challenged.

"What?" Nizzy twisted his face, ready to brag. "Is you crazy? I almost made her pass out from squirting before."

"Come on, Cuzzo, stop faking."

"Faking?" Nizzy repeated. "I don't do no faking, Cuz," he assured, and began to go into great detail about just how freaky Crystal was, as they continued on their way to Baby Mecca to see Adnan.

***

When the soft knock came to the door a second before a prayer book slid underneath the door, Wakal was already up, watching his cell buddy get war-ready. He'd already packed his personal property the night before.

"I got it." Wakal's cell buddy walked over to the door, picked up the book and started talking to the guy outside.

"God bless—" The guy on the other side of the door spoke softly into the crack of the cell door so nobody on the tier could hear him.

Wakal sat on his bunk and listened to his cell buddy and his 'Ghristian' brother, as his cell buddy flipped the prayer book opened and removed a murder weapon. He wasn't trying to be in nobody's business. Not even his cell buddy's. He knew that his cell buddy was about to put in some work when the doors hit, and he couldn't just sit back and let none of his Muslim brothers blindly walk into something that didn't have anything to do with them. Especially not while his cell buddy was swinging a murder weapon like the one the 'Ghristian' guy had just slid underneath the cell door.

"May the power of Jesus be with you, brother—I'll see you when the doors open." The guy on the other side of the door ended the conversation, and Wakal's cell buddy walked back across the cell and finished getting ready for war.

"Ayo, you don't mind if I put the Imam on point, do you?" Wakal asked, cautiously keeping his eyes on the knife his cell buddy had just received. And he'd thought what Kaamil had given him was vicious. But, if truth be told, the steel them 'Ghristian' boys were playing with was straight out of Bethlehem. "I mean, I just don't want him to come walking down here to talk to me, you dig?"

"Do what you got to do. I'm good."

"Listen man," Wakal thought about something else, "when you go to do what you gotta do, be safe Ock. There are a lot of Bloods on the tier."

"There are a lot of soldiers of Jesus Christ on the tier also!" he exclaimed. "But honestly, homie. This what I do. Because I know dudes be thinking Christians weak because we're humble. But watch my work. I'ma make guys think twice before they put their hands on another brother around here. After I give out this blessing."

"Just be careful out there, Ock!" Wakal cautioned.

Ten minutes later, Wakal heard the sounds of the cell doors beginning to open at the front of the tier. His cell buddy stepped to the back of the cell and began quoting ancient scripture, like he was talking in tongues. "For this reason I remind you to stir up like a fire the gift of God that is in you through the laying of my hands on you. For God did not give us a spirit of cowardice, but one of power and—"

When all of the doors on the tier were opened, Wakal bee-lined down the tier to Ameen's cell and told him what was up. "My cell buddy about to go at the Bloods!" Wakal said, as Jihad walked up.

"Yeah, I'm hip," Jihad replied. "That's why I'm right here," he continued. "Look, once them kafirs start working, stay. The only thing we're worrying about is the Imam."

Wakal nodded and turned to watch what would happen next. He saw his cell buddy slowly walking down the tier towards the Blood's shot-caller. If you had to go at somebody, there was no sense in going at a pawn when there was a king available.

Wakal kept his eyes glued to his cell buddy all the way up until he pulled out the murder weapon and moved in for the kill, and that was all he wrote. Wakal's cell buddy's hand went up, but before it came down, one of the little Blood dudes slipped out of the crowd behind him and knocked him out cold on his feet. It seemed like slow-motion as he stood there out on his foot for a moment before crumbling to the ground.

After that, the Bloods just swarmed him and started beating the hell out of him. They fucked him over to the point where Wakal began to feel sorry for him and thought about running down the tier to assist him. Especially, once he realized that none of the other 'Ghristians' were going to do anything to help him.

Damn! Wakal thought to himself, looking away to keep from throwing up. He had shot and stabbed quite a few motherfuckers during his heydays. But, he'd never witnessed a person literally getting slaughtered by a pack of wild dogs. It always looked like a scene from a National Geographic special.

By the time the C.O.'s showed up and got shit under control, it was a mess; there was blood and pieces of clothing everywhere. Most of the Bloods got away, but some of them were committed to the bitter, bloody end.

Chapter 14

I got over the jail Tuesday night, a breeding ground for everything from robbery to murder. A place where challenges came without warning, and you were only able to keep what you were willing to protect. A place where the only things that were respected were blood, unity, and the destruction of state property. I had been hearing about this spot my entire life. Especially, the infamous 'hopper tier'. It was considered to be the original 'gladiator school', and I'd finally arrived. It was after 1 a.m. when I hit the eastside of the section, but niggas were damn sure wide awake. I peeped in damn near every cell, trying to find a familiar face as the guard escorted me down the tier, but I didn't see one nigga I recognized. This was crazy because I knew a few frequent flyers from around my neighborhood.

"Okay, Rhodes, move all that shit off the top bunk. You're getting a cellmate!" the guard ordered, stopping in front of an open cell door before turning to me. "Breakfast is at five— Anything else you want to know, take it up with the next shift!" the guard said to me as I stood there kind of lost. "Well, come on!—Step your ass in the cell—I don't have all day!" the guard ordered, and I complied.

"What's up, yo?" I nodded to the white boy, as he cleared the top bunk off, but he didn't reply. "What's up, yo?" I repeated, tossing my mattress and stuff up on the top bunk, as the guard secured the cell and walked off.

The bag of chips and two lemon cookies I still had from the bullshit ass Central Bookings dinner bag fell to the floor. "Where you from?" the white boy asked, sticking his mirror out between the grill, as if to see where the guard was going.

"North and Pennsylvania," I replied proudly, picking up my chips and cookies off the floor.

"What they get you for? Where they catch you at? They give you a bail? How old are you?" I could feel the white boy checking out my gear and sizing me up as he continued with his one million questions. "What's your name?"

"Charm," I mumbled, climbing up on the top bunk. All I wanted to do was, lay down and get some sleep. The cold ass, funky feet and ass-smelling Central Bookings holding cell had been kicking my ass the last couple of days.

"Charm, huh?" he repeated with a silly smirk on his face, making me instantly wonder if white boy and I were going to have to get it in up in this bitch.

"Yeah, Charm," I repeated, sitting back up to eye him. I wasn't with no games. I already had too much on my mind.

"Why? What's up? You know me or something?"

"Nah, yo, it's ain't like that. I ain't on no bullshit or nothing." He laughed. "I just thought you were playing, 'cause you look familiar—that's all."

"Oh." I laughed too.

"Plus, I like to know who I'm in the cell with," he said. "Because ain't no rats, homosexuals or rapist staying up in here with me, you feel me?"

"I feel you." I relaxed a little bit. "What's your name?"

"Paul-Paul."

"Where you be at?"

"Down South Baltimore. Pigtown."

"Yeah, that's probably where you recognize me from." I was very familiar with Pigtown. "I be coming through there fucking with one of my lil' side pieces all the time. She work at the Urban Reads Book Store up in Mount Clare Junction."

"Yeah, that's exactly where we probably crossed paths at," Paul-Paul agreed. "I done been in there a few times to cop them *street typey* magazines," he explained. "Who your peeps? Mizz Konnoisseur?"

"Nah," I lied, deciding to stake my claim on one of Tia's fine ass employees. "My baby name Lady Blue," I added, not really trying to put my business out there. I wasn't one of them young niggas who wanted everybody to know that I was hitting a boss.

"Oh, 'cause I was going say we're probably not going to get

132

along because I'm chasing Mizz Konnoisseur's bad ass—That's the only reason I go to all her stores," he confessed. "The one on Greenmount, the one up Mount Clare, and the one in Reisterstown Road Plaza. I love 'em thick and gangsta like that."

Paul-Paul paused, like he was about to say something else, when a book tied to the end of some ripped sheets came flying out of nowhere, and hit the grill before landing just outside the cell.

"What the fuck!" I said, jumping, caught off guard.

"Here we go with the dumb shit." Paul-Paul shook his head.

"What's up?" I questioned curiously.

"Nah, these dudes over here always on some dumb stuff," he stated. "I just had to trash one of them the other day about the phone."

"What? Are you clicked up?" I looked at him sideways, wondering if he was with one of them racist white boy gangs I'd heard about.

"Fuck no!" He sounded offended. "I do me," he added, as somebody from down the tier called his name, and I could respect that because I'd never heard of a white boy holding their own over the jail.

"Ayo, Paul-Paul!"

"Wohh!" Paul-Paul went to the grill.

"Ayo, where your cell buddy from?"

"Over west!" Paul-Paul replied, and everything got quiet for a moment.

"Oh yeah!" I heard the voice say. "Tell yo to put them dopes and that G-Shock watch on the line!"

"Man, I ain't got nothing to do with that!—I'm gone back," Paul-Paul replied, turning around to look at me as my face twisted up.

That nigga couldn't be referring to me. I was a fucking Dummie.

"You heard what yo said? They're gonna try to take your shit."

"What? Shiddd!" I hopped off the bunk with the quickness.

"Watch out, yo." I slid past Paul-Paul. It's wasn't no way in the world that niggas were taking shit from me. Not Nicole Johnson's son. Respect was everything to me.

"Ayo! Check this out! Niggas not taking shit from me! And I'm not coming up off nothing, flat out!" I yelled out on the tier, representing myself. "No tennis, no watch, nothing!"

When dudes heard that, they started going off. Threatening to chop me up, calling me out of my name. One nigga even promised to shit me down; in other words, throw feces into the cell on me. Paul-Paul assured him that if he threw something inside the cell, I would be the least of his problems, and that seemed to put an immediate stop to that.

I was catching as many names as I could. *Madd- Don P Body—Eazy—Barfield—Lor'   Rah-Rah—Tator-Man—Little Dinkles—June*. But, most of all, I was trying to figure out when the fuck Deli was going to acknowledge me. I mean, I knew that he was holding it down over this bitch. He'd always been the type of Dummie who rose to the top, no matter where he was at. And thorough niggas always seemed to gravitate towards him.

"Ayo, you don't know where my nigga Deli sleep at?" I asked.

"Nah," Paul-Paul shook his head. "You sure he's over here? Because a lot of dudes be calling home lying like they're holding it down, but they be on the coop."

"Oh, nah, Dummie definitely ain't on no protective custody," I assured. Too many niggas had come uptown talking about how Deli was carrying his mail on the hopper section. "You probably just don't know him."

"What he look like?"

I thought for second. "Like a fake ass Kevin Hart," I finally said, trying to relax.

"Well, he's not on this side—that's for sure." Paul Paul spoke with confidence, as dudes continued talking shit.

Once niggas began to realize that I wasn't about to stand at the grill and go back and forth like a cell-gangster because I didn't do shouting matches, the tier got quiet, and everybody seemed to fall back. But, not before they assured me what time it was. "A'ight, tough guy! We'll see where your heart is at when these doors open for rec, bitch!"

"I hope you go hard yo," Paul-Paul encouraged as I climbed back up on the hunk. "Because they're definitely going to try and call your bluff."

"Yeah, well, when it's time to show my hand, I don't do no bluffing." I tried to sound slick even though my heart was pounding.

Paul-Paul stood there, staring at me for a moment in silence. Then, he shook his head again and said, "Well, I hope you got a good hand 'cause you're going to need it."

I laid back and tried to rest my nerves. There was no more to he said. When the doors came open, I would be ready for whatever.

It seemed like I'd just dozed off, when I thought I heard somebody whispering my name and looked up to see one of my frequent flying city jail homeboys from around the way sweeping the tier, and I couldn't be happier. "Ahhh shit! Lil' Diggs!" I jumped down off the bed with lightning speed. "What's up, yo?"

"Cooling," he replied, ice-grilling Paul-Paul. "I'ma have to come back after they collect trays though."

"That's what's up." I nodded, getting back up on the bunk. There was no way that I was going back to sleep. Not now, I needed to find out where Deli was and get something up off Lil' Diggs. Shiddd, I knew that if he was carrying it the way he had it in the streets, then he had something big and nasty that would hack the average nigga down.

"What's up, Charm?" Lil' Diggs returned as promised, after the working men collected the feed-up trays. "Fuck is you doing over here?"

"You already know." I wasn't really for the small talk right now. We could play catch up later. "But, fuck all that, yo. I need a hawk asap! Niggas talking about taking my shit when the doors hit."

"I ain't nowhere right now. This coochie tight over here. I been trying to get something from my rap-buddy down on K-section, but yo started playing games." Lil' Diggs looked up and down the tier. "You know what, just give me your shit and I'll tuck it off for you. That way, niggas can't get it and you ain't got to fuck around and get hit about no dumb shit."

"What? Give you my shit to tuck off? Fuck outta here!" I looked at Lil' Diggs like he was ten-carat crazy. "Fuck I look like? Niggas not taking shit from me! You got me fucked up, Lil' Diggs. Where Deli at?"

"On the other side. You won't see him until we go to the gym."

"Can you get over there?"

"Not right this minute, probably later. But I can holler at the tier runner over there and get him to go to his cell."

"Man, let Dummie know that I'm over here," I said. "And tell him to send me a hawk asap!"

"Already," Lil' Diggs nodded and dipped off down the tier as Paul-Paul started laughing. I guess he found my situation very amusing. But I could care less because I knew one thing for sure: with or without a weapon, if niggas came at me, they'd better be prepared for a fight.

When it came time for the doors to open, I stepped out with it on my mind. I wasn't about to trap myself in no little ass cell because I was feeling more homicidal than suicidal and needed room to move. Plus, I was hoping to find Lil' Diggs before shit went down. When I looked down the tier and saw a couple of niggas aggressively coming my way, I knew that I wouldn't be so lucky.

"Step back in the cell and strip, nigga!—Your bitch ass know what it is!" the tiniest one of the pack barked first.

This was it. My hopper tier test had arrived. It was time to go dick-hard and use everything that the streets had taught me. Because I didn't have no bail and going home wasn't an option.

"Niggas not gonna ask your punk ass again!" the second wolf growled, pulling out a big piece of sharpened steel.

I don't know if it was fear, heart or something else, but I went straight into Dummie-mode. There was no more time for hesitation. No more time for contemplation, and no more time for Deli to pop up joking. Nah, it was go time. It was time to set the tone for my stay.

I hit the wolf with the knife first and stepped back to square off with the pack. If I couldn't do nothing else, I could rumble. The squad had made sure of that.

The first wolf rushed me, swinging wild as his man tried to recover. However, I was more concerned with getting hit when the wolf with the sharpened steel took another swing at me as I continued to fight the first wolf off. He missed my face and hit the first wolf in the hand. I locked on to his wrist for dear life and started punching the shit out of him, using everything I had. Speed, strength, accuracy and execution. I knew most dudes expected a motherfucker to take flight or freeze up when the knives came out. But I was all heart and guts. All Dummie.

I finally dropped the wolf with the knife and was about to the finish wearing the first wolf out when a third wolf hit me so hard that he made me see stars. *Damn! How many of these niggas I gotta see?* I thought, grabbing a hold of the third wolf to keep from going down. I had just shaken off the punch and started tussling with the third wolf when somebody yelled out that the guard was coming, and everybody scattered.

When the guard walked to the back of the tier, it got real quiet, and everybody tried to play dumb. All the same, the guard saw blood on the rail in front of the cell and called for an immediate lock-down and body-check.

After the second wolf who'd gotten stabbed in the hand and the one whose nose I'd broken and face I'd swollen up were located, Paul-Paul and I were pulled out for questioning. On my way down the tier, I looked inside the cell where the hard-hitting third wolf had ducked off in when the guard showed up, and saw Lil' Diggs sitting on the bunk. I asked him what was up, but he only hunched his shoulders like he didn't know what was going on. *Bitch ass nigga!* I thought to myself and kept on moving.

In the end, I was moved over to the westside because they said my knuckles looked red.

I saw approval in Paul-Paul's eyes, as I gathered my little bit of property and mattress to bounce. "Stay up over there, Charm," Paul-Paul spoke as I walked out of the cell. "I'll see you around."

"Already," I replied.

"If you need something, let me know," Paul-Paul added.

"I heard that." I nodded appreciatively, knowing that we would definitely be seeing each other again. On this side or the other.

When I got on the other side of the section, Deli was already down with what had happened. He just had no idea that I was involved. Turns out that there was a major East Baltimore/ West Baltimore war going on over the jail, and the hopper tier just so happened to be at the heart of it.

Deli recognized a few of the names I could remember—especially, Tator-Man and June: Two rap-buddies who were over the jail for trashing three dudes with them Beretta ARX-160 assault rifles up on Durley Avenue after a neighborhood fight. I remembered the case because the police chief had been all over WJZ 6 o'clock news, going off about juveniles being able to obtain jam-proof weapons with amphibious (both hand bolt, ejector, and action) capabilities. However, I didn't give a fuck about none of that. I was trying to see anybody who had something to say and everybody who was down with the move the wolf pack had tried to bring me. Because there was no way that I was letting that shit slide. Not after niggas tried to rob and stab me. That was just straight up disrespect. I mean, I could co-exist with niggas I fought, banged out with, or even in some cases did not like. But, disrespect could not be tolerated under no circumstances. Win, lose or draw.

"Like I said, Dummie, I don't give a fuck if a nigga is hooked up with the Crips, Bloods, B-G-F or none of them other new 'Sucker Lives Matter' movements somebody done came up with. I'm trying to see em all!" I fired, still heated as Deli tried to explain how shit went on the hopper section.

"I got this, Dummie," Deli assured, as we stood in front of his cell looking at pictures of everybody. "June a straight up soldier. Yo, ain't nothing like Tator-Man. He don't be on that East Baltimore, West Baltimore fuck shit! So, as soon as I holler at him and find out exactly who else was involved, I'ma get with the police and set it up." Deli said those words as I continued to look through his photos.

"Fuck you mean, you're gonna get with the police?" I looked up from a photo of Deli and his brothers. "The police like, the C.O.?"

"Yeah, how the hell else you think you're going to be able to see niggas from the other side without going on lock up?"

"Oh, they're carrying it like that over here?" I asked, impressed.

Deli nodded. "They got a couple of them crazy Cumberland white boys running the tier and they be letting niggas get it in."

"Get it in where?" I looked around. "In the cells?"

"Nah, Dummie." Deli smiled. "See that open space down there?" Deli pointed to the front of the top tier. "That's the square. That's where everybody go to test their 'G' head up with the steel or hands."

"Oh yeah," I stared down the tier at the makeshift ring. "Niggas got their own fight club over here, huh?"

"Something like that."

"Ahhhhh, yo got some pictures of Bucky Love dirty ass," I joked, checking out a few photos of Deli's first love looking good as always.

"Don't get balled up, Dummie!" Deli threatened with a smile. "You know I'm fool about Bucky Love."

"Yeah, you and sport-coat," I teased. "Bucky Love not yours no more, Dummie."

"Yeah, a'ight, nigga. You see this?" Deli pulled his shirt up to reveal Bucky Love's real name tatted across his chest. "Bucky Love will always be mines, believe that. I don't care who she's fucking with."

"It's your book, Dummie. You write how you want." I laughed but honestly, I knew Deli wasn't lying. Since we were children, he and Bucky Love somehow always seemed to find their way back together. "So, when do I get to see these East Baltimore niggas though?" I asked on a more serious note, flipping through a stack of photos of the entire Dummie Squad all hanging out at '6 Flags Great Adventure' last summer.

"It depends on who's working," Deli replied. "If Reed or Lensbrouer got the tier, they're not going to let niggas go too hard if some brass is floating around. But, Durst and Broadwater don't give a fuck!" Deli assured. "Once I tell them what's up, it's a wrap! They're gonna let niggas rock with the hands or roll with the joints as long as they get to see it."

"Set it up asap! I'm tryna trash something," I threw my guards up and started showcasing my skills on the shadow-boxing tip. "It's been a minute since I put these monkey paws on a nigga, anyway."

Deli knew, like I did, that the call for blood had to be answered on some level. Not only was it the Dummie Squad's way. It was also the law of the jungle—be it concrete or steel. It was the only way to truly earn your respect in the animal kingdom. Deli didn't want me to take it personal, but I couldn't help it. I didn't care that everybody basically got the same 'welcoming card'. I didn't give a fuck that some hoe ass Park Heights lame had gotten knocked out, pissed on, and thrown off the top tier. And I damn sure could care less about the last East Baltimore thug who'd ran out of the 'square' with his face looking like a dirt-bike tire. Niggas had violated, and somebody had to be dealt with, period. No ifs, ands, or buts about it.

"I should be cursing your silly ass out anyway!" I fired, remembering the message I'd sent his dumb ass.

"Cursing who out?" Deli questioned.

"You, nigga!" I spat, handing him his flicks back. What the fuck happen to you sending me something over by the working man?"

"What the fuck is you talking about?" Deli looked at me,

genuinely confused, tossing the photos on his bed, and I didn't know if he was playing or not because he played so damn much.

"I told your retarded ass to send me a hawk!" I retorted. "If you would've done that, I could've wore them niggas out. Especially that black ass nigga!"

"You ain't tell me shit! I didn't even know your dumb ass was over here yet," Deli revealed. "Last time I talk to Lor'Homie, he said you were still over the Bookings. Plus, you know I would've never left you over that bitch naked with all them East Baltimore niggas. Fuck I look like?" Deli argued and I could tell that he was being sincere. "I would've sent you the street knife over there."

"Hold up, Lil' Diggs never sent word or nothing over here to tell you what I said?"

"Man, fuck no! Niggas don't even fuck with that lil' bitch! He's a bonafide rat!" Deli exclaimed.

"Who? Lil' Diggs?" I questioned, to be sure, praying that shorty wasn't just another gun-gangster. He had been putting on for the 'Avenue' since we were kids.

"Yeah, that whore!" Deli confirmed without hesitation. "Yo, over this bitch giving the 'Avenue' a bad name."

"Damn, Dummie." I shook my head, drained. It seemed like everytime a fake nigga got separated from his tone, he either started snitching, or the bitch came out. "All that work that nigga put in."

"I know, now he's telling on half of West Baltimore."

"That's crazy," I shook my head again. "That nigga going like that, Dummie?"

"What?" Deli said, as if I knew. "That lil' bitch ratting everybody out. Diesel, Lil' Dirt that look like Snoop from "The Wire", Lil' Curley, all them T-T-G niggas," Deli dropped the name of some real good men through West Baltimore. "His lil' bitch ass was even calling uptown jamming niggas up on the phone."

"Fuck no!" was all I could manage. Now everything started to make sense. I kept wondering why everybody was getting grabbed for bodies and shit all of a sudden.

"See, now you see why I don't be fucking with them phones like that. Niggas be too reckless out the mouth on both sides of the phone."

I felt sick to my stomach.

"That's not the half of it though," Deli revealed. "Remember the lil' nigga Peedy and them from Edmondson Avenue that use to grab niggas with Goo and Lil' Arron?"

"Ain't no question," I assured. "They be right up there on Warwick where the lil' red-bone nurse bitch—Moncy—I use to dig out live at. Yo and them be getting to the paper."

"Yeah, well, Lil' Diggs telling on them too about some two thousand twelve shit."

"Wow! And here it is I just thought his lil' ass was acting like a chump when I seen him. You know this nigga had the nerve to tell me to give him my dopes and shit."

"Hell, no!" Deli bust out laughing.

"That's my word, Dummie," I assured. "Talking about he gonna tuck my shit off so nigga won't get 'em."

"Yo, lil' ass a straight up and down fuck boy for them East Baltimore niggas over there. They stay sending that nigga on crash-dummy missions. They be taking his shit too. I remember his baby mother brought him some court clothes and the lil' nigga Rah-Rah took his shit and spit in his face."

"Hold up, Dummie, now that I think about it. The black nigga who stole me was in the cell with Lil' Diggs." I remembered, massaging my jaw.

"Oh, that's the nigga Barfield then. He ran that Blood shit over east!" Deli exclaimed.

"That's who I wanna see then." I smiled at Deli. He of all people knew how much I hated the Bloods behind the death of my lil' sister. "What you say his name is? Barfield?"

"Yeah, he real nice with his hands too, Dummie." Deli said.

"Yeah, I'm nice with mine too."

"Nah, Dummie, this nigga 'Upton' Boxing Gym nice." Deli warned. "I mean, yo be destroying niggas in the square to point of giving them CTE."

"I got him, Dummie," I assured confidently. "Don't forget I use to spar with Tank and Berry."

"Well, just in case you don't, I'ma bring the hawk."

"And watch me slap the fuck outta of that lil' bitch Diggs when I see him too," I disclosed, still finding it kind of hard to believe that Lil' Diggs would try to play me out for some East Baltimore niggas when he knew how I got down for mine.

"That shit still fucking with you, ain't it? Seeing a nigga who was a cold-blooded killer on the streets getting treated like a hoe in the joint."

"A little bit," I replied, unable to stop myself from laughing at the sad face Deli put on.

"That shit had me tripping at first too," Deli admitted. "I was, like, damn, homie—with that tone, you was the man, homie, what the fuck happened to you?" Deli joked, making me laugh harder. I swear, it felt good to be back around my nigga again. Even under the circumstances.

Delmont Player

Chapter 15

"What up, slick?" Zimbabwe entered Billy Lo's room with a broom, noticing Nurse Edwards. "Oh, how are you doing, Miss Edwards?"

"I am blessed, thank you." Nurse Edwards continued to draw Billy Lo's blood. "And yourself?"

"Same old, same old," Zimbabwe replied.

"What's happening though?" Billy Lo looked up, kind of surprised to see Zimbabwe so late in the day.

"I can't call it." Zimbabwe sneakingly gestured towards Nurse Edwards, like he had something important to tell Billy Lo, and began to sweep. "You was all knocked out up in here earlier when I came through, so I just skipped your room."

"I had a long day. I was down in the visiting room all morning going over my trial strategy." Billy Lo exclaimed. "Then, you got Miss Edwards feeding me all these meds."

"Don't you start with me," Nurse Edwards warned, pressing down on his vein with a gall-pad, before removing the large rubber band and needle. "I am not forcing you to take that medication. Now, hush up and hold this while I get a band-aid."

"Yes, ma'am."

"What? You got the state's discovery?" Zimbabwe questioned, tripping off of Nurse Edwards.

"Yeah," Billy Lo replied, as Nurse Edwards carefully placed the band-aid over the gall-pad and told him to leave it on for at least an hour as usual. "It's so much mess in there, slim. I haven't even finished going through it yet."

"Okay, well, let me get out of you gentleman's way," Nurse Edwards interjected, quickly gathering her things as Zimbabwe started to sweep under the bed. She always got uncomfortable whenever Billy Lo began discussing his case because in her heart, she knew that only God had the right to judge another human being. Because only God was without sin.

"I need to finish my rounds," she added, placing everything on her little metal hospital cart, heading for the door.

"You know your little man is on the hopper tier, right?" Zimbabwe stated the moment Nurse Edwards rolled the cart out of the room.

"Who?" Billy Lo asked nonchalantly, scratching his arm.

"Charm," Zimbabwe said, getting Billy Lo's full attention now.

"Charm?" Billy Lo sat up, all ears. "Charm's on L-section?" Billy Lo looked at Zimbabwe for confirmation and continued after he nodded. "You sure?" Billy Lo asked, wanting to be certain.

"I'm positive," Zimbabwe replied with conviction. "I heard one of them little kids call his name in the gym yesterday. So, I got my little folks to pull his name up this morning. It's him."

"Oh yeah?" Billy Lo couldn't even think straight. Charm was in his arena now, and there was no way he could let him get away untouched. He had to find a way to give him the blues. "That little bitch on the hopper tier, huh?" Billy Lo rubbed his chin, thinking out loud as his mind began to run wild with ways of being able to get at Charm. "Ayo, slim, isn't your little nephew still on the hopper tier fighting that Cherry Hill case?" Billy Lo had an idea.

"Yeah, I think so." Zimbabwe paused to think. "My daughter hasn't said nothing to me about him getting found guilty or being home."

"Find out for sure."

"Why? What do you have in mind?"

Billy Lo just stared at him for a second before responding. "You think you can get him to tear the fur off Charm's little ass for him."

"Most definitely. My nephew live for that drama. You're gonna have to look out for him, though."

"If he's still over there, line it up!" Billy Lo ordered without hesitation. "Let him know I'll put the money wherever he wants it at."

***

146

"I thought your Italian friend had him taken care of before all that other stuff went down?" Tariq continued to rub his temple and squeeze the bridge of nose.

"I thought the same thing. He assured me that he would, even before I took care of Samad. So, you can imagine my surprise when I got the phone cell this weekend telling me that the brother was spotted lounging at some five-star hotel right outside of Virginia." Adnan leaned back in his soft leather recliner and placed his elbows on the armrest, before clasping his hands together.

"That's not good, Ock."

"I know," Adnan agreed, staring into Tariq's radiating eyes of wisdom. "Something like this could really come back to haunt us."

"So, what do you think he's doing in Virginia?" Tariq questioned curiously.

"Hiding—witness protection, maybe. He could be starting over. Who knows? Either way, he has to be dealt with."

Tariq walked over to the mini-bar in Adnan's 'Al-Fatihah' Oil and Incense Shop office, and poured himself a drink. He knew that Adnan wanted action. Not suggestions. Because in their line of work, the truth was often seen, rarely heard.

"I should've let Yah-Yah hit him outside of the Horse Shoe Casino when he first informed me about it." Adnan took a deep breath. It seemed like it just never ended. He hadn't been back from his pilgrimage to the Holy City of Mecca, a week and he was already dealing with past fuck ups again.

"It's not your fault, Ock. Had he told you—"

Adnan cut Tariq off with a wave of the hand. "Nah, it is. Because he told me about it and I should've made sure that it was taken care of. Especially after all of his guys were rounded up by the Feds."

"So what now?" Tariq took a seat. "Because I know you're not about to sit on your hands."

"Of course not. I am going to take a trip out to Virginia and clean this mess up myself."

"I don't think that's such a good idea."

"I didn't ask if you did," Adnan corrected. "What I am going to do is, go out there, find out where he's staying and do whatever's necessary to get the job done."

"And what about the brothers out in Virginia? I am sure they don't need no more unwanted heat. Especially after all the stuff with my son out in Philly."

"Let me worry about them." Adnan looked at the monitors. There was no way in hell that he was letting a cancer continue to go untreated. Not when he had the chance to remove it once and for all. "I am sure they do not want to sit around and wait for disturbing news."

"So, what do you need me to do?"

"Get me a rental. Something good for the road." Adnan knew that he couldn't afford to take a train or airplane. Tariq nodded. There was nothing else to be said concerning the matter. "Now, what was it that you wanted to talk to me about?"

"Oh yeah." Tariq had almost forgotten. "It seems that Charm has gotten himself into a little bit of a jam. From what I gather, he was arrested with a weapon that may or not be attached to a couple of cold cases."

If some of these kids today had brains, they would truly be dangerous. Instead, they wanted to put all their business on social media, spend all their money on nothing but clothes and women, and now he guessed, hold on to murder weapons. "I thought Charm was smarter then that." Adnan shook his head. "What do you need me to do?"

"Maybe call in a favor. Have the weapon disappear or something." Tariq knew that Adnan had a lot of pull within the police department from years and years of working with them within the community as an activist.

Adnan remained silent, as if carefully considering Tariq's words. He wished that he was still in Mecca. It had felt so amazing to be surrounded by millions of brothers from all over the world. "I'll take care of it," he finally spoke. "But make sure that Charm understands that when the time comes, he's gonna pay us back big time," Adnan added, knowing that nothing in life was actually free.

***

"Anything on the time of death?" Detective Baker questioned the lab tech before kneeling down to peel one of the blood-stained sheets back to get a good look at the stiff corpse.

"Not yet. But, from the looks of decomposition, I am guessing two, maybe three days. Won't know for sure until I get them on a table."

Detective Gibson continued to walk around the small basement in shoe-covers, looking for anything that seemed out of place as the crime lab took photos, dusted for latent prints, and collected DNA.

"Anybody hear anything?" Detective Baker stood back up, wondering about witnesses.

"Nope," a nearby uniformed officer replied. "Not a sound."

"You mean to tell me that two people are tied up, tortured and shot two times each in the head and nobody hears a thing? Not even a neighbor?" Baker used a loose glove to pick up a bloody wooden baseball bat. He hadn't seen so much blood since a couple of whacked out kids got high off of some bad synthetic molly and stabbed each other to death in a small apartment located off of Pressman Street a few years back.

"You sound surprised. You know how it goes around here."

"Yeah, everybody honors the code of silence until we get them alone downtown," Baker assured him, slipping the bloody baseball bat into a large evidence bag. "Who discovered the bodies?"

"That would be the daughter, sir—Said she hadn't heard from her father in about a week and decided to drop by," the uniformed officer replied.

"Anything else she could tell you?" Baker waited for a response as Detective Gibson walked back over. "Enemies, debts, threats, etc?"

"Not really. She showed up, noticed that the door was ajar, entered, came upon the bodies and called the police. But then again, she was a little shaken up. So, maybe she'll be a little more helpful once she's had some time to calm down."

"Well, after talking to a few spectators, I did gather that these two were quite the neighborhood duo," Gibson spoke up.

"Ahhhh, don't tell me these guys were another one of those damn up-and-coming rap groups!" Detective Baker fired. It seemed like everybody wanted to be rappers nowadays. "I remember a time when rappers wanted to be gangsters. Now, it's like gangsters want to be rappers. I bet they got them damn cars where the rims won't stop spinning too."

"Nobody has spinners any more, detective." The uniform officer laughed, not understanding Detective Baker's humor.

"Anyway," Detective Gibson continued. "Turns out the duo was pretty feared around here and for good reasons. One spectator said that the duo had shook down so many dealers in the neighborhood, that we'd be lucky if we could find one who didn't want them gone. Let alone one brave enough to pull the trigger."

Chapter 16

"A'ight, you little motherfuckers! If you're going to the gym, you better be ready when the doors open!" one of the tier officers screamed, walking up and down the tier.

By now, I had been over the jail a little over a month and had Deli's lawyer, Elizabeth Franzoso, representing me on the gun and sure to come murder beef. I had finally gotten my day in the square too. The two crazy white boy C.O.'s Broadwater and Lensbrouer had let me see Madd-Body and Barfield head-up with the dick-beaters. Of course, I earned my respect. This was, of course, after I slapped the taste out of Lil' Diggs's mouth and Deli made him go to the tier officer and request to be moved onto the chicken farmer. I can't lie though, the dude Madd-Body's could go with his hands, but he wasn't ready.

The nigga Barfield, however, was a problem up in that square. I had thought the nigga had just caught me off guard when he first snuck me and made me see lights. Now, I knew for sure that the nigga hit hard. We went until neither one of us could move, and our eyes were damn near swollen shut. The guards had to make us stop because both of us were willing to go to the death.

The jail wasn't so bad once you got accustomed to it. My mother and Nizzy made sure that I was straight, and Ebony kept a smile on my face with letters, sexy photos, 92Q Radio shout-outs and weekly visitations. She was like one of them back in the day gangster bitches that young niggas only heard about holding shit down when shit hit the fan.

When we got to the gym, Deli and I went straight up on the bleachers and sat down in our usual spot near a few other West Baltimore niggas. The jail had a way of bringing sworn enemies together and building bonds between niggas who were normally at each other's throats. It was like the men separated themselves from the mutts over the jail. However, there were some relationships that could just never be mended. For instance, like the Murder [Murphy] Homes niggas and us. It was just too much bad blood to have anything more than respect for each other's space.

Every time I saw Lil'Deezy's black ass, I thought about David and Monk, and honestly wanted to bring him a move. I knew that I had to leave that shit in the streets and work on getting Deli and myself back on the bricks. At least for now. But I promised myself that the minute everything was in order, I was going straight at Lil'Deezy—especially if we were still on the tier together. I didn't give a fuck about new charges or nothing. I wasn't going to tolerate no nigga who did something to one of my brothers. Not when I no longer had to, anyway.

"So what's up, Dummie? Fuck was you hollering about last night?" I questioned Deli after hollering at a few good men.

"I got my discovery last night," Deli said, handing me a large manilla envelope.

"That's like all the statements and stuff in your case right?" I acted like I really knew something about the law.

"Yeah, crime scenes photos, police reports, medical records and things like that," Deli replied, reaching over to open the envelope and pull out a stack of papers. "It got the pictures they took of me, Thugg and Lil'Deezy at the hospital. Plus, I got the autopsy on Alien and Monk."

"Let me see the joints of Thugg and Alien, Dummie," I requested excitedly, dying to see my work up close and personal. I didn't want to see my nigga laid out on a cold steel table. "Fuck is this?" I questioned, as soon as Deli handed me a few sheets of paper stapled together. "I'm trying to see niggas laid out, Dummie!" I exclaimed, after flipping through what appeared to be a bunch of names.

"Hold up." Deli pushed the papers back into my hand. "I'ma let you take everything in the cell with you anyway. But—check that out." Deli gestured towards the stapled papers still in my hand. "That's my witness list. Don't even pay the police names no mind. Start on page two."

I turned the page and skipped over the few detective names at the top and started silently going down the list, scanning names. "That's Stacey?" I looked up, recognizing the lil' thot's name we'd all slutted out at one time or another.

"Yup," Deli nodded.

"Trifling ass bitch." I shook my head. Tyree Stewart, I knew, was Thugg's hoe ass real name. "Shawnte Dukes?" I paused. The name seemed familiar for some reason. "Hold up, that's my man Shoe-Lace nephew, Duke." I looked at Deli, bemused.

"Yeah, I know. That's why I was tripping." Deli appeared to be just as surprised as me, as I continued looking for names that rung a bell. "Shoe-Lace a fucking 'G'."

"Who the fuck is Corey Linwood?"

"I'm not sure—I think it's the nigga Scar that be on the Avenue though," Deli replied. "You know he's originally from the projects."

"Oh," I still shook my head in disgust. It was always those dick-riding followers who broke first. The telling shit was really out of control. I could not figure out when the city had become so rat-infested. It just seemed like everybody was dying to snitch all of a sudden. Even some of the niggas from the 'Stop Snitching' movement were jumping on the stand now. "I don't even want to look at this shit no more, Dummie." I handed the witness list back to Deli. "That shit giving me a headache."

I was done. The game was over. Itchy-Man's own brother was telling on him. Our childhood friend was telling on me. And now, you had a band of so-called gangsters jumping on cases that didn't have nothing to do with them. Old bitch ass niggas too.

"Most of that shit I can get around," Deli confessed. "Like the attempt on Lil'Deezy. You already know yo gonna stand up. I just got to figure out how to get around some of these weak ass niggas and that circumstantial shit."

"Shiddd, get that bitch Elinore to come to court for you. She know you weren't at her party, you feel me?"

"Lil'Deezy already tried to holler at shorty for me—She's on some geek shit! Talking about she's not getting involved," Deli replied.

"She think they're gonna get to asking her about some other stuff."

"Don't worry about it. I got Elinore."

I looked at Deli with confidence. "You know that's my nigga Bozack's cousin. Once I get word to him, he'll make sure she comes to court and do right, whether she wants to or not."

"I hope so." Deli spoke like he wasn't too convinced.

"Just have some faith, Dummie," I said, not wanting my nigga to stress or worry too much. I mean, because at the end of the day, he had something that nobody else had: The support of the 'Dummie Squad' behind him. "You know the squad got you."

***

"Man, if you silly ass niggas don't stop playing around and come the fuck on," Nizzy fussed, sticking his head out the window of his truck as Lor'Homie and G-baby continued to slap-box in the middle of the gas-station parking lot. "I'ma leave y'all dumb asses, watch!"

"You lucky, Dummie!" Lor'Homie said, backing up towards the truck before letting his guards down. "I was about to get in your ass," he added, before opening the passenger side door to climb back inside.

"Fuck outta here, nigga! You the lucky one. I was popping the fuck outta your slow ass," G-baby retorted, climbing into the back seat. "Fuck is you talking about?"

"I let you do that 'cause it's your birthday," Lor'Homie said, as they pulled out of the gas station. "Don't get it fucked up."

Nizzy turned the music up and headed for their next destination as Lor'Homie and G-baby continued to argue about who had the sharpest hands.

"So, what's up now?" G-baby asked, looking at his watch. They'd been hanging out all day, smoking, drinking and strip-club hopping.

"You already know." Nizzy smiled over his shoulder.

154

"Remember the lil' after-hour bitch you were sweating?"

"Yeah, he remembers," Lor'Homie said when G-baby started smiling.

"Well, you already know how we do."

"Don't play, Dummie!" G-baby warned. He played about a lot of things, but pussy wasn't one of them. "You know I was all over that bitch."

"You know I don't play about money and I don't play about no pussy!" Nizzy spat.

"That's what I'm talking about." G-baby rubbed his hands together like he'd just won a prize. "Take notes, Dummie, that's how you set your man out for his b-day nigga!"

"Ahhhh, nigga, fuck you," Lor'Homie replied, as they passed what looked like the same apartment complex for the second time. "Give me my five bands back then, nigga."

"No, no, no," G-baby joked, leaning forward to squeeze the back of Lor'Homie's head.

"Come on, Dummie, before you fuck up shit!" Lor'Homie complained, slapping G-baby's hand away before gently running his hand over his fro-hawk to make sure the two cornrows were still perfectly in place.

"Stop crying, nigga. Ain't nobody gonna fuck up your lil' hair." G- baby laughed.

"Ayo, I thought that lil' bitch had a husband?"

Nizzy answered: "She does. That's why she told us to wait till after midnight when her dude went to work, before we came through. You know you can't stop these thots from fucking."

"Do you even know where the fuck you're going?" Lor'Homie questioned. "We done went past that pool three times."

"You wanna do this, nigga?" Nizzy looked from one apartment complex parking lot to another, as they drifted down the street. "If not, shut your dumb ass up."

"If you need me to, I will," Lor'Homie replied, turning the music down. "Cos you know I can sniff a bitch out better than a blood hound."

"You hear this nigga?" G-baby shook his head.

"I'm not paying that nigga no mind." Nizzy continued looking for something familiar. "I'm looking for bitch car."

"Ayo, if your girl text me one more time, I'ma start to think she's tryna give me a birthday present too!" G-baby exclaimed, holding his phone up to Nizzy's face so he could see the screen.

"Don't get fucked around, Dummie," Nizzy said, snatching the phone out of G-baby's hand to read the message. "Nigga, she only texting your funny-looking ass 'cause she can't find me," Nizzy said before replying, as if he was G-baby: *I left dummie & 'em at the club*, Nizzy texted.

"That's how it always starts," G-baby joked. "Stupid nigga leaves his phone somewhere and his girl think he's fucking around and needs a shoulder to cry on. Next thing you know, her head falling into your lap." G-baby leaned back and pretended to be getting some slow-neck.

"You already!" Lor'Homie egged G-baby on with some dap.

"You a dumb ass nigga," Nizzy directed his comment at Lor'Homie, reading Butta's response. "You left your phone in the club too, nigga!" Nizzy reminded Lor'Homie as he replied to Butta one more time before aimlessly tossing G-baby's phone back over the driver's seat.

"Fuck is you doing, Dummie!" G-baby almost didn't catch the phone. "You about to break my shit!" He juggled the phone a few times before it fell in his lap. "I just bought this phone, nigga!"

"Fuck you, nigga, see if I get any of you niggas some pussy in the future. Birthday or not." Nizzy brought the truck to a complete stop when he saw the car he'd been looking for. "There go shorty's car right there!" Nizzy said the moment he laid eyes on the red Hyundai Sonata parked at the back of one of the complexes' parking lots. "I know what the fuck I'm doing."

"Ahhhh, nigga, you don't know shit!" Lor'Homie challenged.

"Where you going at?" G-baby questioned, confused when Nizzy pulled off again instead of turning into the parking lot.

"It's a parking spot right there."

"Didn't I just say the bitch didn't want her dude to find out she was creeping?" Nizzy shook his head. "Why would I park right in front of her building so her nosey neighbors can be all in her business!"

"You can tell this nigga don't get no pussy, Cuzzo." Lor'Homie looked at G-baby over his shoulder and laughed.

"I get more pussy than both of you niggas put together!" G-baby retorted, as Nizzy made a left and drove around the back of the building. "Watch how I handle this big butt bitch when we get up in here."

Nizzy pulled the truck all the way behind the apartment complex, and parked beside a dumpster before they all exited the truck, still joking with each other.

"Nah, she supposed to have a few homegirls and her sister here." Lor'Homie addressed G-baby's concerns. "If not, we're banking that bitch up in there."

"Nigga ain't running no train on my bitch on my b-day," G-baby argued.

"Fuck outta here." Nizzy just continued to lead the way as they cut through a path that ran between the building and the woods. "This nigga sound like Murdock," Nizzy said over his shoulder. "He in love with the pussy and he hasn't even gotten it yet."

"I don't love nothing but money, Dummie," G-baby assured, looking around as he tried to watch his step. "It's dark as fuck back here. You better hope I don't get no mud on these Gucci's, nigga!" G-baby felt something smash into the back of his head before he fell to his knees.

"Judgement day, bitch!" Lor'Homie stepped over top of G-baby, as Nizzy looked around for any signs of life. It was better to be safe than sorry when it came to witnesses.

"Ahhhh, nigga!" G-baby whined, as his hands shot to his now bloody head. "What the fuck is wrong with you?" G-baby looked from his bloody palm to Lor'Homie.

"Why you do it, Dummie?" Nizzy eyed G-baby with no

emotion. "You shouldn't have broken your oath," Nizzy added, as Lor'Homie raised the .40.

"What? What the fuck are you talking about, Dummie? I didn't break my oath." G-baby played dumb, but honestly, he knew exactly what Nizzy was talking about. He'd given Charm up to the peoples for another day of freedom. "Hold up, Lor'Homie!" G-baby pleaded, putting his hands up as Nizzy walked back towards the truck. "We're family. Don't do this. You know me."

"Why you do it, Dummie?" Lor'Homie really wanted to know what could make a nigga sell his soul.

"I swear to God, Dummie. I ain't say shit!"

"Stop lying, bitch!" Lor'Homie spat. "The police recorded you." He lied.

G-baby dropped his head, defeated. "I wasn't going to testify, Dummie. You know that." G-baby reasoned, looking off into the darkness where Nizzy had disappeared. "Nizzy! Nizzy!" G-baby called out. "Come on, don't do this, Dummie. I swear, I wasn't going to testify. I would never go out like that."

Lor'Homie shuddered to think of the harm G-baby could have brought to the squad. "I know, Dummie, I know."

Lor'Homie pulled the trigger the first time and shot G-baby right in the face with the Chrome Glock 40. Then, he just emptied the rest of the clip.

Nizzy had just reached the truck when he heard the unmistakable echo of a suppressed gunshot. He stared in the direction of the shot and saw the. illuminating flashes of light a few seconds before Lor'Homie emerged from the darkness alone and climb back into the truck.

"Who the fuck you think you are, nigga? Frank White or somebody?" Lor'Homie questioned with a laugh, as Nizzy backed out and pulled off. "You gonna walk off into the shadows and shit while Dummie begging for his life."

"Keep it a hundred though. That shit was gangster." Nizzy smiled.

"Hell no! You was stiff as shit!" Lor'Homie joked. "Nah,

Cuzzo, all jokes aside. You did that."

"What that bitch say?" Nizzy inquired, wondering to himself if he'd ignored any warning signs that should've told him G-baby would eventually go the wrong way.

"That he wasn't going to testify. He sworn to it."

"Good, we just made sure."

"That shit was crazy though," Lor'Homie confessed, slowly wiping his tone down.

Nizzy peeped over at his cousin. "I know you aren't getting soft on me, nigga?"

"Of course not. It's just that—we went to school together. So, it felt funny killing one of my day one niggas—my childhood friend."

Nizzy frowned. "Fuck that skunk! Family, friend or foe—He was dead weight," Nizzy fired, using Dummie Squad lingo for a snake, rat or pig. "And for that he had to go." Nizzy knew his cousin and G-Baby were close, but G-Baby violated everything they stood for. "You know like I do, Cuz, that it was only a matter of time before he gave all of us up to them peoples. That's how them rats works after they break. They'll use whoever they can think of as a scapegoat to remain free. Nobody's safe!"

"Already." Lor'Homie nodded. Still, it felt weird that he had to be the one to blow his day one nigga's brains out and take his life. "And you already know how we're living."

"Honor over everything!" Lor'Homie replied, knowing that any organization that didn't honor their own laws were destined to fail. Because they would be easily torn apart by betrayal

"Exactly." Nizzy looked over at his cousin and smiled as they turned onto the expressway. "Any Dummie who forsake that honor knows what he's losing, but not what he shall find."

"You already," Lor'Homie agreed, knowing that G-baby was the only one who could say Charm cracked Xavier that night and give so many details. "So, what are you getting into?"

"Nothing, really. Why?"

"Nah, I was thinking about them Longwood freaks we were messing with last week."

Nizzy looked at his cousin, shook his head and laughed. "If you was as focused on getting money as you were on getting pussy, you'd be a rich young nigga."

"Look who's talking!" Lor'Homie retorted. "Nigga, if you wasn't as in love with killing as you are with them Mexican bitches, you'd have a conscience"

Nizzy just continued to shake his head and laugh because it was easy to tell that they were family.

***

"Good afternoon," a cute, little, round-faced Mexican chick looked up from her tattoo magazine, as the unique-sounding door alarm made her aware of my presence as I entered 'El Pie del Caballo' (The Foot of the Horse) House of Ink and headed towards the mirror-covered counter. "How may I help you?" she questioned with a very friendly and outgoing disposition.

"I'm here to see Roofy," I replied, looking around as the memory of Leon and I getting matching tattoos on his birthday came back to me. *Sneaky ass bastard!* I thought, smiling. I'd really believed that we were there simply to obtain tattoos.

I watched as the cute, little Mexican chick walked a few feet over to a black beaded curtain-covered doorway and pulled it back before yelling something in Spanish. I eyed the large yellow dragon tattoo that completely covered her exposed back and appeared to end somewhere beneath her shorts.

"Gracias," I said to the chick.

A model-like Mexican woman appeared a few moments later from behind the bead-curtain in a pink tank-top. "Hola, senorita," the Mexican woman said, looking at me.

"Roofy?" I questioned, surprised when she nodded. I'd expected to see some tattoo-littered, El Chapo-looking motherfucker. "Peanut," I extended my hand. "Black's wife."

"Si, si." She smiled, shaking my hand gently. "Mikey Mumbles girlfriend, Cat, said you would be stopping by. Come, come." She waved, gesturing for me to come around the counter.

"Tu sei bella, bella sei tu!" she mumbled softly before winking at the cute counter girl, as I came behind the counter.

"What was that?" I questioned curiously. I wasn't for all the Spanish language, especially since I couldn't understand it.

"I just told my little sister that you are beautiful, beautiful you are." She smiled softly.

"Yeah, well, I would appreciate it if we—you—just spoke in English," I said, removing my metal clip-front MGM sunglasses. Honestly, I wasn't offended. I knew I was a bad bitch. Especially today with my tight, curve-fitting, cocaine-white Fendi outfit and matching white Red Bottoms to show off the curves of my legs and thick thighs. I had my lips nice and glossed up, and my hair done up in a fresh Peruvian 'Straight wrap'. I made sure that I was oozing with sex appeal before I left the house, because Leon had taught me a long time ago that most men were visual. They couldn't see with their third eye once they were blinded by beauty with their first two. But now that Roofy turned out to be a woman, I realized that it was all for nothing.

"Si, I mean, yes," she agreed before holding the bead-curtain open for me, as her little sister appeared to roll her eyes. Roofy led me down a small, dimly lit hallway with hundreds of photos, tattoo patterns and designs plastered all over the walls. We entered the next-to-last room, which—strangely enough—was brightly lit.

"So, what is it that you would like, Peanut?" she questioned, picking up a huge black, loose-leaf notebook to hand to me. "If you can't find anything in there up to your liking, I'll have to draw something up," she continued, as I looked at her like she was crazy. Roofy must've realized that I was about to say something. So, she put her finger up to her lips to shush me before pointing up towards the ceiling, mouthing something about somebody listening. Then she reached over to program an MP3 Player.

"Oh," I nodded, understanding, ready to play along. "I only want something small on my lower back. Probably my daughter's name." I played along as Roofy turned the volume completely up.

"You can never be too careful," Roofy said.

"I understand." I sat down. "So, why are you here, Peanut?" Roofy's eyes slowly roamed over my body.

"Well, I got some cousins who are looking to purchase some weight. And I was—"

"Let's not bullshit each other, okay? It's a waste of time," Roofy cut me off. "Just let me know exactly what it is that I can do for you."

"I need insurance," I revealed. "I want to be sure that if something goes wrong with the guy that I'm in bed with, you'll cover me."

Roofy seemed to consider the idea. "Sounds like you have a problem." Roofy smiled, and I nodded. "Why not just let me get rid of it for you?"

"It's a little more complicated than that," I confessed, honestly hoping that Roofy would not press me for more information. I didn't feel like explaining that I too wanted to make Charm suffer for joining the same team that was responsible for the death of my daughter's father.

"Okay." She appeared to be in agreement. "Let's say I give you an insurance policy, what's in it for me?"

"What is it that you want?" I shifted slightly. I'd noticed the way Roofy had began to stare at me. So, I now knew her weakness. And I plan to exploit it to my advantage.

Roofy giggled like a school girl and walked over to the door. "Well, you talk a good game, baby." Roofy closed the door and locked it. "Let's see if you know how to play one too."

Chapter 17

"Damn!" I said, cutting my neighbor off. "Hold up, yo!" I added, pressing my face to the grill, trying to get a better look at the chocolate-drop who'd just strutted past the cell in a body-hugging uniform with her ass jiggling like it had a mind of its own. "Who the fuck was that?"

"What?" Whoopie questioned, confused. "I'm talking about Carilyn Cosby, nigga!"

I was no longer paying Whoopie no mind. My focus was on the chocolate dime piece who'd just left the intoxicating smell of her perfume lingering in my nose. "And I'm talking about shorty on the tier."

"Who?" Whoopie asked, as I stuck my arm between the bars and used my mirror to watch her walk down the tier.

"You didn't see that bad ass C.O. who just walked by?" I questioned seriously.

"Nah," he said. "I was zoned out."

"Them pills got you fucked up."

"I know," he admitted. "That's what I been trying to tell everybody. I'ma use that shit in court when I see my red-bone too. I'm—"

"Hold up real quick!" I interrupted him again. We could finish chopping it up later about his so-called wifey and how much he couldn't wait to see her in court when she tried to bury his retarded ass in prison for the riots. Right now, I was stalking shorty on the tier. "I'm trying to find out who this is doing count."

"That's Sellmen," my cell-buddy volunteered, as Whoopie's arm came out of the grill with his peeper blocking my view. "She doesn't usually come through like that," he added, hopping down off his bunk as the female C.O. screamed something about niggas being 'some nasty little bastards'.

"Move your arm, Whoopie!" I had my eyes locked on her nice ass. I couldn't imagine what else she expected from a bunch of horny, hard-dick hoppers who would do just about anything for a shot of pussy at the moment.

"Oh, that's my baby Sellmen—sexy, chocolate ass." Whoopie exclaimed, and I smiled. Whoopie's lil' funny-looking, knotty-head ass sworn every bad bitch was his girl. "She phat to death too."

"I see," I mumbled, readjusting my mirror. Either her thong was all the way up in her ass, or she did not have any draws on. I bit my bottom lip and kept my mirror locked on Sellmen's jiggling ass cheeks. To me there wasn't nothing in the world more attractive than a nice-looking, thick, chocolate honey-dip.

"I think she from around the way too," Whoopie added. "I saw her with my baby mother before."

"Oh yeah." I stared at her reflection as she strut back down the tier towards us. But, she didn't look familiar at all.

"She's definitely *U-T-P!*" Whoopie assured, and I could not agree more.

"You ain't lying." I licked my lips. Shorty was definitely what we liked to refer to on the hopper tier as 'up town pussy'. Simply meaning that a nigga would fuck with her in the streets and not just on the section.

"I love you, Miss Sellmen!" Whoopie's fool ass yelled, snatching his mirror inside the cell.

Scared nigga! I thought, twisting my mirror to look inside Whoopie's cell to see him laying back in the bunk, pretending to be reading.

"You a bluffing nigga, boy! All them baby mothers you got!"

"Ayo, Charm!" I heard Deli call out from the bottom tier.

"Whoa, Dummie!"

"You better not be up there gun-slinging, nigga!" He laughed and my chump ass cell-buddy giggled. "I mean, I know you're from the wild, wild west and all!"

"Don't even play like that, Dummie," I yelled back, honestly wishing that I didn't have a cell-buddy at the moment. Because although I wasn't a gun-slinger or nothing, my dick was as hard as jail-house steel, and I would've damn sure jumped out there.

A month without no pussy was like torture to a young nigga. "You know I ain't out that tree jumping mob." I eyed my cell-buddy until his giggle turned into a throat-clearing cough. *Sucker*! I thought.

"Yeah, a'ight, Dummie!" Deli hollered as Miss Sellmen stopped right in front of the cell.

"What did you just yell out the door?" Ms. Sellmen challenged.

"I didn't yell nothing!" I countered.

"Which one of y'all last name Johnson?" she inquired, looking from my cell-buddy to me curiously.

"Huh?" I replied, stuck on stupid as Deli continued to say something.

"Is one of y'all last name Johnson or not?" she repeated, and I guess my clown ass cell-buddy gave me up because then she eyed me. "What? You don't know your name or something?"

"Huh?" I repeated, trying to recover. Damn! I hadn't even realized that she had a blue diamond stud in her pierced eyebrow that only managed to enhance her beauty when she first walked by. "I mean—ummmm—yeah," I replied nervously. "Why? What's up?"

"Nah, my homegirl asked me to make sure you were okay over here." She lowered her voice secretively, which made me look at my nosey ass cell-buddy.

"Who's your homegirl?" I smiled curiously after my clown ass cell-buddy recognized the look and climbed back up on his bunk. I couldn't lie. I felt like a real big boy, knowing that shorty was posted up in front of my cell while everybody was watching. I even heard a nigga tell Deli to fall back when he kept calling my name.

"Tiphani," She leaned towards the grill and whispered, after looking up and down the tier.

Oh shit! I thought, when it hit me. Shorty must be Tiph's homegirl—Shekey—Miss Glover from North Avenue. "I heard that. Tell sis everything Gucci on my end."

"Well, I'ma be coming to check on you from time to time to

make sure nobody's messing with you," she teased, and I couldn't tell if she was smiling or blushing.

"I'll be looking forward to that," I assured her sexy ass sincerely. I was gonna have tell Tiphani to hook a young nigga up when I touched down.

"Then, you better keep watch." She smiled, winked and strutted off the tier as I pressed my face against the grill again and stuck my mirror back out the grill to get one last look at her nice, round ass. Damn! I gotta get the fuck up town.

"Ayo, Dummie!" I called out to Deli. "Ayo, Dummie!"

"I ain't got no rap, nigga!" Deli fired. "I know your dumb ass heard me calling you."

"I was talking, nigga!" I defended, ignoring his fake ass attitude. "I gotta holler at you up close." I could barely contain my excitement.

"Yeah, whatever, Dummie!" Deli retorted. "Are we still hooking up?"

"Hell, yeah!" I exclaimed without hesitation. I was hungry as a runaway slave, and I already knew that dinner was going to be some garage. "I got everything you asked for right here on the bed." I looked back at the food items on the bunk. I had two tuna fish, four cups of shrimp noodles, some cheese and mayonnaise.

"Did you find any crackers?"

"Ole shit! I forgot all about the crackers. I'ma ask Whoopie's scared ass right now!" I said.

"Cool, I'll get up with you when we come out after dinner then!" Deli said, falling back.

The cell doors couldn't open quick enough once I got my legal mail. So, when the doors popped for rec, I said *fuck the steps*, climbed over the rail, hung down and dropped to the bottom tier before quickly making my way to Deli's cell. "What's up, Dummie?"

Deli embraced me with a weird look. "Fuck the hook up shit at?"

"Man, fuck that hook up!" I fired, handing him the letter I'd just received from the lawyer's office, stepping back. I wasn't even hungry any more for real. "Read that."

I stood there and watched as Deli sat down on the bunk and began to read the letter. I could instantly tell when he got to the part I really wanted him to see concerning the gun ballistics because his whole facial expression changed.

"Yooooo," Deli's head shot up with a big ass smile on his face. "So, you only basically got the gun charge now?"

"Yeah, that's what it seems like the lawyer is saying." I shook my head, hoping what I'd read was true. Deli and I both already knew about G-baby's bitch ass. "But, I'ma call Franzoso in the morning to find out for sure."

"Yo, how the fuck you beat the ballistics?" Deli asked, as curious as I was.

"I don't know, Dummie," I replied honestly, drawing a blank. "That shit got me fucked up. Because I know that's the tone Nizzy cracked ole boy with."

"That shit crazy, Dummie." Deli handed the letter back. "Whatever the case, them bitches messed up somehow," Deli added. "And I thought Nizzy was a lucky motherfucker. But, you're the one with the horse shoe."

I'd honestly thought that the state would try some funky shit after G-baby's body was discovered out in Baltimore County. I had even gotten Franzoso to hold off on petitioning for a bail because I was convinced that the prosecutor would still try to use the ballistic results against me.

"You can definitely get a bail now," Deli suggested, reading my mind.

"I was thinking the same thing, Dummie," I confessed honestly because rather it was a fuck up on their part, or luck on mine. I definitely wasn't going to miss the chance to use it to my advantage.

"Damn yo, a nigga gonna be over this bitch by himself again." Deli sounded sad, and I could tell that the news was kind of bitter-sweet. I mean, shiddd, I hated to leave my nigga too. But, I had to go because it wasn't no good to either one of us sitting over the jail.

"Don't even trip, Dummie. 'Cause you already know what time it is when I touch down. I'm all over that situation. So, you're right behind me."

"Already." Deli smiled and gave me some love because if my nigga didn't know nothing else, he knew that with me in the streets, everything would be okay. "I'm still hungry though, nigga," Deli reminded me, as we broke the embrace.

"Well, you better go grab that shit off the bed then," I countered. "'Cause I'ma bout to go jump on this bike real quick and tell my girl the good news." I dipped down the tier and picked up the phone that was reserved for gangsters only—a luxury few had. I dialed Ebony's number. I knew that she was going to be happy as shit once I gave her the news— especially since she had been holding a young nigga down with flicks, pre-paid calls and stuff.

I had just heard Ebony pick up the phone on the other end and began to turn around to put my back up against the caged-grill when I felt a blow to the side of my head and stumbled sideways into catwalk beside where the phones hung at. *What the fuck!* I held on to the phone to keep my balance and shook myself off a little bit before I realized that I was surrounded by a couple Park Heights niggas.

"Bitch!" I swung on the closest motherfuckers. A tall, ugly ass nigga with a curly bush. Once I began to get out on him, the rest of his homies rushed me. We were rocking and rolling for a few seconds before I noticed that I had blood running down the side of my face and realized that somebody had cut me.

When I slipped or got hit and went down to the ground, I started swinging and kicking like crazy, as they continued working me over. That's when I saw exactly who had the straight-razor. A lil' bitch ass nigga I could not stand from up Park Heights. It took me a moment to get back to my feet and break down the tier towards Deli's cell.

"Dummie!" I hollered, tripping over a dinner tray laying out in the middle of the tier, falling as I struggled to get my hawk out. "Work call, Dummie! Work call!" I yelled out to get Deli's attention, as niggas swarmed me again like a pack of hungry hyenas. I felt hands and feet hitting me repeatedly as I finally got my hawk free.

"Bitch!" I caught one nigga's leg as he tried to kick me. I tried to take that motherfucker off.

"Fuck is you whores doing?" Whoopie came flying out of nowhere, hitting everything in sight as Deli ran out of his cell with his hawk already out.

"Get up off my man, bitch!" I heard Deli order, stabbing the tall dude. And just like real hyenas, niggas began to scatter when the wounded lion was able to get to his feet.

By now, my adrenaline was in overdrive, and I was ready to kill something. I got to my feet with one thing on my mind. The nigga who'd cut me across my head with the straight-razor. "Nah, bitch, don't run now!" I barked, locking eyes with the nigga I wanted the most after searching the crowd before chasing him down the tier.

"Ahhhh!" the fleeing hyena cried out in pain, as my hawk slid in and out of his back repeatedly when I caught him trying to escape to the top tier and began hawking his ass up.

"Shut up, bitch!" I ordered, snatching him out of the air. "Stop crying!" I hawked him a few more times, as he stumbled into the catwalk. I saw Deli going at it with two dudes down the tier and went to assist him. One of the dudes was a nigga Deli didn't like. So, I hawked his man and let Deli do his thing. Whoopie's lil' ass was all over the place. Every time I looked up, he was hawking something. It was strictly iron slinging—no tussling.

It seemed like a lifetime before the C.O.'s blitzed the section, spraying mace, tackling niggas and shit as we chased Park Heights dudes all around the tier. They were locking themselves in niggas' cells and everything because there was no way out. The funny part was that when it began getting funky, only a few Park Heights were truly committed to the cause.

I was hand-cuffed and dragged off the tier as I choked to

death on mace. They laid me in between Deli and Whoopie out in the hallway in front of the section. I couldn't catch my breath for shit. Whoopie kept telling me to calm down and breathe. But I hadn't been over the jail eating mace like his crazy ass.

"Yo, that shit fucking me up, Dummie." I squeezed my eyes shut, trying to stop the burning. It felt like I had been cutting fresh onions for hours.

"Stop whining, nigga!" Whoopie spat, making me laugh. "Look at this nigga, Deli. He got tears coming out of his eyes."

"Yo, I'm still trying to figure out where you came from," Deli said.

"Me too," I said. "I looked up and you were flying through the air."

"I jump off the top tier nigga!" Whoopie said, and I knew his crazy wasn't lying.

"Fuck no!" Deli retorted, laughing as I looked over at him laying on his stomach, hand-cuffed, covered in blood with his face on the floor, and smiled. A motherfucker couldn't tell me that we weren't gangsters. North Avenue stand up!

As the guards began taking us to medical, I was taking a mental note of who was all involved and trying to figure out why they had brought me a move out of the blue—especially after I thought we were all on some West Baltimore versus East Baltimore shit.

In the end, despite all the blood, when we all finished at the infirmary, most of the wounds were artificial. Well, one of the dudes Whoopie hit did receive a countless amount of stitches. But, other than that, we all basically lived to die another day.

***

"What? You aren't going out, Ock?" Ameen asked when the doors opened for the big yard and he noticed Wakal approaching with a laundry bag full of clothes slung over his shoulder.

"If I can make it back in time," Wakal replied. "They just called me for property—So, don't think that I'm ducking no rec," Wakal added, knowing that all the brothers were required to work out together whenever they had big yard. "Where Jihad at?" Wakal questioned when he noticed the Imam was without security.

"They called him and Kaamil up front," Ameen said, adjusting his workout gloves, as they began to walk down the tier. "You know Shabazz and them got into it last night with them jokers down in housing unit five."

"Yeah, Jihad told me about it at breakfast this morning." Wakal switched his laundry bag to his other shoulder. "Plus, I saw the police running to the code."

"Did you see who all they grabbed?"

"Not really," Wakal thought back. "I did see Latif and Shaheed though," Wakal confessed. "Oh, yeah, I saw the brother Davenport and the other big, light skin brother he always be with."

"Mango?" Ameen questioned.

"Yeah, Mango. That's his name. The brother who work down lock-up."

"By the time I made it to the window, they were gone—So, all I saw was their work," Ameen disclosed. "*Inshaallah,* none of them little jokers died," Ameen added, knowing how Davenport and Mango got down.

"Yeah," Wakal said.

There were already multiple stories floating up and down the compound. Some dudes were saying that there had been a joker's body found, rolled up in a blanket, stuffed up under Shabazz's bed. Others were saying that one of the brothers had died en route to the hospital after his lungs had collapsed. The *nigga-net* was vicious. However, the administration had shut the housing unit down for now. So, nobody really knew anything unless they had a direct line of communication to somebody on the tier.

"Right now, everybody is just speculating." Ameen knew how things went when something major happened in prison. A lot of people got rounded up, and everybody wanted to play like they were involved somehow. "And I just don't want a bunch of brothers getting put on administrative lock-up behind this foolishness."

"Inshaallah, that doesn't happen." Wakal was very familiar with the kind of foolishness that came from spontaneous shake-ups. He'd been knee-down in the middle of the situation with Suf'yan and them, when both the Imam and assistant Imam had been removed from the compound and shipped out of the institution without warning, after a couple officers got jumped on when he was still next door.

"Inshaallah, you're right." Ameen stopped to give Wakal a brotherly handshake and hug. "Assalaam alaikum."

"Waleikum assalaam," Wakal replied, breaking the embrace. "You sure you're good, Ock? Because I can walk you down to the yard."

"I'm good, Ock." Ameen smiled. He didn't fear anything but Allah.

"I'll see you later," Wakal added before Ameen disappeared into the crowd of dudes on their way to the yard. After seeing one of the brothers on his way to commissary and cracking for a 'Butter Peacon' ice cream, Wakal entered the multi-purpose building and headed on towards the property room to pick up his clothing package.

"Good morning," Wakal spoke, walking up to the officer behind the counter, laying his ID down on the counter. "White," Wakal volunteered his last name, looking towards the holding cell. "Is there anyway that I can get out of here before movement ends?" he questioned, since nobody was in the holding cells. "I'm trying to catch the yard."

"We'll see," the officer replied, picking up his ID. "Have a seat in the bullpen."

Wakal took a seat in the holding cell and waited. Several other inmates came and went, but Wakal's name was never called. So, eventually he decided to find out what the fuck was going on. "Ayo," Wakal addressed the working man, as he approached the counter. "I've been up here all morning and y'all haven't called me yet."

"What's your name?" The white boy looked up, acknowledging his presence.

"White," Wakal replied. "Donald White."

"I been called you," the white boy said. "You were the first one I called."

"Damn." Wakal felt stupid. "I didn't even hear you."

"It's all good." The white boy looked up at the clock." Give me your list and I'll see if I can get you out of here before lunch."

"Oh, mmhhh, give me medium t-shirts, two-X boxers and thirty-four/thirty-two pants." Wakal paused for a minute to look at his own feet. "And make the boots an eight."

Wakal kept watching the clock as the white boy dipped into the back and returned with another red bearded white boy, pushing his boots and clothes on top of a laundry cart.

"Here you go," the white boy said, picking up the boots off the laundry cart and sitting them on the counter top. "I got you a nine, 'cause they're cut small. And my Dawg put some extra underclothes in the bag for you too."

"Thanks," Wakal nodded as the other white boy with the red beard placed the brown paper bag up on the counter next to the boots. "I appreciate that."

"It ain't nothing," the white boy assured, sliding the property clothing form and pen across the counter. "Sign right here," he added, marking the spot with an X.

Wakal picked up the pen, pulled the property paper across the counter and leaned forward to sign it. He knew that yard was over. So, the best thing that he could hope for now was, being able to catch one of the brothers in the yard working out later on. "Do I sign it twice where the—"

The white boy reached across the counter and grabbed Wakal by both of his wrists.

"Fuck is you doing, yo?" Wakal tried to pry his wrists free as the red bearded white boy jumped over the counter. "Get the fuck off me!" Wakal ordered.

The white boy with the red beard hit Wakal and dazed him. Then, he grabbed his head and slammed it into the counter repeatedly until he was semi-unconscious.

"Come on, Dawg! Hurry up before somebody comes," the other white boy said, still holding Wakal's wrists.

Wakal felt a strong thick arm snake its way over his face before his head was pulled back slightly. Just enough to expose his throat. "Ple-ease! I didn't do nothing," Wakal pleaded, using what little strength he had left to try to pull his wrists free.

"Hurry up and shut his ass up, Dawg," the white boy ordered his red bearded friend.

The white boy with the red beard pulled out a nice, factory-made, sharpened blade, reached his hand completely around to the opposite side of Wakal's neck, before slowly jamming the blade in.

Wakal's eyes went wide as his throat was carefully cut wide open from one end to the other while he kicked and struggled, trying to get free. When the white boy released Wakal's wrists, his hands immediately shot to his neck. He tried to stop the bleeding, but it was no use. The blood continued to seep between his fingers as he fought for air and got weaker and weaker.

The last thing Wakal saw before he passed out was the smiling face of the yellow-teeth white boy who had been holding his wrists. "When you get to paradise, tell Allah Shabazz sent you." He laughed devilishly.

Once Wakal's body collapsed on the floor, the red bearded white boy quickly scooped Wakal's limp body up and rolled it across the counter into the waiting laundry cart. "Make sure he's not breathing while I clean this blood up!" he commanded, pulling a piece of towel out of his back pocket.

The white boy stood over top of the laundry cart for a minute to see if Wakal moved. When he didn't, he began tossing arms full of clothes on top of his body.

"What the hell are you doing?" the red bearded white boy questioned, wiping up the last bit of blood on the counter top.

"Covering him up," the other white boy replied. "We can't

leave him here, Dawg," he added, sounding nervous.

"Where the hell else we going to leave him?" he inquired, double checking the floor and counter for blood splatter.

"Outside one of the housing units like dirty laundry," the white boy suggested.

"You're fucking crazy, Dawg, you know that?" The red bearded white boy shook his head. "But, it's your call. Just get me some bleach real quick so I can mop this floor and wipe this counter one more time before we go."

***

"Cuzzo, what the fuck are you up to?" Lor'Homie questioned, checking the rearview mirror for the umpteenth time, as they sat outside of a Park Heights night club.

"Just keep this bitch running, Cuz," Nizzy ordered, watching the club's exit. Lor'Homie was confused. His cousin wasn't telling him nothing. Yet, he was stretched across the back seat of a recently stolen car with a fully loaded sub-machine gun. "Get ready to drive, Cuz!" Nizzy whispered, cracking the back door of the car, as a small crowd of people came out of the night club.

"Ayo!" Nizzy called out after pulling his Dummie mask up. "I got a message for the P.H. niggas on the hopper tier." Nizzy laughed, extended the gun out the cracked door and opened fire. Nizzy let the weapon go without caution, hitting anything he could. The goal was to send a message over the jail that 'every violation brought vengeance' when it came to the 'Dummie Squad'.

"Go, Cuz! Go!" Nizzy pulled the door shut and slapped the back of the driver's seat.

"Oh, shit, Cuzzo!" Lor'Homie exclaimed, burning rubber. He hadn't known exactly what Nizzy was up to, but he was down for whatever. "You're a fool with it!" Lor'Homie laughed. "I fucking love you, Cuzzo!"

Nizzy laid down across the back seat and began breaking the gun apart, dismantling it. He would never slip like Charm had.

175

"What the fuck was that about?" Lor'Homie asked, watching the mirrors as he sped through the back streets of Park Heights. Nizzy explained how Charm had told him it was a bunch of Park Heights niggas who'd pulled that fuck shit over the jail. So, he wanted to send a message to let niggas know that the 'Dummie Squad' were off limits, even over the city jail. "Man, Cuzzo, why the fuck you didn't put me on point?" Lor'Homie argued. "I could've robbed them niggas. They were dripping too."

"Well, when I was over Peaches' house yesterday, fucking with her and Ebony, she said Charm goes for bail review next Thursday. So, once Dummie hit the bricks and tell us exactly who was who, you can rob all them niggas."

"You went over Peaches' house by yourself, huh?" Lor'Homie joked.

"Don't start playing, Cuz!" Nizzy warned.

"I'm just saying," Lor'Homie laughed.

Now, Nizzy couldn't help but think about how nice Peaches had filled out since she stopped getting high. "Nah, you playing and shit, but I swear Ebony caught me checking Peaches out."

"What's up with her?"

"Mannnnnn, that bitch crazy, Cuz," Nizzy said. "She tried to hook me up with some faggy nigga, playing."

"What?" Lor'Homie exclaimed. "I'd slap that bitch brains out. That's my word."

Nizzy just shook his head. "I said she was playing, Cuzzo. Anyway, I didn't know Peaches could cook like that. She made some mac and cheese, boy! I'm telling you, Cuz." Nizzy's mouth began to water as he went on to tell his cousin about the meal he ate over Peaches' house.

***

After all the 'he said, he said', Shabazz and them lost their visits and received six months on lock up. But, he was cool with that because he had finally been able to tighten this little one joker up that called himself claiming one of the phones in the dayroom. It never creased to amaze Shabazz how quick fools were to claim things they could never own.

On the other hand, Doug and Hoark got a couple of savages to give Wakal exactly what he had coming to him without his name being involved. Unfortunately, the two crazy white boys had gotten caught pushing Wakal's body across the compound in a laundry cart. Somehow, Wakal's blood had managed to seep through the bottom of the laundry cart and leave a trail of blood all the way up the compound. Shabazz didn't know whether he should attribute their fuck up to ignorance or arrogance. Especially, once he found out that Wakal survived.

Shabazz wasn't surprised when he received word from Ameen on lock-up that the community was going to retaliate if the white boys didn't deal with their own. Nor was he surprised a week later when a small war kicked off because the white boys refused to back down. Ameen, Kaamil and Jihad were all grabbed and put on administrative lock-up. One white boy was knocked unconscious in the kitchen's tray room, placed up on the tray-belt and ran through the dish-machine. By the time he came out of the other side, all of his skin was gone. Shabazz swore by Allah that he heard him screaming a half of a mile away on lock-up.

Whatever the case, Shabazz just wanted to make sure his name stayed out of it. As far as he was concerned, he'd did his part. All the extra shit was on Doug and Hoark.

"You eating, Ock?" Latif asked, grabbing the first of two trays coming through the feed-up slot into the call they shared on lock- up.

"What is it?" Shabazz asked, looking up from the book he was reading.

"P and J," Latif replied, sitting the trays on top of the sink, before grabbing the two milks off the slot and wiping it down.

"I'm good," Shabazz sat the book down on the bed and sat up. "Give me one of them milks though."

"You still reading that 'Penitentiary Incarcerated, Gang Affiliated' joint?

"Nah," Shabazz got up off the bed. "I'm reading that 'Ultimate Sacrifice' part six you gave me."

"That's that, ain't it, Ock?" Latif bragged. He'd been going on and on about the book since his cousin had sent it in from his store.

"Yeah, I ain't gonna lie the brother can write, Ock," Shabazz admitted. "I'm impressed. I like how he be breaking the game down."

"You gotta read one thru five," Latif suggested, having read them all. "He got some more heat too."

"It's a part I just read that reminds me of the conversation we were having last night about how much things have changed."

"What conversation?"

Shabazz shook his head. "You're too young to be that absentminded, Ock." Shabazz smiled. "The conversation about how the rules of hate have really switched."

"Oh, yeah," Latif recalled now. Shabazz had spent the better part of an hour explaining to him how instead of dudes being hated for being rats, snakes and chameleons, many were now being hated for being stand-up, outspoken, independent and authentic. "I'm with you, now."

"Man, watch out," Shabazz demanded, opening the milk, walking over to look out the window. "I bet if we were talking about Shabree, your little bubble belly ass would've remembered everything I said." Shabazz teased, referring to Latif's wife.

"You already know." Latif laughed.

What nobody knew was that the for the last few months, everyday after dinner, whether he was behind the door or in general population, Shabazz would stare out the window to observe and study every inch and detail of the prison within sight. He'd count every guard that came through. Time every security truck that drove by outside the gates. And weigh the pros and cons because he had absolutely no intentions of being like the guys who worked out or kissed the police's ass for nothing. The ones that ran the yard for hours, did all the sit-ups and push-ups in the world for nothing. The ones who could outlift or out-slave the whole jail just to walk around looking good until the day they died. Nah. Shabazz had other plans. He was going to get free or die trying.

"What's on your mind, Ock?" Latif inquired. He could always tell when Shabazz had something on his mind.

"Nothing, just thinking about my daughter that's all." Honestly, he really wanted to bring somebody in with him, but history had shown him that telling one person, would be one person too much. Worrying about himself and going alone was the only way to assure that he would make it. A lot of good men had failed to make it 'one way or another' by trying to be helpful. Shabazz, however, had no plans of making the same mistake. He didn't need or want no more buddies, even it they were his Muslim brothers. Because as far as he was concerned, everything in prison had a price. And another partner could potentially sell his escape plan to the highest bidder without a problem.

Chapter 18

I really couldn't believe that the state was even trying the bullshit ass circumstantial case against Deli and Lil'Deezy. Especially together, let alone after Deli had requested a separate and 'speedy' trial. Thugg's statement had been suppressed at the motion hearing, and all the charges against Itchy-Man had been dropped once the Feds indicted him on some Rico: Continuing Criminal Enterprise shit. Yet, here we were, four days into trial with the state using a bunch of spineless motherfuckers to run their little game. The game where they used the 'impression of guilt' to convict innocent men, women and children. The strongest evidence that the state had produced so far was the fact that Lil'Deezy had been arrested with the gun that shot Deli and Stacey's fat, funky, funny-built, freak ass and the bitch ass nigga Scar. What tripped me out the most, though, was the fact that the freak Stacey had the nerve to try and come up in the courtroom, looking like something in a pair of rundown Red Bottoms, some dusty ass looking, skin-tight, knock-off Ferragamo jeans, and a two-size-too-small dollar store halter-top that exposed all the black stretch marks and Swiss Rolls looking rolls around her mid-section. I just kept peeping over at Stacey's boyfriend as he sat comfortably in the courtroom giving her hot-mess looking, dick-eating ass his support as she testified. I mean, what kind of so-called street nigga would sit up in the courtroom and encourage his bitch to tell lies in the name of testifying? All I could do was, shake my head. I was really starting to hate these old niggas. They were so phony. Always talking that 'young nigga' this, 'young nigga' that shit. Young niggas fucking up the game. Then, turn around and be the first one to harbor a rat or jump on a nigga's case. Old stiff ass fuck niggas! Yeah, young niggas were definitely out of order for making 'being stand up' an exception instead of a rule. But, when it came to that telling shit, the old niggas were in class all by themselves.

Deli's attorney, Elizabeth Franzoso, caught the hoe ass nigga, Corey Linwood, in so many lies during cross-examination that it wasn't even funny. And this was even before Elinore reluctantly took the stand on Deli's behalf and said that she knew that Deli had never entered her party or been outside when the shooting started because she was the one outside collecting keys, changing the five dollar parking fee before eveything jumped off. Reaching out to my nigga Bozack had paid off.

"Mister Whack, do you see the person who shot you on the night in question in this courtroom today?" Elizabeth Franzoso backed away from the witness stand to give Deli a clear view of the entire courtroom.

Deli paused for a moment to slowly scan the room as all the jurors sat on the edges of their seats curiously. Deli had already explained how he'd gotten shot on North Avenue near Longwood waiting for the bus. "No," Deli replied, looking to his attorney. "I don't see the guy who shot me."

"Please let the record reflect that my client has not identified Desmond Bright," Elizabeth Franzoso pointed to Lil'Deezy as the jury watched her closely. "The state's alleged shooter."

I looked at the jury and smiled inside as I realized that I was in the wrong line of work. Defense attorneys had to be some of the shrewdest motherfuckers in the game. Prosecutors too. They would sell a jury a good story, buy a lie with blood money, or make Satan look like a Saint if the price or benefit was right.

"Okay, Mister Whack, tell us, if you can, why do you believe that you were charged in this—" Elizabeth Franzoso stopped mid-sentence as if something had just occurred to her. "No, no, no Mister Whack. Before we even get that far. Let me ask you this. Did you shoot yourself?"

"No, I've never even seen a real gun before." Deli replied so innocently and convincing that I had to think about if I ever witnessed the nigga holding a tone.

"Did you ever attempt to assist the police with their investigation when it came to identifying the person or persons responsible for shooting you?"

"Yes," Deli looked at the jury-box as the entire courtroom got silent. "I asked to look at some photos several times, but I kept getting the run around." Deli looked back at Franzoso and I almost burst out laughing. "One detective even went so far as to tell me that they had who they wanted, so it wouldn't matter if I looked at photos or not."

"No further questions, Your Honor," Elizabeth Franzoso exclaimed, walking towards the defense table. "The defense rests."

I knew the jury had to be on Deli's and Lil'Deezy's side. Especially, after the accumulation of slip-ups, lying witnesses, and exposed detectives' cover-ups during trial. The jury had to have realized how desperate the state was for a conviction. They had to see how far the state was reaching. There was no way that the jury could've brought the bullshit the state had been selling for the last four days. I studied the jury for a second and wondered who in the hell had come up with the bright idea to place a nigga's life in the hands of twelve complete strangers, who knew absolutely nothing about law and almost nothing about the streets a nigga was forced to grow up on.

After, the state decided not to cross examine Deli, he returned to his seat and it was Lil'Deezy's lawyer's time to present his defense and put on a show. Both Lil'Deezy's aunt and his brother testified to his whereabouts during the shooting. And the state went at them hard. But, they both held up and maintained that Lil'Deezy never left their sight during all the chaos. In fact, Lil'Deezy's brother said that he had taken the stray-bullet, shielding and protecting him.

It was around a quarter to four when both Lil'Deezy's lawyer and the state decided to call it quits and let the case go to the jury for deliberation. As the jury retired to the jury room, I wondered how long it would take for them to reach a verdict.

***

"The verdict's in!" Someone opened the courtroom door and yelled out into the silent, waxed halls of the courthouse. It was quiet as shit as the jury filled in their jury seats less than an hour later and passed the bailiff the verdict for the judge. I tried to read the judge. But, he didn't give up nothing as he took the verdict in. It felt like I was watching a bad episode of 'Law & Order' when the bailiff handed the forewoman back the verdict, and she began to read the verdict into the record. My stomach was so queasy that I had to say a quick prayer to the gangster Gods to let my nigga walk.

"As to count one, murder in the first degree," the forewoman paused to clear her throat, "we, the jury, find the defendants, Desmond Bright and Delvon Whack, not guilty. As to count two, attempted murder—"

When the forewoman kept repeating the two most exciting words a gangster could ever hear at the end of a criminal trial, the entire squad went crazy. Nizzy and Young Danny jumped up and dapped. Lor'Homie started talking shit and JuJu's dumb ass jumped up on the aisle seat in the courtroom and held his dick. They didn't mean no harm. They were just happy that Deli was coming home, so they couldn't help themselves. Our nigga had just beaten the State of Maryland at the murder game.

I hugged and kissed Deli's mother and was about to go mess with Bucky Love when the judge looked over the rim of his eyeglasses and started threatening to clear the courtroom and hold niggas in contempt. The jury went on to find both Deli and Lil'Deezy 'not guilty' of everything, including the attempted murder charges they both had on each other. The jury did, however, stick Lil'Deezy with the gun charge but by the look on that nigga's face, I could tell that he was good with that. Shiddd, he probably wouldn't do no more than another 9/10 months tops.

The judge excused the jury after thanking them for their services and ordered that Deli be released immediately. Of course, we knew that it was too late for them to run Deli's name through the juvenile system for any outstanding warrants or probation violations and get his papers in order before the courthouse closed. So, we just told Deli that we'd see him in the morning and bounced over to JuJu's house to figure out how to bring Dunmie home in style. Some of the squad wanted to get fresh, go out and hit the strip club or something. Others wanted to chill, get twisted and call up a gang of bitches. We knew that whatever we wanted to do, we had to do it before Bucky Love got a hold of that nigga.

In the end, we decided to grab a room, buy some drinks and have a sex party with all the baddest thots we could think of. JuJu called his cousin and before the night was over, we had a suite reserved at the exclusive downtown glass 'Marriot' and a line up of bad bitches from all over the city, who'd promised to stop by and show Deli a good time.

***

"What's up, Dummie?" Deli yelled, throwing his hands up the instant he stepped out of the release building and spotted Nizzy leaning up against his truck just outside the gates of the jail. "Fuck everybody at?" he questioned, looking around as the prison gate began to open. "It's not everyday that a real nigga get released!"

Nizzy just started laughing as he watched his nigga walk through the open gates with a bag in his hand. "Ahhhh, man, niggas got more important things to do than sit outside the jail all day waiting on these peoples to release your stiff ass."

"Oh, yeah," Deli looked around again to see if the rest of the squad was hiding behind some cars or something. "I been gone almost five months and niggas ain't come to welcome the king home. That's fuck up."

"Nah, nah, Dummie," Nizzy said when he saw the hurt look on Deli's face. "Charm had to take care of something and we're gonna hook with JuJu and them later," Nizzy assured, embracing him.

"Already." Deli smiled, stepping back.

"Damn, nigga," Nizzy squared up and slapped Deli on the chest with the back of his hand. "You done got all swelled up and shit."

"Yeah, Dummie, I'm beating bodies now." Deli squared off

and shot Nizzy a few quick body-shots.

"Come on, nigga!" Nizzy hollered, curling up a little bit to block the blows. "Before I put that tone on your dumb ass."

"I missed you, Dummie." Deli stopped playing and spoke sincerely. "Niggas were over that bitch getting found guilty back to back. And I was like, damn, I might not ever see my niggas again.

"Don't start that mushy shit, Dummie," Nizzy laughed.

"Nah, I'm serious, Dummie. Them whores were trying to give a young nigga football numbers." Deli shook his head. "Nigga ain't even got no kids yet."

"Who you wanna have a baby with? Bucky Love?"

"Who else was there the whole trial, nigga?" Deli smiled.

"Sucker for love ass nigga," Nizzy said, taking the bag out of Deli's hand before opening the passenger side door. "You're still shooting blanks."

"Fuck outta here." Deli laughed.

"Fuck is this?" Nizzy questioned, opening Deli's bag. "I know you didn't bring a bunch of dumb ass jail shit home."

"Nigga, that's my release papers, some pictures, and the shit I got locked up with."

"What about this?" Nizzy reached inside the bag to pull out a handful of envelopes.

"Oh," Deli smiled. "That's a few broken promises from all these fake ass, phony bitches out here I want to give back!" Deli retorted, climbing into the truck as Nizzy ravaged through the bag some more.

"Man, fuck all that, you're home now," Nizzy closed the door, tossed the bag towards a pile of trash and walked around the truck to the driver's side. "So, you can show all them no loyalty having, money-hungry, sack-chasing bitches, why we carry 'em like we do."

"Yeah, that shit sound slick," Deli teased, knowing that Nizzy was probably the most tender dick Dummie in the squad. "But, you know you ain't built for that life, nigga!"

"I'm telling you, Dummie, shit done changed," Nizzy started

186

the truck. "I barely even feed a bitch."

Deli laughed because honestly, when it came down to it, he was the only one whose honor was bigger than his heart. His number one motto was: 'keep your mind on your money, and don't trust the bitch'. "Tell me anything, nigga. But, we both knew who the real player is."

"Yeah, until it come to Bucky Love," Nizzy teased, reaching for the CD player.

Deli couldn't argue with the truth, so he just ignored Nizzy. "Oh, yeah, Dummie, I almost forgot. Lil'Deezy said he show enough respect how niggas carried it."

"Mannnn, that shit ain't about nothing." Nizzy checked the rearview before slowly pulling out.

"Yeah, that's what I told him," Deli replied. "It's wild though. We would probably be on our way to spank them niggas right now, if Lil'Deezy had beat the gun beef and Itchy-Man hadn't gotten snatched by the Feds."

"You already fucking know!" Nizzy nodded. During war the law of the streets was to 'self-preservation first'.

"Ayo," Deli fired, tapping Nizzy on the arm, "when the last time you seen that bitch Pepper?"

"Come on, Deli, man," Nizzy looked at him seriously. "I know you aren't stalking that pussy? You worst than Cuz. That bitch body count, double digits. She on the gram eating dick and everything."

"Yo, as good as Pepper's pussy was and as bad as she is, you know I don't chase nothing but Bucky Love, nigga. Pepper's chump ass brother beat me out of two bands though."

"Man, chalk that shit up," Nizzy slowed down to take a left at the top of Eager Street. "You out here now and niggas ain't hurting for nothing."

"Yeah, you're right." Deli considered Nizzy's words and fell back in his seat. It was just hard to let a fuck nigga get away with something that he knew that he wouldn't have tried had he been in the streets. "But, a nigga ain't officially home until he get some of that sweet, that nasty, that gushy stuff."

"Give it to me!" Nizzy sang along in unison. "You already know Dummie and 'em gonna do right," Nizzy revealed. "But, before niggas get off into all that and get all fuck up, who do you wanna see first?"

"One love, nigga," Deli replied without hesitation, referring to his mother. "Anything else would be uncivilized."

***

I stood for moment with a bottle of Ace in my hand and watched as my niggas enjoyed themselves. There were naked bodies everywhere, and niggas were truly having a ball. Deli had two bad bitches in nothing but heels and thongs all over him. Nizzy was off in the corner eating the pussy of the thickest thot I'd ever seen. Young Danny and Murdock were tag-teaming a phat butt red-bone on the bed. JuJu was stretched out in the middle of the floor with a blunt in one hand and a bottle of Patron in the other, talking shit, getting his dick sucked. Shaggy was passed out naked near the mini-bar, and I didn't know where the hell Lor'Homie and O had disappeared to with the camcorder and all the damn white girls.

I raised the bottle in the air when Deli and I locked eyes from across the room. "Cheers, Dummie," I tilted my head slightly. "May we get what we want and—"

"Never what we deserve!" Deli finished with a smile before stuffing his whole face back between the breasts of the chocolate bitch riding him.

We had brought Dummie home in style, but the surprises were far from over. A lot of shit had changed since Deli had went in. The squad had expanded and some more shit. We were touching everything from coke to heroin, and the Wheels of Fortune had been rolling for a while. I grinned and watched Deli have the time of his life. This was how I'd always imagined it would be for my niggas and I. All of us being loyal to the strong empire we'd built growing up. Ready to fall for each other. Being more than our Dummie's keeper.

"I love you, nigga!" I shouted to Deli as the stripper in Deli's lap pushed him flat on his back, went up on the balls of her feet and started riding him froggy-style.

"There you go with your fine self," a rich deep chocolate stripper, in nothing but a sexy ass pair of strawberry-red 6-inch stilettos walked up behind me, reached around my waist and took hold of my dick. "I been looking all over for your big dick ass."

"Is that right?" I inhaled deeply as she gently, yet professionally stroked my dick. The Grey Goose and Ace had a nigga feeling good all over and the night wasn't the only thing that was still young and restless.

"Mmmh hmm," she purred, pressing her soft lips up against my ear seductively before teasing me with her long-wet tongue.

"Well, now that you've found me, what is it that you plan on doing?" I turned around in her arms as her hard-nippled, soft breasts rubbed across my chest.

"Eat you alive." She bit her lip devilishly, cupped my balls gently in the palm of one hand and began stroking my dick again with the other. "I'ma show you why they call me Pleasure," she added, kissing me on the lips. "Follow me."

The combination of her confidence, beauty and scent was enough to increase my intoxication and make me dizzy. I took one more look around the suite at all my niggas, my brothers, my squad. Dummies I'd gladly kill or die for. Then, I sat the bottle of Ace on the counter and followed Pleasure like a thirsty dog.

I admired Pleasure's breathtaking, tattoo-covered ass cheeks as they did a dance of their own until we reached the heart-shaped jacuzzi that was occupied by a pretty, little Snow-White looking bitch, smoking what looked like a Black & Mild smiling at Pleasure.

"I found him." Pleasure held my hand as we went up a few steps. Then, she led me over to where Snow White was playing in the water and directed me to sit down on the edge of the jacuzzi.

"Right here, baby," Snow White said flirtatiously, patting the spot where she wanted me to sit. "Here you go." She handed me three 'smiley face' stamped Molly's and a bottle of Hennessy before taking Pleasure's hand and helping her into the jacuzzi. "Let us take care of you." Snow White smiled mischievously as she pulled Pleasure down beside her in a kneeling position between my legs.

"Oh, nah, baby, I don't fuck with no pills," I confessed honestly. It just wasn't my thing. Sure, I'd fed pills to bitches, even stick 'em up a thot or two asses, but every time I considered taking 'em, all I could think of was Lor'Homie's dumb ass riding around the city butt naked with the 'K' on his lap, spaced out off the pills.

"Pleaseee, daddy," Pleasure pleaded, staring straight into my eyes before dipping her head low, stretching out her tongue and slowly licking up the toe-curling line between my ass and nuts.

"Damn, girl," Snow White exhaled, reaching for my dick impatiently. "You ain't tell me his dick was this big!" She blushed, wrapping her soft fingers around my dick, squeezing it. I swear it seemed like the bitch was exuding sex appeal from every pore. "I swear, if you do some pills with us, I'll let you put this big mother fucker wherever you want."

Fuck it! I thought, raising my head, tossing the Mollys into my mouth. A young nigga only lived once. I swallowed all three of the Mollys and quickly washed them down with a sip of Henny.

"What you been feeding this thing?" Snow White quizzed, tying her long, dark hair back into a ponytail. "Pussy, ass and brains," I replied as Pleasure forced my legs open wider so they both could sit between them comfortaoly, then she began planting soft kisses on the inside of my thighs.

"Well, he might not get to eat that good today, baby," Pleasure declared, gently caressing my nuts as the white bitch teased the head of my dick, like she was playing the flute before she suddenly stuff me into her mouth, taking me straight to the back of her throat.

"Damn!" I thought out loud, leaning back on my elbows, and

I closed my eyes as Pleasure intentionally pressed the claws of her other hand into my skin and careful ran them down across my chest and stomach, driving me crazy. If I wasn't in heaven, then I had to at least be very close to it. Because I swear, between the way Snow White's greedy ass was gobbling me up, and Pleasure was playing with my nuts, teasing me with her tongue, running her nails up and down my flesh, I felt like I was being eaten alive.

Within minutes, everything began to intensify. It was like Pleasure had a hundred tongues and a thousand hands. And the inside of Snow White's silky throat kept getting hotter and wetter and tighter. It got to the point where I had to open my eyes to make sure that them bitches hadn't snuck two or three more of their nasty ass friends into the jacuzzi. However, what I witnessed almost blew my mind.

Pleasure was gripping Snow White by the back of her head while she continuously engulfed my saliva-coated dick. I had never experienced slow-neck like that in my life, and I was a nasty young nigga. Pleasure allowed the white bitch to have a little more fun, deep-throating me and shit before abruptly snatching her bobbing head out of my lap and pushing her out of the way as she swirled her tongue around her pretty glistening lips, and wiped her shiny, saliva-stained face, popping the thin liquid cum-string, that stretched from my dick to her bottom lip.

Pleasure stood up, and slowly spun around until she was looking at me over her shoulder. Then, she reached between her legs, grabbed my dick and held it steady as she began to ease back onto it. I inhaled quickly, bit my bottom lip and zeroed in on the 'Fit 4 A King' tattoo that ran across the arch of her lower back. All I could do was, shake my head as Pleasure dropped all that ass down on me. I'd fucked some phat bitches, but I'd never hit a bitch whose ass was so big with a pussy so tight.

"Damn! You got a big dick!" Pleasure whined breathlessly, leaning forward to place her hands on my knees as I reached out to palm one of her ass cheeks in each hand and squeezed it. "I haven't been split open like this in a long time," she confessed with a broken cry as her claws dug into my legs and her ass suddenly jerked and backed off. "Ohhhhh, I gotta slow down."

"You better take your time," Snow White warned.

"I know," Pleasure acknowledged, slowly winding her hips. After she seemed to adjust to my thickness, she started taking the dick an inch at a time. Before long, she was riding a nigga like a professional. "Get it, daddy," Pleasure encouraged as her phat ass bounced all over the place. It was almost like a nigga was dribbling a basketball or rather two in his lap. "Yes, daddy, you gonna make me—" Pleasure's pretty, chocolate ass started mumbling some shit I didn't understand until I saw Snow White's face and long pink tongue licking up the thick, pearly looking cum that escaped the edges of Pleasure's pussy, leaving a glaze trail all up and down my dick as she continued to ride me backwards.

After Pleasure came again and got up, Snow White went straight back to work, attacking my dick feverishly. Once Pleasure squatted back down to help her, I knew that it wouldn't be long before I nutted. I watched excitedly as Pleasure and Snow White took turns passing my dick back and forth, long-necking me. Every time it was Snow White's turn, Pleasure would force her head down until she gagged, while she was licking my ass and bells.

"Y'all bitches trying to turn me out!" I cried out in pure estasy. I was on cloud nine thousand, if there was such a thing. And just when I thought that them bitches couldn't take me higher, Pleasure slowly slipped a finger into my ass while Snow White deep-throated me and it was over. I nutted so hard that I knew it would take both of them bitches a while to swallow all shit. "I swear to God, I love you bitches!" I proclaimed as I watched them use their hands, fingers and mouths to clean up all my cum.

"We're just getting started, daddy," Snow White informed, using the flat part of her tongue to lick the cum off of Pleasure's cum-smeared chin.

"Okay," I said, pulling them both up for kisses and handfuls of ass after a brief rest. "Since it doesn't seem like my dick is getting soft," I added in between tongue-kissing them both, "which one of y'all gonna let me get some of that ass?" I questioned, squeezing both of their nice, phat asses.

"Oh, not me," Pleasure shook her head when I looked at her. "Your dick is way too big!"

"Come on, shorty," I begged, using my hand to shake her phat ole ass. "I know you got that tattoo back there for something. I'll throw you something extra!" I exclaimed, trying to dig up in something extremely tight.

"Hell no. I told you your shit is too big." Pleasure kissed me again and ran her hands down between my legs to play with my dick and balls.

"For another five hundred, I'll let you put that big mother fucker in my ass daddy," Snow White volunteered in a whisper in my ear, and that was all I needed to hear. I stood up, flipped her lil' pretty white ass over on her stomach and got down to business. "Ahhh—hold up, baby!" Snow White's back arched up as she tried to re-position herself when I started stretching that tight, little pink asshole open. But, I wasn't having none of that, not today. Especially, while these bitches had me turned up on Molly.

"Stop trying to run!" I ordered, slapping her across the ass, leaving a red hand print before grabbing her by the waist and pinning her already wide spread legs against the inside of the jacuzzi.

"It's too big!" she confessed, but I wasn't trying to hear that shit. Even if I'd to pay the bitch again, that tight, white ass was getting stretched out tonight. "Just relax, shorty," I encouraged, twisting my hand up to wrap her hair around my fist. "I'ma give you another five." I pushed her head down and held her in place.

"Shiddd, I'll do it for a band," Pleasure spoke up smiling, and I knew them bitches were gaming. But, at the moment, I didn't give a fuck. I promised them both that I would go out to my car in the morning and give them both a band each for the ass.

After that, we got busy all night. I had them bitches eating each others pussies, going ass to mouth and all that. Snow White had a throat like a snake and the nasty bitch was down for anything. She even talked Pleasure into eating her cum-filled ass while I laid back with my head in the palms of my hands, talking shit, watching her make love to my dick with her mouth. I swear I was in love. There wasn't anything in the world more beautiful to me than a nasty woman who wasn't shy about getting down for her crown.

After everyone passed out, I was the last man standing. Pleasure, Show White and all the rest of the thots got me on the floor and freaked me damn near to death. I learned a valuable lesson that night. Men fucked until they couldn't, women fucked until they died.

The last thing I saw was a bunch of bitches, running around the hotel room, searching niggas pockets and shit. But, I was so physically drained that all I could do was smile. They had fucked us into submission. It was the oldest trick in the underworld, robbery by a nigga's own permission.

I tried to speak, I wanted to buck. But, all I could muster was a very slurred alcohol and Molly-induced, 'Bitch!' as Pleasure held up my car keys and blew me a kiss goodbye before my head became too heavy for my neck, and slammed back into the plush carpet, and the lights went out.

Chapter 19

Nizzy pulled up in his brand-new metallic silver Range Rover with the mirror tints and climbed out fresh. After dropping O off at the airport.

"Damn, Dummie, B-Day not until next weekend and you're already out here shaggin'," Young Danny said, getting up off his dirt-bike to give Nizzy some love.

"No bullshit!" Murdock seconded, moving towards the Range to get a better look.

"Shiddd, I had to do something. I wasn't just gonna sit back and let you niggas drop y'all nuts on me." Nizzy pointed across the street to where Murdock's Ford Explorer XLS was parked. Everybody had been busting out, holding their nuts. Charm and Deli had twin powder-blue 745 BMWs. Shaggy had just copped the Lexus ES 350 he'd been dying to get. Lor'Homie jumped on an all-black, tinted Ford Mustang GT. JuJu had a pearl-white Chrysler 330. And Young Danny was bragging about the Infiniti he had coming. "So, I said fuck it. Traded the truck in and upgraded."

"This joint sick, Dummie," Young Danny admitted over his shoulder, opening the passenger side door. "You make me wanna say fuck the Infiniti and grab something else."

Nizzy knew he was killing 'em with the black oak dashboard and butter-soft gray leather interior.

"Oh, this joint got the navigational system in it too, huh?" Young Danny stated, smiling. "JuJu seen this joint yet?"

"Nah, not yet."

"Dummie gonna flip!" Young Danny said. Everybody knew how much JuJu loved the Range.

"That joint a straight pussy magnet," Murdock nodded, admiring the wide wheels and silver rims. "Niggas going to have to handcuff their bitch for real now."

"Yeah, you know it cost too much money to chase these hoes," Nizzy said, "so, I figured I would bust with the Range. That way, the hoes could chase me."

"You a bluffing nigga, boy," Young Danny laughed, shutting the Range Rover's door. "But, you definitely about to fuck everything moving."

"And you know I don't discriminate." Nizzy stepped back with his hands raised, as if he couldn't help himself. "So, watch your bitch!"

Nizzy, Murdock and Young Danny stood around, tripping for a good minute. Nizzy convinced them to keep the Range Rover a secret because he wanted to fuck the city up and shut B-Day down. Everybody knew 'Baltimore Day' was the biggest car and fashion show of the year. It always drew the slickest niggas and baddest bitches in the city. So, if Charm or JuJu got wind of how he was coming, they'd both play the game dirty and go for the spotlight.

Nizzy gave Young Danny and Murdock some love before climbing back into the Range Rover and pulling off. His plan was to park the Range outside of his lil' Mexican bitch's house and drive Butta's car until he was ready to bust loose on B-Day.

As Nizzy was coming through the intersection of Broadway and Orleans, he could have sworn that he spotted Ebony in the passenger's seat of one of those low-riding trucks. So, he quickly turned around to double back and make sure that she was okay. After all, they were in East Baltimore where everybody had to 'B-more Careful'. When Nizzy pulled alongside the red low-rider at the next light and hit his horn, he noticed a Mexican dude behind the wheel and another bitch sitting in between him and Ebony running her mouth.

"Ebony! Ebony!" Nizzy called out, waving his hand out the window before laying on the horn until the driver pointed to him.

Ebony looked at Nizzy like she didn't have a clue who he was, before saying something to the dude to make him pull off before the light even changed green.

"What the fuck?" Nizzy got out of the Range and stood there watching the low-rider speed down the block. *I know this bitch not creeping on my man.* Nizzy thought, knowing something was off. Nizzy wanted to follow the low-rider to find out exactly what the fuck was going on, but something told him to mind his own business. Then, he remembered how his cousin had gotten all defensive the last time he tried to warn him about a lil' bitch he was smashing around the way. So, since he didn't know exactly what was up with Ebony, he decided to just leave it alone. He'd let Charm find out on his own accord. Whatever it was, he didn't want no part of it.

The light changed and the car behind Nizzy started blowing its horn. So, Nizzy just slid back into his Range, turned around and headed on for his lil' bitch house up near Johns Hopkins Hospital.

***

"I always say, the Lord ain't never gave us more than we can stand to bear. And though he might let us bend some times, he'll never let us break." Nurse Edwards spoke excitedly as she watched Billy Lo continue taking small steps on his own with the help of a wooden-cane.

"He's definitely recovering quicker than I expected," the physical therapist added, as Billy Lo turned around too fast, causing himself to stumble a little bit.

Billy Lo looked from Nurse Edwards to the physical therapist and smiled. He didn't know if God was truly with him or not, but he knew that Satan was, because the thought of revenge was surely one of the driving forces behind his quick recovery. His thirst for blood and the knowledge that when you really wanted something done right, you had to get off your ass and do it yourself was also inspiring him.

"I think that's it for today," the physical therapist suggested, as Billy Lo completed his last lap around the room. "That's thirty-two laps."

"I'm good!" Billy Lo snapped when Nurse Edwards and the physical therapist came over like they wanted to assist him back to the bed. "Plus, I'm not finished anyway,"

Billy Lo pulled his arm free and started to walk again. He

was still upset that Charm's little punk ass had been able to survive the hit he'd put on his head, basically unscathed. He felt like had he been out in general population, he could've snuck over to the hopper section and did Charm dirty himself. "I'ma do some more laps." Billy Lo knew that he had to get into general population as soon as possible. Especially now, since Zimbabwe and Little Dinky had been released. Billy Lo hated depending on people he didn't know and wasn't sure he could trust. It gave them control over his fate, and that alone made him feel more helpless than not being able to walk.

"Okay, Izzard, a few more laps and that's it." The physical therapist stepped back, sensing Billy Lo's frustration.

Billy Lo's mind started running as he forced himself to push through the pain. *No pain, no gain.* He thought. There was no way in the world that he was going out without a bang. He had already lost everything he truly gave a damn about anyway. His parents were gone, Lotti was gone, Lakeria and the baby were gone. Everybody was fucking gone. And deep down, Billy Lo knew that he should be gone. He even wished he was at times because he knew that everybody was gone because of him. However, since he wasn't gone, he was going to raise hell on everybody else until the day he was.

***

"Is Wayne home?" I walked up to the steps on Lombard Street, questioning nobody in particular, after parking in front of the bar.

"Ummmm, excuse you—" the homosexual in the pink cat-suit and matching heels, who could be easily mistaken for a bitch, snapped, flipping his hair over his shoulder all dramatically. "First of all, I know you see us talking. Secondly, don't nobody by that name live here."

I paused for a second to gather my thoughts. I didn't want to have to drag this wannabe all up and down Lombard Street. "Look *boy* friend," I said, intentionally putting emphasis on the word 'boy', "can you just go tell Wayne somebody's at the door for him?"

"Oh, no this bitch didn't—" He began snapping his fingers and waving his hand all in the air like he was at a gay-parade.

"Yes, she did, gurl," the heavy make-up covered, manly-looking friend sitting on the steps beside him placed his hand over his mouth, like he couldn't believe that I hadn't acknowledged the obvious fact that his friend wanted to be addressed as something he clearly was not—a woman.

"See, that's exactly why I stay cutting these goofy ass bitches up," he argued reaching for his earrings. "They don't be knowing what to say out their mouth."

"Well, if you're feeling like a panther, boyfriend, go ahead and leap!" I encouraged, unzippening my handbag "I guarantee you won't leap again!" I threatened, ready to catch a homocide if need be. I mean, I wasn't stupid or nothing. I knew that up underneath all the make-up, eye-lashes and lip-gloss was still a man. And before I'd let any man—whether he was playing the role of a bitch or not—put his hands on me, I would catch another case.

"Peanut!" I heard the certainty in Wayne's voice and looked up to see his fine ass standing in the doorway, holding the screen-door open in a white, silk robe with his hands on his hips.

"Wayne! You better get this little panther before he end up in a lion's mouth," I said with my hand still inside my bag.

"Tonya, you know this bitch?" The nigga finished removing his earrings before sitting his heels on the steps to work on his pink wig, like he was getting ready to rumble.

"Gurl, you better cool your hot ass down," Wayne cautioned with his man voice. "That's my family."

"And for the record, boyfriend, you need to get neutered 'cause you ain't fooling nobody but yourself!" I taunted looking down. "While your silly ass out here doing all that neck popping and heel tossing, your little ass dick came untucked."

"Uh-uh, see, Peanut—bitch, come on." Wayne laughed, signaling for me to come inside the house as the cat-suit gangster bit his tongue, turned his back to me and tried to readjust his little package. "Your ass is still crazy."

I smiled at the homosexual's embarrassment. Then, I rolled my eyes and switched on into the house, as his friend watched jealously.

"Gurl, didn't I tell your ass to stop calling me Wayne?" Wayne questioned, putting some softness back into his voice once we were inside. "My name is Tonya, bitch." He laughed.

"Whatever," I replied, not paying his dumb ass no attention. He of all people knew that there was no way in hell that I was ever going to call him Tonya. I didn't care how many niggas he flipped, dicks he'd sucked, or sex changing meds he took. He would never be a woman in my eyes, and I would never address him as one. "You just better keep your little happy ass Pink Panthers on their leashes."

"Oh, them bitches know better than to try me," Wayne assured. "But, you on the other hand—" He joked, but I knew he wasn't playing.

Wayne had a whole stable of homosexuals and transexuals— who fucked everything from homo- thugs to state officials—on his command. Wayne had become famous for taking a bunch of down-low, gangster, switch-hitters on the 'Jerry Springer' Show back in the 90's to expose them to the world for exactly who they were—After they tried to act like they hadn't knowingly and intelligently been fucking him for years.

"Anyway, I need your help locating—"

"Can a bitch at least get a hug first? Damn." Wayne cut me off. "I haven't seen your skinny ass since the funerals." Wayne opened his arms.

"My bad," I apologized, giving him a warm hug.

"Damn, bitch, your little skinny self still got all that ass," Wayne said, looking me up and down. "I use to tell Black all the time. That if there was ever a bitch to make me go straight, it would've to be you."

"Boy, bye," I laughed. "You lucky he didn't shoot you dumb ass."

"Seriously though, you know I ain't never been with a woman. And I love the way your ass is so perfect," Wayne confessed. "I done took it up the ass hundreds of times, got about ten butt-shot and brought every color of spanx there is and my shit still don't sit up like that."

"This real beef, baby," I palmed my ass and shook it for Wayne. "You can't buy this on the black market."

"I can't with you." Wayne shook his head.

"So, like I said, I need your help." I changed the subject.

"Who is it?" Wayne asked, smiling. "Cos he probably done ran up in me or one of my panthers. I'm telling you, Peanut, these niggas so phony out here. I wish you could see some of the guys who come through here creeping on the late night. You'd be surprised." '

"Wayne, ain't nobody checking for you like that," I teased.

"Don't let this hangover look fool you, gurl," Wayne said, raking his hand through his wild hair. "I got lit at the club last night, but niggas be fighting over this ass. Call my bluff."

"Look at you, always ready to put somebody's business in the streets. So, they're fighting over you, huh?" I eyed Wayne seriously.

"That's what I said," Wayne retorted, staring at me as if daring me to challenge him. "You better ask somebody. I just had to check a bitch in the club last night about her man. Like, *bitch, don't no man hang around the Pink Panthers unless they're trying to fuck.*"

"You know what," I paused. "I'm not even going to ask."

"Trust me, you don't want to know," Wayne said. "Anyway, like I was saying, I ain't worrying about no clown ass niggas or bitch for that matter doing nothing to me. You know, I know karate and I'll Jet-Li a motherfucker's ass quick. So, what's on your mind, family?"

"Do you remember the bounty-hunter dude that you turned your cousin and them on to?" I asked ready to get to the point of my visit.

"Who? Herbert?" Wayne looked at me questioningly.

"Yeah," I confirmed. That was the name Billy Lo told me. "You still be hooking up with him?"

"Of course, why?" Wayne's fond smile let me know that he had absolutely no idea that Herbert was partially responsible for his cousin's downfall. "You looking to get in the hoe game or something?" Wayne laughed. "I mean, no disrespect, Peanut, but he'll pay extra for an ass like you got."

"Set it up then," I instructed.

"Are you serious? 'Cause I'll set that shit up for real."

"I'm not playing—Set it up," I repeated. "Tell him that I'm one of your new girls. 'Cause I need the money."

"I can do that."

"When?" I questioned.

"Well, one of the panthers and I see him every other Wednesday. So, not this Wednesday, but the next one."

"Make it happen," I said, moving for the door. "I'll call you for the details in a few days."

"It's two things I don't play with, Peanut," Wayne seemed to warn as he followed me to the door. "That's my clients and my money, so if I do this, you can't stand him up, and I want my cut."

"I got you," I assured, stopping to turn and face him. "I only have two requests."

"What's that?" Wayne raised his eyebrow and stared at me curiously.

"That I go alone and that you keep this between you and I because it's only going to be a one time thing."

"Tssk," Wayne sucked his teeth. "Bitch, you know your secret is safe with me." He winked. "But you better represent like a panther."

I gave Wayne a hug, assured him that I would indeed represent, and bounced. I had to meet up with Billy Lo's partners again. However, this time I'd be telling them something I knew they wanted to hear. Something that had everything to do with money, and nothing to do with sitting on their hands. Something to do with robbing Herbert for all the money he had from taking pay outs and setting up licks. Shiddd, as far as I was concerned, his undercover faggy ass deserved it. Because not only was he a crooked cop, but—according to Billy Lo—he'd violated their business agreement. Because, under no circumstances should he have given up his business associates.

***

I pulled up on Zimbabwe and Little Dinky on the corner of Park Heights and Woodland Avenue as planned and waited for them to get in.

"You said one o'clock," Little Dinky reminded me, as he and Zimbabwe climbed into the car.

"I got held up." I said, pulling back out into traffic. "Everything okay though?"

"Everything's good. Just waiting on you." Zimbabwe seemed to make sure that I understood his disapointment.

"Anybody talk to Billy Lo?" I looked into the rearview mirror before changing lanes.

"I did last night," Little Dinky said.

"What did he say about what we talked about?" I questioned rhetorically, having already talked to Billy Lo myself.

"He said to follow your lead," Little Dinky admitted, looking at Zimbabwe. I knew that both Little Dinky and Zimbabwe were ready to just hit Charm where it hurt the most and call it a day. But, Billy Lo and I wanted to use the art of deception to ruffle some feathers. We wanted to use our puppet-master skills to test the bonds that Charm and his little squad believed that they had.

"So what now?" Zimbabwe questioned from the passenger seat.

"We wait," I replied, knowing that Charm wouldn't be ready for the curve ball I planned to throw him.

"So, what are we meeting for?" Zimbabwe asked, as if he was irritated.

"I got something else in mind. Something that's going to put some money in our pockets and prove to you both that I ain't the average bitch." I smiled, knowing that they were both still trying to figure out what I had up my sleeve!

"Fill me out. Must be something almost unheard of. The type of shit you read about in books."

"You line it up, we'll knock it down," Little Dinky spoke up from the back seat. "My pockets need fattening up."

"Nah," I shook my head negatively. "It's gonna take all three of us to pull this off."

"What does it involve?" Zimbabwe questioned, as if it mattered.

"A crooked pig and his bacon," I replied.

"Well, you know I hate the police," Zimbabwe looked over at me. "But, I'm very fond of money."

"Hell—in that case, you're about to cash in." I assured, about to do some unheard of shit. The type of shit people read about in books.

Chapter 20

My mind was racing and my hands were shaking, as I continued speeding through Dru Hill Park, looking for the squad. I was ready to kill something behind the disturbing news Ebony had just given me. My brother, my nigga, one of my men had crossed that line. Ebony hadn't even wanted to tell me. She even tried to hold it in, but I knew something was wrong by the way she'd been acting. And yet, even though she said she felt like I deserved to know, she refused to reveal anything until I promised her that I wouldn't do nothing silly.

I can't believe this nigga! I thought, shaking my head. It was crazy how you never knew the truth about your niggas until money, power and women came into the picture. Although the city had gotten 'B-Day' pushed back this year due to the riots, it was still in full swing. There were niggas and bitches everywhere, and you could tell that summer was still in effect.

When I came around the bend near the tennis courts, I spotted Deli first. Standing under a big ass oak tree with everybody else in some throwback black and silver Bo Jackson's with the matching Tim Brown Oakland Raiders Jersey, trying to catch some shade. I pulled over and parked behind a money green Tahoe and jumped out with it on my mind. I saw Lor'Homie's Mustang GT and Shaggy's ES 350 parked on the grass near JuJu's pearl white Chrysler and some fat dude's black 2015 Jaguar F Type R Coupé. It was a true car show, but I was too heated at the moment to truly take it in the scenery or enjoy the excitement of the day. Then, I saw the whip that made everything that Ebony had told me official. It looked exactly how she'd described.

"What's up, Dummie?"

Deli tried to give me a pound as I brushed past him and threw a straight right off my back foot that caught Nizzy just above his left eye and made him stumble backwards. I let the left fly next. But, Nizzy slipped it and hit me with a solid kidney-shot before we both stepped back to square off. The scratch line was set.

"Whoa, Dummie!" Deli jumped in between us as the rest of the squad rushed over. "What's up with you?"

Before I could respond Nizzy ducked under Deli's outstretched arm and had me airborne. When we hit the dirt, it was on again. We exchanged blows until Deli and JuJu managed to pull Nizzy off top of me. Young Danny and Murdock tried to help me to my feet, but I snatched away and began brushing the dirt off my clothes.

"Nigga, I'ma crush your bitch ass!" I barked, trying to break past Young Danny and Murdock just as somebody hit me from the blind. I saw Deli let go of Nizzy and rush over as I went down to one knee. But, JuJu grabbed him.

"Fuck is you doing, nigga?" I heard Deli interrogate and looked up to see Shaggy holding Lor'Homie in a tight bear hug.

"You put your hands on me, Dummie?" Nizzy questioned, checking his brow for damage. "You know you gotta answer for that."

"Fuck you, nigga!" I stood up, spitting blood into the dirt, looking from Nizzy to his cousin. "And Lor'Homie bitch, you's a dead man."

"Hold up, Charm," Shaggy looked at me over his shoulder. "You need to chill, Dummie, seriously."

"What?" I moved towards Shaggy. I wasn't really feeling his tone or stare. "Fuck you mean, Dummie? When you get crazy, Shag? You can get it too nigga."

Shaggy immediately released Lor'Homie as Juju got in between he, Lor'Homie and I. "You don't want it with me, believe that."

"Shag, you ain't nobody!" I fired, realizing that sides were being chosen. But, I didn't give a fuck. I was ready to get off into some gangster shit anyway. "Niggas been carrying you for real."

"Yo! Yo! Come on, y'all!" Murdock tried to calm everybody down. "We're family, man." '

"This shit is crazy," JuJu agreed, shaking his head. "I don't even know what the fuck is going on."

"Ask that bitch ass nigga what's going on," I suggested, pointing at Nizzy. "He's the one that can't hold his liquor."

"Come on, Charm, Dummie," Young Danny pleaded with me. "Chill with all that for a second," he requested before turning to Nizzy. "What's up, Dummie? Fuck is y'all niggas out here acting stupid for?"

"Man, I don't know what the fuck is on that nigga's mind, Dummie." Nizzy stared at me. "But, his punk ass is going to pay for putting his hands on me, you can bet that!"

"Let's do it then, nigga!" I challenged, tussling with Murdock, trying to get past. "I'm right here!"

"Come on, yo," Murdock looked around. "Niggas out here causing a scene."

"So!" I didn't give a fuck about the gathering crowd. "Fuck that!" I continued. "This nigga the one going at my girl, showing off his new truck, talking all this wild shit about taking over and shit."

"Nigga, what? I ain't even seen Ebony, fuck is you talking about?"

"Oh, you ain't seen her, huh?" I looked at Nizzy with hurt in my heart. He was supposed to be my brother. "Then, tell me how the fuck she know about the plug, nigga?"

"I don't know, nigga. Probably pillow talk. You the one got your head stuck up her ass!"

"Oh, and you fucked my mother, nigga?" I had to pause to mentally process my thoughts and physically keep myself from pulling out my tone because under different circumstances, guns would be blazing. "You took advantage of my mom at her weakest point, nigga. You talk all that *brother and honor over everything* shit. But you a snake for real, nigga! You ain't got no honor."

"Say it ain't so, Dummie," I saw Young Danny look at Nizzy like everybody else. And I knew what he was thinking. The same thing I had thought when I first found out. Ebony was one thing. I mean, baby mother or not, a bitch was still a bitch.

But Mom Dukes was an entire different story. "Tell me you ain't cross that line."

"Dummie, mannnn, yo," Nizzy appeared to be considering his words carefully, before dropping his head in shame. "That shit was when Peaches was still getting high," he defended himself as if it made things okay. "But, I swear Dummie, I'm telling you that bitch lying."

"How she know all that then, Dummie?" I questioned, honestly wanting to know.

"I don't know," Nizzy replied. "But, I caught her out of pocket over east. I just ain't want to say nothing. She was in a red low-rider with some Mexican dude."

"You can miss me with all that bullshit, nigga!" I barked, cutting him off as he tried to make up some lame ass excuse because I knew that a liar's greatest fear was being exposed.

"Damn, Dummie," Deli shook his head disappointedly.

"Bitch!" I broke loose and hit Lor'Homie with a wicked overhand while everybody's focus was on Nizzy. "I'ma kill your whore ass!" I tackled Lor'Homie to the ground and started getting the best of him. Nizzy peeped what was happening and wrestled free from JuJu and came over to assist his cousin, but Deli dropped him as I kicked out at him to keep him off my back.

"Oh, so, that's how niggas doing it, huh?" Shaggy exclaimed, backing up like he was about to reach for his tone.

"You definitely don't wanna do that, Shag." Murdock threatened, as park security and Baltimore City's Armed Thugs pulled up, looking for someone to fuck with. After the police assured that nobody was hurt or wanted to press charges, the line was drawn. Deli, Young Danny, Murdock, JuJu and I on one side. Nizzy, Lor'Homie and Shaggy on the other.

"You got that, Dummie!" I acknowledged. For some reason, I'd always known it would come down to this. It always did when your friends were more ambitious than honorable. I just never believed in a million years that it would be one of my day one niggas.

"So, you're gonna believe that bitch over me, Dummie?" Nizzy questioned, like he was hurt. "Your own brother? After all the shit we done came through, nigga?"

"Brothers don't do what you did, nigga!" I argued. To me it was bigger than Ebony. To me it was about honor and respect. Discipline, even. "And for the record, nigga, that bitch is my baby mother," I added, ready to go harder than 'Django' to defend Ebony's honor.

"Man, fuck them niggas, Cuz," Lor'Homie spoke up, always looking for a reason to throw someone to the wolves. Be it friend or foe. "You already see what it is. Let's bounce."

"Yeah, them niggas aiding with Charm," Shaggy added, walking off behind Lor'Homie.

"The truth don't take sides, nigga!" JuJu fired, as Lor'Homie and Shaggy headed for their cars. "It's just the truth."

"I heard that—I see where niggas at," Nizzy said, shaking his head before turning to leave. I watched them with murder on my mind and fire in my eyes, until they got into their respective vehicles and pulled off. Baltimore Day was official ruined. At least for us, it was.

"Yo, I think we should bounce too, Dummie." Murdock suggested, probably not trusting Nizzy and them no more than I did.

"Yeah, you're right," I agreed, giving everybody some love. "Let shoot over JuJu's."

I didn't know where we all stood as far as Lor'Homie, Nizzy and Shaggy were concerned, or how shit would unfold the next time we all crossed paths. However, I did know that things would never be the same again. Because not only had lines been drawn and blood been shed, but Nizzy had exposed himself.

***

Adnan didn't know what to do at first when Charm came to him about the situation with Nizzy and the girl, but he knew that he had to use sound judgment. So, he gave it some thought for a few days before deciding to summon both Charm and Nizzy to have an old-fashioned sit-down—a meeting of the minds. If not for peace, then at least for the sake of business. Everyone didn't need to get along to get money. As long as Charm understood that there would be no need to cut Nizzy off, nor lighten Charm's delivery.

"I am glad you could make it," Adnan snook Nizzy's hand firmly and patted him on the arm. "Now that everybody's present, we can all lay our cards on the table and see who has the best hand."

Nizzy nodded, but Adnan noticed that his facial expression never changed. He figured Nizzy was still wondering about the sudden summons. "Good," Adnan looked at Rashid Salih and signaled to him that he had it from there before leading Nizzy into his private office with Tariq in tow.

"Hold up, Adnan," Charm shot to his feet the instant he saw Nizzy entering the office. "Fuck is this nigga doing here?"

"Have a seat, Charm," Adnan ignored his concerns and made his way around the desk. "You can have a seat too, Nizzy," Adnan added, pointing to an empty chair in front of the desk next to Charm and waited for Nizzy to comply.

Nizzy pulled the chair further away from Charm. Placed it in a defensive position and sat down before Adnan continued.

"Now, let's get one thing straight before we even begin. I called this meeting, so there will be no disrespect to me or my place of business, understood?"

"Yeah," Charm replied reluctantly after Nizzy nodded in argeement.

"I am trying to bring some kind of order to this little problem you seem to be having, so that we can all continue to make some money." Adnan looked from Nizzy to Charm again to make sure that he was making himself crystal clear.

"No disrespect or nothing, Adnan, but I don't fuck with no snakes!" Charm spat, ice-grilling Nizzy. "As far as I'm concerned, they're all dead weight."

"Dead weight?" Nizzy repeated, with a sarcastic laugh.

"Nigga, you the one that ain't a hundred."

"How you gonna up and say I'm not a hundred when you ate of my plate?"

"Ebony really got you gassed up, huh? You that blinded by love? Or is the sex that good?" Nizzy stared at Charm and tapped on his temple lightly with his index-finger, as if telling him to think. "Come on, Dummie, you're smarter than that. Use your logic. The bitch lying."

"I'm not going to keep telling you about that bitch word!" Charm warned. "But she knows too much to be lying, Dummie."

"You're really a fool, Dummie." Nizzy sat up in the chair and shook his head again.

"And you're really a snake, nigga!" Charm barked. "And you know how we deal with snakes."

"There you go with your lil' threats again." Nizzy stood up.

"You of all people know that I don't make idle threats." Charm got up.

"Sit down." Adnan's patience was beginning to run very thin. "That's enough."

"I'm telling you, Dummie—You're gonna stop threatening me," Nizzy said, slowly easing back down into his seat. "I let that shit slide at first because you were in your lil' feelings. But, that's your last warning. Next time, you're gonna stand on that."

"You don't want no smoke, nigga! You know how I get down!" Charm challenged.

"I said, *enough*!" Adnan slammed his fist down on the desk top, rasing his voice to cut Charm off. He could tell from the evil in Charm's eyes that the little reunion he had hoped for was a lost cause. The blade had sliced too deep. So, the next step had to be taken. "I have heard enough. Nizzy, you are a good soldier, but you're out." Adnan brought his hand up when Nizzy attempted to protest. "Save it, Ock. It's over." He turned to Tariq. "Do me a favor and see Nizzy out."

"That's crazy, Adnan," Nizzy stood up, shaking his head. "I ain't never been nothing but one hundred with you niggas. Now, this nigga got you on some fuck shit! And he knows it."

"It is what it is, Ock," Adnan replied, waiting for Tariq to escort Nizzy out of his office.

"I'ma say this to you before I go, Dummie," Nizzy began. "You know I'm one hundred. I never crossed you or none or my niggas. Your bit—I mean, your girl lying. I'm telling you she's lying. And if you don't see that nigga, you're going to end up dead."

"Yeah, whatever, nigga," Charm waved Nizzy off.

"Well, you got your wish, Ock," Adnan addressed Charm once Nizzy exited the office, and he watched the smile spread across his face. "I know you asked me not to do this. But, I had to try to get you both in the same room together to see if there was any chance to move on. I see now, there's not." Adnan stared at Charm. "Now, you know what's expected of you, right?"

"Already." Charm nodded.

"Good. Now, if there's nothing else, you can see yourself out." Adnan rose to his feet and extended his hand across the desk. "We'll meet up again in a couple of days."

"Already." Charm shook Adnan's hand.

Adnan smiled at Charm as he left the office. But honestly, his money was on Nizzy. He had watched Nizzy the entire meeting. There was no way he was lying. There was no way he was stupid enough to tell some female all his business. Charm had let emotions cloud his judgment. But, if he knew like Adnan knew, he'd have woken up and cut his loses. Because, there wasn't anything waste than a woman who couldn't be trusted.

Adnan walked over to his personal mini-bar and picked up No. 23 of the 785 individually numbered bottles of Remy Martin, Black Pearl Louis XIII, limited edition Cognac and sat it down on the desk, before pulling out his cellphone to call Tariq. "Assalaam alaikum, Ock— Did you do what I told you to do?— Is he still with you?—Good—Yeah—well, bring him back in." Adnan ended the call. He knew that he was making that right decision. Because, not only was Nizzy definitely about his paper. He was also about his work.

"Adnan, what's going on, man?" Nizzy walked back into the office, looking confused. "You tell me to leave. Then, refuse to let me go."

"Why don't you have a seat and let me explain?" Adnan gestured towards one of the empty chairs again. It was time to separate the left hand from the right.

"I'm good," Nizzy replied, watching Tariq like a hawk.

"Suit yourself," Adnan smiled, poured himself a shot of Cognac and took a seat behind his desk. He didn't have any hard feelings. "Here's what's going on. A good friend of mine once told me to never bet on a man who doesn't know how to tell when he's being played. So—what I want to do is, put my money on you."

Adnan went on to explain the situation to Nizzy in great detail. He expressed that he didn't believe Charm's story about him revealing their dealings. He also settled Nizzy's concerns about being out before they went over quality, quantity and delivery as if they'd just met. By the time they finished, Nizzy was sitting down in one of the empty chairs, rubbing his hands together with a huge grin on his face.

"—So there you have it, Ock. You're still in the same league as Charm. You're just batting for your own team."

"That's cool with me," Nizzy stood up to seal the deal with a gentleman's handshake. "Can I ask you something though?"

"Sure," Adnan came around the desk and placed his arm over Nizzy's shoulder as they walked towards the door.

"What happens if the right hand finds out about the left hand? You know, like if our teams end up playing against each other or something?"

"In that case—" Adnan looked at Nizzy seriously. He knew exactly what he was getting at. "There's only two things to do. Either, cut off the one of less value, or I let the best man win."

Chapter 21

I was happy as shit Ebony had left a plate in the oven for me when I got to the crib because the blunt I'd just finished smoking with Deli had given me the munchies like shit. I poured myself a jumbo glass of ice tea and sat down at the kitchen table to destroy the fried porkchops, gravy smothered rice, and cheesy broccoli plate that my baby had put together. Then, I picked up the remote control and turned to ESPN on the old box television that Ebony kept on the kitchen counter. I wanted to catch some highlights from my man Gervonta Tank Davis' fight.

I got up to wash my plate and straighten up a little bit after I finished eating. Then, I pulled up my Twitter account and posted something about Tank. It felt good to see another homie from the city winning—especially when he was keeping it one hundred.

I went live from the kitchen for a minute, talking shit about how I'd taught 'Tank' everything he knew. Then, I liked something on Lor Scoota's I.G. and headed on upstairs to lay my high ass down. Remembering how I use to go round for round with Tank and Berry.

—dont forget what i said, dummie!

I read Deli's text message as I walked up the steps, and knew he was right. Some changes needed to be made quick because, as Deli had expressed, Nizzy knew too much about the day-to-day operation and could no longer be trusted. Especially, since I'd gotten him cut off from the plug. I respect what Adnan said, but I also knew Nizzy. If there was food out there, that nigga was going to eat one way or another.

I tip-toed into the bedroom to find Ebony laying across the bed under the fan in nothing but a pair of white boy-shorts that made her chocolate skin look even more enticing. I slowly admired her body from head to toe. The slopes of hips, the softness of her ass cheeks, the curves of her legs. The view was stunting. I made my way around behind the fan, geeking, ready to play.

"Hey, beautiful," I mumbled into the back of the fan,

allowing the spending blazes to alter my voice. "Daddy's home," I added, laughing at my own robot sounding voice.

Ebony stirred, readjusted her pillow and rolled over onto her side, causing her sexy boy-shorts to cut deeper into the crack of her butt, as I began to get nasty ideas. I got undressed and leaned across the bed to softly kiss Ebony on her exposed ass cheek.

"Charm, stop." Ebony tossed a pillow over her back at me. "I'm not in the mood."

I figured she was probably still upset that I hadn't made it home early enough to eat with her. But, I wasn't trying to hear none of that. Not while she was laying there looking all tasty and tempting, like a McDonald's Sundae. "Don't be like that, baby," I whispered, easing in behind her, slowly snaking my hand over her hip, down into her boy-shorts. "I just wanna taste you." I gently ran my finger between the folds of her wet pussy lips before teasing her clit and sliding two fingers into her hot pussy. "Can I taste you, baby?"

"Sssss!" Ebony moaned, arched her back and shivered like she was on the verge of cumming. I teased her clitoris again and smiled. Most women's power lie between their legs. Strangely, it's also where her weakness lays. If you can make her cum, she'll submit every time, because it's in nature to sumbit to a man who is taking care of home. So, whatever you fuck up, go home and play to her power. By taking it in one sense, catering to it in another. My mother had explained that to me the first time I told her about my women problems.

I kissed my way down Ebony's back before gradually casing the boy-shorts over her firm hips and down her pretty legs. Once I got Ebony out of her panties, I rolled her over, propped her up on pillows, hooked one of her legs over my shoulder and went deep sea snorkeling inside her.

"Charm, I'm serious, you—you—mmmmhhhhh!" Ebony let out a breathless, high-pitched sound and gripped my head with amazing strength. "Ohhhh, my Godddd!—Wh—where did you le—learn to eat pu—pussy like that?"

I wasn't the type to talk with my mouth full. So, I continued to devour her until her legs began to shake hard. Then, I kissed my way back up to where she was holding the flesh of her breasts in her hands, as if offering them to me. I rolled my tongue back and forth across her bullet-sized, hard nipples and nibbled on them.

"You gonna let me get mine now?" I questioned, then went on licking and sucking her dark nipples in my mouth, as she continued to shake, moan, squirm and cum.

"Yes, daddy," Ebony submitted, wrapping both legs around me.

I could literally feel the heat oozing from her pussy.

I continued to massage and gently teased Ebony's breasts until she was pressing and rubbing her pussy up against me almost feverishly with her eyes slightly out of focus. Then, she began begging me to beat that pussy up.

I slid into Ebony nice and deep. Damn! She got some good pussy! I slowly pulled out until only the head of my dick remained. Then, I gradually entered from an awkward angle. I was going to knock the lining out of her pussy tonight. I was going to fuck her until we both collapsed into each other's arms and passed out.

***

The fire-alarm was going off as I made my way down the hallway to the unguarded hospital room and eased inside. I moved as silently as a shadow. Yet, as quickly as a cat until I reached the hospital bed that Billy Lo was lying in. Then, I raised the gun, snatched the sheets back, and pulled the trigger repeatedly without a moment's hesitation. However, nothing happened.

I was about to pull the trigger again when Billy Lo's hand came from under the sheets and pointed a big ass motherfucking gun at my head, causing me to freeze up. I could see the tip of the bullet sitting at the other end of the barrel just before he squeezed the trigger.

Bang! Bang! Bang!

"No!" I screamed, shooting up to a sitting position in bed before realizing that Billy Lo was haunting my dreams again. "Huh?" I questioned, trying to gather my thoughts as Ebony pushed me out of the bed with a concerned look on her face.

"Somebody's banging on the door!" Ebony said a second before the *'Bang! Bang! Bang!'* came again.

"What time is it?" I looked at the clock and wondered who in the hell could be banging on her door at three o'clock in the morning like they were crazy. "You expecting company?" I questioned, picking up my sweat-pants off the floor to check my right pocket to make sure my tone was still there, as Ebony got up and walked over to peep out the window. There were only a few things that showed up in the middle of the night, and none of them were good.

"It's Keystone!" Ebony exclaimed over her shoulder.

"My mother's boyfriend?" I questioned, to be sure.

"Yup," Ebony nodded. "Peaches' boyfriend."

"How the hell he know where you live at?" I questioned, slipping on my sweats.

"I don't know, but he's definitely at the door." Ebony seemed more relaxed, as she walked back over to throw herself across the bed.

"Let me go see what's up." I hurried from the room, taking the stairs two and three at a time because I knew something had to be wrong for Keystone to show up at Ebony's house at this time of night.

Downstairs, I snatched the door open. "What's up, Keystone?"

"Man, I been trying to reach you all night," Keystone spat. "What? You lose your phone or something?"

"Nah, I just got a new one when I came home," I confessed. I'd learned something new about how cell-phones and cell-towers were being used to place niggas near or at crime scenes when G-baby's bitch ass gave that business up. So, I'd let my old phone go. "What's up, though?"

"It's Peaches," Keystone paused to take a deep breath. "She's in I-C-U."

I swear that was all I heard before my mind and body went into shock mode.

***

I burst into Maryland University's Intensive Care Unit with Keystone hot on my heels and demanded to see my mother, but she was still in surgery. All I could do was, sit out in the waiting room with Keystone and wait. Which was only driving me crazy. Because, despite all the things my mother and I had went through over the years when she was still getting high, that was my baby. When nobody was there, she always was. I couldn't count how many times she'd made a way out of no way. Or how many times she'd comforted me when nobody else could. She was all I had left, and losing her would be too much.

"Keystone, tell me this shit again," I ordered, pacing a path into the waiting room's carpet, unable to sit still. "You say some niggas grabbed my mother?" I questioned, unable to believe it. Anybody who knows me, knows that I don't play about my mother. Especially, since I lost my sister. I'd go against God Himself and lay my life down for Peaches. Niggas had witnessed me tear the city up before looking for the stick-up boy who'd made the mistake of robbing my mother and snatching a chain off the neck of my five-month-old lil' cousin last year.

"Yeah," Keystone replied. "I mean, that's what the police told me when I got down here earlier."

It couldn't be niggas from around the way. They knew better. They'd seen first-hand or at the least heard about the way I'd wore the stick-up boy out behind my mother. On top of that, my mother was like the neighborhood aunt who everybody knew, loved or respected because she knew everything, but told nothing.

"The girl on her job told the police that two guys jumped out of a dark-colored van and grabbed Peaches when they got off work. They don't know if they were trying to rape her or what." Keystone closed his eyes as if to try and calm himself down. "Whatever they had planned though didn't work because about four or five blocks away, Peaches somehow managed to get loose and jump out of the back of the moving van. The doctor told me that they were going to have to remove a large piece of glass from her arm." Keystone wiped his eye to keep a tear from falling, and took a few deep breaths. "Can't nothing happen to your mother, Charm. I'm telling you, can't nothing happen to Peaches. Motherfuckers don't want to see that side of me."

"I hear you," I said, wondering if Keystone's old ass had it in him. I mean, I knew how much he cared about my mother and I'd heard rumors about how he may or may not use to get down. But, honestly, I was the one niggas didn't want to see the other side of because they knew my other side didn't take no prisoners.

Where the fuck are Deli and them at? I thought to myself. The squad couldn't get to the hospital quick enough.

"Don't even think like that," Ebony said softly, trying to comfort Keystone. Honestly, I had forgotten that she was even sitting over in the corner.

I saw a nurse pointing Keystone out to an older black dude wearing a long white hospital coat with a clipboard in his hand and got Keystone's attention as he approached. "Heads up, Keystone."

"The rest of the Johnson bunch, I assume?" the doctor said as he came over while Ebony began to rub my back slowly.

"Yes," Keystone confirmed. "My wife's son and daughter-in-law," Keystone added, as Ebony came up beside me and gently took my hand.

"Well, I have some good news," the doctor smiled softly before looking at his clipboard. "Missis Johnson is out of surgery and she's stable. As I said earlier, there was a large piece of glass lodged into Miss Johnson's forearm that was threatening to cut a main artery, but we were successfully able to remove it and stop the bleeding before it caused more damage."

"What about the glass that was in her hand?" Keystone

questioned.

"We removed that also. It really didn't cause any damage, just a lot of blood loss. Miss Johnson will need her rest. So, we'll be holding her for a few days to run some more test and make sure that we've recovered all the glass."

"So, she's going to live?" I questioned because honestly, that was all I cared about.

"I don't see why not." The doctor smiled again. "Minus a few scars and stiffness, I expect Miss Johnson to make a full recovery in a couple of weeks."

"Can we see her?" Ebony spoke up.

"I don't know about that," the doctor shook his head. "It's hospital policy that the police be the first one to—"

"Come on, Doc," Keystone grabbed the doctor's hand, went into his jacket pocket, pulled out a fistful of bills and stuffed them into the good ol' doctor's hand. "Five minutes, I promise."

The doctor stared at the pile of twenties and fifty dollar bills in his hand for a moment, as if to consider the request, before looking around and replying. "I suppose that I can sneak you in for a few minutes before the detectives return. Seeing as though you all have been so nice." The doctor slipped the bills into his pocket.

"Hold up," Keystone looked confused. "I thought the police were already here?"

"They were," the doctor confirmed. "But, we needed to rush Miss Johnson into surgery. She was also refusing to answer any questions at that time anyway. So, I told them that I would give them a call once Miss Johnson was out of surgery and we'd collected DNA simples. I just got off the phone with them."

I couldn't help but smile inside. If my mother wasn't nothing else, she was a fucking soldier. "So, when can you get us in?"

"It's going to have to be now because once Missis Johnson is moved upstairs, nobody except detectives will be able to see her for twenty-four hours."

"Let's do this then," Keystone suggested, taking the words right out of my mouth. He probably wanted to get to mom just as bad as me.

"You picked my pockets, Keystone," I acknowledged the fact that I'd been thinking the exact same thing.

"I'll be right here, baby." Ebony squeezed my hand and kissed me on the cheek.

"Okay," I replied. "If Dummie and 'em show up, tell 'em I'll be right back."

Ebony nodded. Keystone and I followed the doctor on down the hallway.

"Right this way," the doctor mumbled, as we passed the nurse station. "Now, I have to warn you, Miss Johnson is a little banged up," the doctor revealed, looking back over his shoulder, as we neared the hospital rooms. "Her left wrist is broken and her right shoulder is skinned almost bare. There are also lacerations covering about twenty percent of her body and some slight head trauma. All of which we assume she sustained during her struggle and eventual escape."

The doctor stopped in front of room #1. "You guys ready?" The doctor looked from Keystone to me with kindness. "You have five minutes!" He exclaimed after a brief pause. Then, opened the door and stepped to the side. "Five minutes or I'm calling security."

When I stepped into the hospital room and saw my mother, tears instantly began to fall from my eyes. I was crushed. I didn't know what to say. If there was God, how the fuck could He have allowed this shit to happen to my mother? Especially, after she had been submitting her life to Him, working, staying clean, attending church service, giving charity, all that! Now, mom was laid up in Maryland University all battered and bruised. Come hell or hot water, somebody was going to pay for what happened to my mother, you can believe that.

"I'll leave you all alone," the doctor whispered, pulling the door close.

"Ma!" I shot straight over to her bedside. "What happened?"

"Baby, who did this?" Keystone gently took my mother's bandaged hand.

"I don't know," my mother couched. "But, it was two of them. A tall, stocky one with golds. And a short, lightskin one with real pretty eyes. They were waiting outside my job."

"Did you see their faces? Was it anybody that be around 'The Avenue'?" I questioned anxiously.

"I didn't get a real good look at them. But, I'll definitely know either one if I ever saw them again." Plus, I bit the hell out of one of them right on the cheek."

"You got any ideas?" Keystone looked at me.

"Nah," I confessed honestly. I couldn't figure out who would be brave enough to attack my mother. "But, it gotta be some niggas with a death wish."

"You say you bit one of them on the face, baby?" Keystone questioned my mother, and she nodded. "Then, that's where we'll start. We'll put some money on the streets and see what turns up."

"Hold up," I smiled. I had another idea. "The doc said the detectives are on their way to question mom, right?"

"Yeah, so?" Keystone stared at me curiously.

"We can have mom do the photo line-up so that we—"

"What? Man, hell no!" Keystone fired, cutting me off. "My woman isn't no snitch! I'll find these little niggas myself!"

"That's not what I was saying!" I spat, balling my face up.

"Well, you're talking about line-ups and shit!" Keystone argued.

"Trust me, Keystone, baby, Calvin knows he was raised by a soldier!" my mother interjected thankfully before I went on Keystone.

"You got to hear me out first, Keystone." I looked from Keystone to my mother and couldn't help but laugh. "What I was thinking definitely didn't have nothing to do with telling," I assured. "I just know that a bite mark will heal. A nigga can stay in the house for a few days, you feel me? So, here's what I was thinking."

Once I knew I had Keystone and my mother's attention, I walked them through my master plan of saving time and getting everything we needed to find and fry the niggas who'd been stupid enough to violate the number 1 law of the streets: Never fuck with a man's family.

"I got to admit—I like that, soldier," Keystone nodded after I finished explaining exactly what it was I was trying to do. "I got to stop sleeping on y'all little kids out here."

"I like it too," Mom seconded, smiling. "You are your mother's child."

"You know the apple don't fall far from the tree, Ma."

"Sorry, guys, but your time's up." The door opened and the doctor poked his head inside. "They just paged me from the front desk downstairs. The detectives are on their way up."

"A'ight," Keystone gave him a slight nod, kissed my mom and promised that he'll not leave the hospital without her, as we made our way from the room.

"I love you, Ma," I said, ready to go duck-hunting.

"I love you too, son!" She smiled. It had been a long time since either one of us has used those words with each other.

When we got back to the waiting room, the Dummie Squad was in full force. I hugged Ebony tightly, then embraced my niggas one by one and gave them a quick update.

"What it is, Dummie?" JuJu asked after I gave everybody the rundown. It was no secret that he would go about Peaches. He'd been right by my side when I fucked the stick-up boy over behind her the last time. "How many niggas we gotta crack?"

"I don't know yet," I admitted. "First, we gotta find out who's responsible for this shit."

"What about Nizzy?" JuJu questioned seriously.

"Nizzy ain't that crazy, Dummie."

"Yeah, but Lor'Homie is!" JuJu retorted.

I stared at JuJu for a moment. I'd be lying if I said that the thought hadn't crossed my mind. But, after some deep consideration, I didn't believe that Nizzy would let nothing like that happen. "Yeah, but there's nothing to be gained." I shook my head. "This wasn't them. This was probably some ransom shit."

"Charm!" Keystone called out from the other side of the waiting room. "Don't forget the detectives are on their way up." He reminded me with a knowing look.

"Damn," I looked around. I'd almost forgot. There was no need for the detectives to show up and find a room full young goons. Especially, if we wanted my plan to work. "You got Mom?"

"Of course," Keystone replied.

"Cool, I'll see you in the morning." I grabbed Ebony's hand and told my niggas to come on because the police were on their way up, and no more needed to be said. Everybody in the waiting room was strapped up.

"I'm hitting the stairs, Dummie," Deli spoke up, and everybody followed him into the stairway exit. Because, despite how young and wild niggas were, they were not dying to run into the police. Especially, with our tones on them. I, on the other hand, walked towards the elevators with Ebony, because I didn't want to be nowhere near them niggas. Not with my hospital history. With everything going on I had forgotten all about the shit with Billy Lo on the ninth floor. But, more importantly, there was no way in hell that I was going to allow Ebony to walk down a ten flight of stairs while she was pregnant with my child.

***

"Ayo!" Nizzy was coming out of New Identity's when he spotted Ebony pulling up in Charm's 745 BMW. He hadn't seen her since the day he'd peeped her trifling ass over East Baltimore doing what he now knew was something out of order. "That's some real fuck shit you pulled!" Nizzy walked up on Ebony as she got out of Charm's car. "You're lucky I don't slap your stupid ass!"

"Don't be mad at me because my pussy is tighter than you and Charm's little friendship," Ebony retorted, sliding the yellow purse strap up over her shoulder before locking the car door. "Shit, I just beat you to the punch."

Nizzy shook his head, disgusted. He still couldn't believe Charm could be so blind. "I don't know what Charm sees in your crusty ass."

"Come on now, Nizzy, you don't have to lie no more. I done seen you goosing. But, now you can take a better look," Ebony slowly spun completely around. "Now, add that to the fact that I do everything in bed. And I do mean *everything*, baby."

"You ain't nothing but a snake in sheep's clothing!" Nizzy declared, and Ebony poked her tongue out and started hissing. Again, he wanted to slap the shit out of her. Maybe then, he could wipe that funky ass smirk off of her face. But, he didn't want to have to end up really having to spank Charm. "But, Dummie's going to figure you out, and once he does, you're gonna wish you'd never started all this mess."

"You really think Charm's going to hurt the mother of his child?" Ebony questioned, rubbing her belly gently. "Come on, Nizzy baby, even you know better than that."

"Shorty, you don't really know Charm," Nizzy assured her with an odd laugh. "But, I grew up with that silly nigga. And his hate for snakes is just as blinding as his love, but you're gonna learn."

"What about you, Nizzy?" Ebony stepped dangerously close and grabbed Nizzy's hand. "How allergic are you to reptiles?"

"Don't put your fucking hands on me, bitch!" Nizzy snatched his hand away from Ebony and started for his truck. Personally, he could deal with the snakes because he always kept his grass cut low. It was the rats that he had a problem with, but he didn't let Ebony know that because he knew that in the end he would have the last laugh.

"Ahhhh, come on, Nizzy," Ebony called behind him seductively. "I was just dying to give you a real taste of power." Ebony patted her phat pussy print. "Plus, I wanted you to feel what it's like to put your dick down a snake's throat," Ebony added with a laugh before slowly running her long tongue across her top lip.

Nizzy took one more look at Ebony, shook his head, climbed

into his truck, and pulled off. He hoped that when Charm discovered exactly what Ebony was, he would cut her open from belly to brain and feed her to her own fetus.

Nizzy drove around to Warwick and double-parked when he saw one of Shaggy's little soldiers leaning up against his ES350, bobbing his head to some music. "Where Shag at, Al-Qamar?"

"In the trap," Al-Qamar replied over the music, gesturing to the house across the street.

"Do me a favor and go get him while I park." Nizzy requested, before driving down the block to find a parking spot. Nizzy watched through the rearview mirror as Al-Qamar entered the stash house to get Shaggy for him.

About two minutes later, Nizzy saw Shaggy limping out of the trap-house looking around with his lil' sexy ass midget, and shook his head. He'd told Shaggy a thousand times about having her in the trap. She wasn't no more then fourteen at the most on his arm. Anyway, Nizzy watched as Shaggy began tonguing her down. He couldn't lie, though. Shorty lil' ass was phat to death.

Nizzy hit the horn and continued to watch as Shaggy slapped the lil' midget on her big butt before sending her on about her business and making his way up the street to where he was parked. "What's up, Dummie?" Shaggy questioned, climbing into the Range Rover, giving Nizzy some love. "Fuck you doing up here this early?"

"I just came from New Identity's," Nizzy touched his fresh Boosie fade. "I see you still letting that lil' school girl play hooky in the trap."

"I can't help it, Dummie," Shaggy smiled. "She got that torch between her legs," Shaggy admitted, looking over his shoulder. "Go around the block, Dummie. I'm not trying to keep sitting here. The jump-out boys out and it's work all up and down the block."

"Come on, Dummie, I done told you about that shit!" Nizzy contended, peeping into his driver side mirror before pulling off. "That's what the trap is for."

"You run your shit your way. And I'll continue to run mine

my way."

Nizzy didn't even reply. He just couldn't reason with hard-head, know-it-all niggas.

"I just ran into that bitch—Ebony."

"Oh, yeah?" Shaggy looked at Nizzy curiously. "What's up with her?" Shaggy wanted details. Especially if Nizzy was trying to fuck her because he knew deep down Ebony was a freak. He could just tell. Plus, she had those 'head doctor' lips.

"Nah, Dummie, it ain't nothing like that." Nizzy recognized Shaggy's glare.

"Shiddd, if it is, it doesn't matter now," Shaggy assured. "It's all fair in love and war."

"It ain't ever that fair!" Nizzy retorted. He would never be caught thinking with his dick. "But, I'll school you on that later. Right now, I need to get in your ear about something else."

"I knew your ass wasn't up here all early for nothing, nigga. I ain't stupid." Shaggy continued to observe the streets as Nizzy circled the block. "What's on your mind?"

"You know what's on my mind, nigga, don't play dumb!" Nizzy declared. "You and Lor'Homie with this silly shit about moving in on Gold Street."

"Laurens and Division," Shaggy corrected.

"Don't play with me, Dummie," Nizzy looked over at Shaggy seriously. "You know what the fuck I mean. I told y'all niggas to fall back and be cool for now. We got Warwick, North and Pulaski, Popular Grove and Braddish. Plus, you know I already spoke to my cousin about South Baltimore."

"We deserve Laurens and Division," Shaggy pulled a blunt from behind his ear. "Lor'Homie and I built that corner ourselves. Besides, Charm and 'em basically got the whole Avenue. Why can't we get some of it?"

"We aren't hurting for nothing, Shag. We got four strips that doing numbers," Nizzy argued.

"Man, fuck that, Dummie! Homie and I want Laurens and Division." Shaggy paused to light the spliff. "Charm the one that started all this fuck shit anyway! All behind a dumb ass bitch.

Tryna take food out of a nigga's mouth." Shaggy hit the blunt hard and choked a little bit. "Damn, that's fire," Shaggy held the blunt out to look at it before continuing. "Charm on that fuck shit, Dummie, not us. And you already know my feelings about fuck niggas."

"I just wanna keep moving slow for now," Nizzy took a left at the corner. "Everybody's eating. But, I promise when the time is right, we're gonna move in for the kill."

"The time is right now, Dummie!" Shaggy reasoned. In his mind it was already on. It was just a matter of time before everybody else realized it. "There's no sense in letting that nigga get away with no goldmine."

"You know Charm or JuJu not just going to sit back and let us take Divison."

"So, if them niggas want some smoke, I'll give it to 'em!" Shaggy fired. "These our stumping grounds too. Niggas can get down with the lay down or you already know what it is."

"You and Cuzzo boy," Nizzy reached for the spliff in Shaggy's hand. He hadn't even realized that Shaggy was a megalomaniac like his cousin. But, Nizzy only pulled the tones out when he was out of options. "Can you just convince Cuzzo to chill for the time being and trust me?" Nizzy pleaded. He didn't want to have to cut his own flesh and blood off.

"I'll try." Shaggy nodded.

"I'm telling you, Dummie, we're going to come out on top after everything is all said and done." When they moved on Charm, Nizzy wanted to make sure that they finished the job. Until then, he wanted Charm to continue to think that he was untouchable because of Adnan. "After that, you and Cuzzo can have any strip y'all want."

"That's what it is then," Shaggy agreed, satisfied. All he wanted to do was, remind Charm that he did a grimy nigga, like he did a grimy bitch. "But, you have to promise me one more thing, Dummie."

"What's that?" Nizzy eyed Shaggy.

"That when it's time to barbecue these nigga, you'll let me

be the one who set Charm ass on fire."

"You got my word, Dummie." Nizzy agreed, hitting the spliff because for him, it was a lot easier to kill a friend than it was to kill a brother.

"Oh yeah, did you get a chance to get up with O?" Shaggy asked.

"Yeah," Nizzy replied.

"So what he say? Where he stand?"

"He said that he wasn't taking sides," Nizzy admitted.

"Yeah right," Shaggy fired, knowing what that meant. "I told you that nigga was loyal to Charm! All them niggas are."

"You were right, Dummie," Nizzy confirmed knowing there was no such thing as neutrality in war. Sides were always chosen.

"So, you know what that means, right?" Shaggy looked over at Nizzy.

"Yeah. When we put our lick down, O has to be got too."

"Ain't no question."

Chapter 22

Well, my plan hadn't really worked like a charm. However, in the end we still got the results we were looking for. When my mother first identified her attackers from the photo-array line-up, we were all over them. But, the detectives just so happened to know exactly who both of the suspects were very well and suddenly rushed out into the streets to arrest them. Little Bobby and Larry High were two West Baltimore old heads, who had been terrorizing niggas all up and down North Avenue since the 80's. They were both known to kidnap and rob. But, word was that they would also murder, if the bread was right.

After Little Bobby and Larry High were arrested inside the Red Fox Lounge just off Fulton Avenue, we quickly had to improvise. We got Mom to write a two-page statement and sign a sworn affidavit saying that she'd made a terrible mistake. Then, she called the state's attorney office and had the charges dropped. Which was why we were now sitting outside of the J-I-Building, across the street from the city jail on Madison Street in the pouring down rain, waiting for Larry High and Little Bobby to be released.

JuJu and I had attended Larry High and Little Bobby's preliminary hearing earlier when the Judge had ordered them both released. Now, we were about to give them exactly what they deserved.

"We been out here since these niggas came from court." I broke the silence, keeping my eyes on the J-I-Building exit. "I hope these stiff ass niggas didn't have no detainers."

"Shiddd, you're right," Deli said, leaning forward to stick his face between the seats. "If they got detainers, we're fucked!"

"Hold up, Dummie," JuJu mumbled, hitting the windshield wipers. "They're letting some dudes out now."

"Yo, I think that's them, Dummie," I informed, straining my eyes to be sure as an officer held the J-I-Building's door open so guys could get out.

"Which ones?" Deli questioned, as the crowd continued to

spill out of the J-I-Building into the rain.

"The lil' lightskin nigga with the throwback jersey on." I referred to Little Bobby. "And the big nigga in the skinny jeans and Jordan's with the patch on his face. The one pumping his fist in the air like he's Tank or something," I added, tripping off how Larry High's old ass wanted to be young.

"You sure that's them, Dummie?" JuJu questioned as the crowd of men began to use paper-bags, shirts, and any other excessive property they'd been released with to shield themselves from the relentless rain.

"Yeah, that's them niggas," I confirmed as the C.O. secured the door and everybody began to make their way down the J-I-Building steps as the windshield wiper swiped the water away from the windshield, giving me a clear view. I could even see the slugs in Larry High's mouth that my mother had mentioned.

"Text Keystone." I kept my eyes locked on Larry High. He would not feel like a champion when the night was over.

"What's up with the fat nigga?" Deli questioned, as a fat dude appeared to be with Little Bobby and Larry High.

"I don't know," I replied as JuJu pulled out his phone and began texting Keystone. "But, if his fat ass is with them, then, he's getting it too." I noticed that fat boy was busting all out of his tight, skinny shit like a tube of biscuits. These old niggas be killing me. They talk so bad about a young nigga. Then, turn right around and start cutting their hair, dressing and sounding like us.

Little Bobby, Larry High and the fat dude walked past and stepped out into the street to try to flag down a taxi. "I hope these niggas take the bait," JuJu said to no one in particular.

"If not, we may just have to smash 'em Commacosi Style," I said because under no circumstances were Little Bobby and Larry High getting away with what they'd done to my mother.

"Here come Keystone now," JuJu informed, making me check the rearview mirror on his side. I saw Keystone coming down Madison Street and held my breath. He drifted past us and came to a complete stop in front of Little Bobby, Larry High and the Fatboy.

"Don't get in that cab, fat man," Deli mumbled, although the fat dude couldn't hear him. "You get in that cab you're fair game."

Almost as if he could hear Deli, the fat boy gave Larry High and Little Bobby some love and wobbled on up the street. Larry High exchanged a few words with Keystone before climbing into the back of the cab, followed by Little Bobby. "Got 'em." I smiled finally, exhaling. *So far, so good*, I thought.

"You think we going have to come back and do that to fat boy?" JuJu questioned, as Keystone pulled off.

"Nah, Keystone's cab company is legit," I said matter-of-factly, starting the car. "So, even if fat boy tries to give that business up, Keystone got it covered," I assured, knowing that Keystone and I had dotted all the i's and crossed all the t's.

I slowly pulled out into the oncoming traffic and followed Keystone at a caution distance through the semi-dark city streets. I didn't know if Larry High or Little Bobby were the type of dudes who paid attention to what was going on around them or not, and didn't want to chance being spotted. Keystone drove like a true cabby. Slow enough to run the meter. Yet, fast enough not to draw the customer's attention. We kept a safe distance until Keystone texted us an address. At that point, I sped off into the night.

Roughly eleven minutes later, I turned down Ashburton Street and parked as close as I could to the address Keystone had text. "Y'all niggas ready," I looked over at JuJu and Deli, adjusting my black baseball cap. "It's go time then," I added after they both nodded, opening my door to step out into the pouring rain. It was time to get into position.

We saw some headlights flashing across the parked cars at the top of the block and faded off into darkness, just in case. "That's them, Dummie!" I alerted, pulling the tone from my pocket.

Once Keystone came to a stop, I emerged from behind the tree and lightly tapped on the cab's window with the business end of my Glock, catching Little Bobby off guard as Deli and JuJu came from behind the car they'd hidden behind, snatched Larry High's door open, dragged him out onto the wet street and started working him over to set the tone.

"Get your big ass up!" I heard Deli demand, and smiled as Little Bobby locked the door and ordered Keystone to drive off.

"It's too late for all that, Bobby-boy," I said as Keystone unlocked the back door. "Y'all did my mother dirty. Now, it's time to see me."

I opened the door as Keystone turned around and pointed a big ass, old, ugly Magnum at Little Bobby's head. "Get out!" Keystone ordered, using his thumb to pull the hammer back on the Magnum.

Little Bobby grinned and mumbled something under his breath. He'd been playing the game long enough to know when he'd been caught slipping. Little Bobby slowly got out of the car with his hands up in defeat as I pressed the tone to the side of his head. "Do something stupid and I'ma leave you right here!" I warned through clenched teeth. "Park a few blocks away and come back." I turned to Keystone. He nodded and drove off quickly.

"Stop faking, nigga!" I heard Deli bark a second before he punched Larry High in the gut, forcing him to bend over in pain, trying to catch his breath. "You're too young to have a heart attack!" Deli aimed his tone at the back of Larry High's head. "How you wanna play this, nigga? The hard way or the healthy way?"

We quickly marched Little Bobby and Larry High into what turned out to actually be Little Bobby's older brother's crib. JuJu and I busied ourselves binding and gagging Little Bobby and Larry High while Deli searched the house top to bottom to make sure that no one else was home. Then, we waited for Keystone. When Kestone showed up, we started what he called the 'Eliot Ness' G-Men Interrogation. We were pistol-whipping, stabbing, brass-knuckle punching, water-boarding, and doing all kinds of other old-school shit Keystone came up with. The tone was set, and Larry High and Little Bobby knew that we weren't playing games, but these old niggas were old-school taught, so they didn't break easily.

"Look, yo, all we want to know is who sent you niggas after my mother," I repeated for the umpteenth time, standing over top of a bloody faced Little Bobby as he laid on the floor, tied to a chair with his gag dangling from his neck. "Just tell me that and this shit will be over."

"I don't know nothing, man." Little Bobby struggled against his restraints. "I swear!"

"What about you, big man?" Keystone pulled the gag out of Larry High's mouth again. "You ready to talk now?"

"Fuck you, nigga!" Larry High fired with a mouth full of blood-covered teeth. "I ain't telling you shit!"

Keystone hit Larry High again with his brass-knuckled covered hand and sent his chair crashing to the floor before kneeling down beside him. "Oh, you're going to tell me something, big man, I promise you."

"Man, fuck this shit, Dummie!" Deli exclaimed! walking over to aim his tone at Little Bobby's head impatiently. "These niggas aren't going to talk. Let's just handle this shit and bounce."

"Hold up, soldier," Keystone stuffed the gag back into Larry High's mouth and stood up straight. "I got something else I wanna try first." He sounded excited. "Somebody find me some pliers. I'ma remove this nigga's golds one by one."

"Nah," JuJu spoke up. "Let's boil some water and make them drink it."

I looked at JuJu crazy. "How the hell they gonna talk after they drink hot water, Dummie? We might as well just cut out their fucking tongues." My suggestion was hypothetical, and this stupid nigga smiled.

"I got an idea." Deli walked over to the coffee table and picked up the small, clear, plastic ziplock bag he or JuJu had removed from Larry High's pocket. "Bingo!" he said, tossing me a key-chain. "Check that out." He continued to pull contents from the ziplock.

I flipped the key-chain over and saw a photo of Larry High, a sexy ass big girl, and two pretty little girls. "What are you up to, Dummie?" I looked up to see Deli holding up Larry High's driver's license, smiling. "Ohhhhhh!" I exclaimed, understanding where Deli was going with this now. I caught Larry High's license and read the address out loud.

"I knew exactly where this at," I assured. "So, since y'all niggas want to play gangster, I'ma turn what was initially just justice into vengeance. You know, sometimes it's hard to tell the difference."

Larry High instantly began fighting like crazy to get free, saying some shit into the gag that nobody understood.

"Nah, y'all wanna play games?" I questioned. "Game on! First, we're gonna wait for your brother to show up so we can kill him," I informed Little Bobby before turning to Larry High. "Then, we're going to drive over to Webb Court and kill your kids. But, first I'ma rape that sexy bitch of yours. Dummie, did you see how thick shorty is?"

"Hell yeah," Deli smiled."

"Shiddd, let me see," JuJu grinded, reaching for the key-chain like he couldn't wait. "You already know I love 'em nice and thick."

I saw the lights come on in Larry High's head as I tossed JuJu the key-chain. I knew he was starting to think like a father instead of a gangster. So, I went in for the kill. "Come on, Larry High, all I want is a name and a neighborhood. I mean, y'all niggas opened the door by going after my mother. Yet, I'm still willing to keep it in the streets. But, only if you tell me who sent you." I assured honestly as Keystone walked over to remove his gag. "But, I'm warning you homie, if I gotta go to your house, it's not going to end good."

"Look, man, I don't know where the nigga be at or nothing but—" Larry High began before being cut off by Little Bobby.

"These niggas bluffing, Heezy! They aren't going to hurt no innocent woman and kids! They aren't cut like that. They're just trying to—"

I snatched a cushion off the couch and laid it over Little Bobby's head and pulled the trigger twice to shut him the fuck up. It was a gun-fire muffling trick Mumbles had taught me during the murder of the two Jamaican 'Shower Posse' Blood dudes responsible for killing my lil' sister.

"What's it gonna be, big boy?" Keystone questioned, knowing we had Larry High on the ropes. On the scale of life, family always outweighed everything else.

"My daughters, broh," Larry High pleaded.

"Ain't nobody going to touch your kids," I assured sincerely. Honestly, Little Bobby had been right. Under no circumstance would any Dummie harm an innocent woman or child. Especially, without consequences. We just didn't get down like that. But, I couldn't afford to let Larry High know that. "But, you got to give me the name," I added. "Unless of course, you wanna be a fool and continue to remain loyal to a dead man?"

"You gotta give me your word that nothing will happen to my girl and daughters." All the gangster was gone from Larry High's voice.

"You have my word." I stared at Larry High until he nodded.

"A'ight," Larry High finally submitted. "It was a darkskin dude name Nizzy. But, like I said, I don't know where the nigga from. He gave the hit to Little Bobby and we split the bread. We were suppose to slump her and dump the body on the Avenue."

My head started spinning. I couldn't believe what I'd just heard. Nizzy had really just taken shit to a whole new level. First, this bitch ass nigga goes after Ebony, and now, he turns around and sends some wolves for my mother. *I'ma kill that nigga!* I thought. *Betrayal never comes from your enemies, champ. You always know where they stand. It's your friends you gotta be careful of.* Money Cola's word echoed in my ear.

"Did you say Nizzy?" Deli questioned, addressing the elephant in the room.

"Yeah, Nizzy," Larry High repeated, nodding. "But, that's Little Bobby's man. So, I don't know what—"

Keystone silenced Larry High with three nasty head-shots. "You need me to handle that little bitch Nizzy?" Keystone stared at me with blood in his eyes.

"You already know I got this bitch!" I replied, knowing that it was about to be on because I never changed on my niggas, especially my day-one niggas, until they exposed themselves. "I'ma take it to that nigga and anybody that stand with him." I clenched my teeth and took a deep breath as the last little bit of love I had for Nizzy turned into hate.

"If we don't bounce now, you aren't going to be doing nothing—Because all of our dumb asses are gonna be over the Bookings for murder," Deli said, reminding everybody that we were standing in the middle of a murder scene.

Keystone set the couch and curtains on fire before we left the house, climbed into the car and drove off. "Y'all know we gotta crush Nizzy, right?" I broke the silence as we drove to where Keystone parked. The plan was to tail Keystone to Baltimore's favorite dumping grounds to get rid of the car. "That nigga violated to the fullest."

Nobody responded, and I knew why. Nizzy was like a brother to all of us. We'd all come through the trenches together—especially Nizzy, Deli and I. So, the fact that we were now actually going to have to crack him was a hard pill to swallow. I know it was for me.

"If y'all don't, I will!" Keystone spat, as I pulled over to let him out near the cab.

"We got 'em, Keystone," JuJu spoke up, looking over at Deli.

"It's all good, Keystone," Deli agreed, shaking his head in agreement sadly, as Keystone closed the door and jogged over to the cab. "Dummie, y'all know once we crack Nizzy, we're gonna have to accept the full weight or fury this nigga Lor'Homie going to try to bring. I mean, that's Dummie's cousin."

"That's why we're going to hit all them niggas together," I said, following Keystone as he pulled out. "Nizzy, Lor'Homie and Shag."

"That's what it is then," Deli said, falling back. He of all people overstood that nobody really wins when you have to go to war with those you loved.

"Well, we gotta hit these niggas hard," JuJu added. "Cos we know they aren't going to just lay down for us. Especially, if they see us coming or we fuck around and miss."

"Oh, I don't do no missing," I assured, already seeing Nizzy's funeral in my mind. "Plus, I know some of the lengths Nizzy will go to to get his man."

"They're not going to see us coming because we got one thing that they don't." Deli spoke up again.

"And what's that?" JuJu and I questioned in unison, looking at Deli.

"Knowledge they don't know that we possess, and opportunity they don't know we're about to utilize."

"I'm with it," JuJu professed. "All y'all got to do is say when, and I'll put Dummie's dick in the dirt myself. Miss Peaches is like a mother to me."

I just nodded and continued to tail Keystone because I already knew that my squad was down to ride with me to the end. Win, lose or draw. "Let's get everybody together over the house first, because once we knock these niggas off, we're moving in to take back all our turf."

Chapter 23

Despite Young Danny's feelings about Nizzy being like family, it took about three days to put together a hit that would change the game and put us completely on top. "You ready to pop these niggas coochie, Dummie?"

Deli glanced over at me. "You already know."

I nodded, keeping my eyes locked on Nizzy's and 'em main trap house. Not much had changed around Warwick since the squad had split up. A new fuck nigga here, an old fuck nigga there. Shaggy had always been a creature of habit. His shooters were too far from the trap-house to protect it. And his look-outs were too close to see what was about to take place. The only words that kept running through my mind were, 'We were suppose to slump her and dump the body on the Avenue'.

"It's go time, Dummie," Deli spat, pulling up his 'Dummie' scarf the moment we saw Nizzy coming out of the trap we'd been stalking all weekend.

"Where the fuck Lor'Homie at?" I questioned when I saw Shaggy's goofing ass limping out behind Nizzy, tying something around his dreads.

"Fuck if I know," Deli muttered through his scarf. We'd both definitely saw Lor'Homie go in the trap when they all first arrived. "But, we're not waiting for him."

"Let's do it then," I agreed, pulling my 'Dummie' scarf up without waiting for a response. If all else failed, we could always run up in the trap and handle Lor'Homie after we smashed Nizzy's and Shaggy's snake asses.

Straightening my BMX up, I saddled the bicycle seat and used my feet to push myself forward before I started pedaling my way down Warwick, followed by Deli.

Once we got halfway up the block I eased the brand new Daewoo DP51 Triple Action 9mm Calibre out and tucked it behind my leg. As soon as we got close enough to knock Nizzy and Shaggy's head off, I brought the DP51 up and started letting them niggas have it.

Nizzy immediately dashed behind a parked car, and Shaggy took off running down the block. I saw Deli fly by as I hopped off the BMX and went after Nizzy, who instantly sprinted for the trap-house when he heard the bike crash to the ground, but I was on his ass. I wanted the head off the snake.

I came around the car, dumping, determined to wear Nizzy's snake ass out just as he grabbed a pretty little bitch in a pair of fancy leggings and colorful boots, and pushed her towards me. I didn't know what Nizzy thought that would do and honestly, I didn't care because I wasn't taking no prisoners. I blasted the bitch and kept coming. All the Facebook-fighting, Snapchat-shit-talking, and Instagram-insults were over. I was out for blood.

Nizzy missed his step, stumbled and tripped into the doorway as what I believed was an Xbox 360 came flying through the living room window, almost taking my head off. I turned to shield my face as glass went everywhere, and the Xbox just missed my head. I looked up to see Al-Qamar before sending a few shots in his direction. Then, I ran up on the steps to put an end to all the death-selling. However, just as I cleared the top step, raising the tone to finish Nizzy, Lor'Homie peeped around the wall and hit me with a taser.

"Ahhhh!" I screamed out in pain as the metal-prongs bit into my chest and sent just enough electric bolts of fire through my body to stop me from moving momentarily so that Nizzy could get away. "Bitch!" I spat, firing wildly into the trap-house, still unable to completely feel my arm or focus my aim as Nizzy quickly scurried inside. *Fuck*! I wobbled before crumbling to the floor. I could still feel the electric current running through my body a split second before the trap-house vestibule was rattled with bullets.

Panicking, I dropped my gun, ducked down and dove outside, fucking my ribs up on the front steps. Once I rolled to the ground, I crawled around the car and took cover as either Lor'Homie or Al-Qamar continued to fire relentlessly. I prayed to the gangster-Gods, and Deli came riding back down the block with one hand dumping lead from his tone to bail me out because by then, I was out of options.

Staying low, I snatched the bike up off the ground and sprinted up the street towards Deli until it was safe enough to hop back on the bike. Then, I leaped on the BMX and took off, as Deli continued to let his shots ring.

I came off Warwick with my heart pounding and saw Shaggy laying behind some steps on North Avenue trying to steady his aim. "Watch out, Dummie!" I warned, diving to the ground as Deli came flying off of Warwick as the first shot went off.

Blop, blop, blop—

Sparks jumped off Deli's bike as I ducked behind a car and watched Deli dip out into oncoming traffic, confusing Shaggy. Shaggy didn't know which one of us to watch. Deli crept all the way around and ran at Shaggy from his blind side. Hitting him with at least a half of a clip. Then, we hopped back on the bikes and fled the scene, leaving Shaggy for dead.

"I heard that business all the way around this bitch!" Murdock informed excitedly, after we tossed the bikes into the back of the waiting van a few blocks over and climbed inside.

"You already know niggas were gonna drop their nuts." Deli slid into the front passenger's seat.

"Did y'all trash them niggas?" Murdock checked all the rearview mirrors.

"We let them niggas have it! But, I think Nizzy got lucky," I confessed, pushing the latch down on the rear door of the van as Murdock slowly pulled off. "I had his hoe ass down bad too," I added, unwilling to volunteer that I'd gotten tasered and dropped my tone.

The sound of sirens increased to an ear-piercing, heart-stopping level as flashing lights glared through the side and back windows, illuminating the inside of the van. Everybody got silent for a second as five or six police cars surrounded the van. The looks on Murdock's and Deli's Faces said it all. We'd fucked up. Then, the police cars split up and sped of in opposite directions.

"Mannnnn," I finally breathed. "I was about to shit on myself."

"You—" Deli laughed. "Scared ass niggas," Murdock kept his eyes on the road. "That's probably how Nizzy got away."

"You know I had to save this nigga, Dummie," Deli revealed, as the sirens began to fade into the distance.

"Oh, yeah?" Murdock replied, like he believed him.

"Fuck outta here!" I retorted.

"So, what about Lor'Homie and Shag?" Murdock questioned again. "Did y'all get them?"

"I don't know what the fuck happened to Lor'Homie—But, Shag a done deal," Deli assured, as I looked out the back window of the van for any signs of danger, paranoid as fuck. "I trashed that nigga!"

Fuck! I thought, kicking myself in the ass when another cop car got behind us. I quickly laid on the floor and held my breath. We couldn't afford to get pulled over in no stolen van. Especially, not while we were riding extremely filthy with guns, masks, duct-tape and rope.

"Stay cool, Dummie," I heard Deli whisper to Murdock, as he continued to drive. "The plates should still be clean," Deli added before a long period of silence. "A'ight, he's turning off now."

"Y'all niggas were about to panic!" I exclaimed, sitting up to peep out the window again. I saw the tail of the police chump's car as he took a right and disappeared down a side street.

"You heard that old rapper nigga!—I ain't never scared," Murdock said, but the look on his face had told another story. "So, did y'all get Lor'Homie or not?"

"Nah," I admitted, making Murdock look back at me over his seat. "Lor'Homie is the one that saved Nizzy's bitch ass. Him and that lil' nigga Al-Qamar."

"Are you serious? Al-Qamar got with that?" Deli seemed surprised. "So O was right?"

"Yeah," I nodded. "That's who was cranking from the house," I said. "This lil' wild bitch Al-Qamar threw the Xbox at me through the window and everything."

"That's not going to end good." Murdock shook his head, and I knew that he was right. Now, Nizzy and Lor'Homie knew we were gunning for them.

"I know," I agreed. "And we gotta get Al-Qamar too."

"Yo, tell Dummie how I walked that nigga Shaggy down," Deli suggested.

"Nah, nigga, tell him how Shag almost cracked your shit if it wasn't for me," I replied jokingly. "Watch when you see this big ass hole Shag put in the frame of this nigga's bike."

"Man, that nigga outran me," Deli argued. "I didn't even know that I hit his dumb ass until we came off Warwick and he started bucking from behind the steps. I wore his ass out through."

"That nigga wasn't fast enough to outrun them hot-rocks." Murdock laughed because Shaggy always thought that he was faster then everybody in the squad.

"Damn, yo!" I fired, kind of under my breath, mad at myself. "We should've waited so we could've gotten all three of them niggas at once. Well, four now."

"Don't trip, Dummie," Deli said, fidgeting with the old ass radio. "We're gonna get at them niggas again and wear their asses out. Al-Qamar dumb ass too."

I nodded, sure hoping that Deli was right because the game that we had just intiated was for keeps.

Delmont Player

Chapter 24

"Fuck that! We need to go around there and let them bitch ass niggas have it!" Lor'Homie suggested, watching his cousin stare out the window. He felt like a sitting duck, and was severely fed up with waiting to get back at Charm and them. "And, don't give me that *patience is a virtue* bullshit!"

Nizzy turned around and looked at his cousin. It had only been a week since two shooters he instantly recognized as Charm and Deli had come through and tried to end his career. "Come on, Cuz, you know we gonna see them niggas about what they did." Nizzy spoke, using his crutches to make his way back across the room to the couch to sit down.

"Shit!" Nizzy grunted in pain as one of the three slugs he'd taken sent a bone-chilling ache up his leg.

"Then, what's the hold up?" Lor'Homie questioned curiously. "I been creeping through there heavy. That coochie wet, Cuzzo. Let me go handle that."

"I just don't wanna make the same mistake Charm did," Nizzy explained, feeling his cousin's rage. "When we get at them niggas, I want to make sure we don't miss," he added. Unlike his cousin, Nizzy had never been the type to indulge his pride at the expense of his life.

"Then, just let me handle my business, Cuzzo," Lor'Homie begged. He had some new heavy metal, and he was ready to party with it. "Them bitch ass niggas already drew first blood when they did that fuck shit to Shag! At least let me take a couple lil' soldier through there to spank some shit. I don't want these niggas to think we laid down."

Nizzy thought hard for a moment. He felt his cousin's pain and knew that he was dying to be let off the leash. Especially, behind Shaggy, but he wanted to approach this shit from a different angle. One that Charm and them would never expect.

"Listen to me, Cuzzo," Nizzy pleaded softly. "Hitting them niggas not a problem. But, I wanna be able to kill two birds with one stone. That way, we can handle Charm and them and take over the whole 'Avenue' at the same time."

Lor'Homie took a deep breath and ran his hand over his fro-hawk in frustration before replying. "A'ight, if you say so." Lor'Homie wasn't in agreement with nothing that didn't end with him standing over top of Charm's and Deli's dead bodies. But, he respected and trusted his cousin's ability to call the shots. At least for now, anyway. "I just want to know how the hell you plan on doing it."

"Who's running all them niggas, Cuzzo?"

"Charm," Lor'Homie replied without a second thought.

"And what's the one thing we know will make Charm react without thinking?" Nizzy stared at his cousin.

"Ebony." Lor'Homie smiled.

"Exactly," Nizzy nodded in argeement. Between Charm's little outburst at B-Day and Ebony's little stunt outside the beauty salon, Nizzy realized just how valuable a piece of commodity Ebony could be used to bargain with. "So, all we need to do is figure out a way to grab that bitch, and we can probably make Charm handle Deli and 'em for us."

"I like that, Cuzzo," Lor'Homie smiled. He knew, like his cousin did, that Charm was a fool for Ebony. "That kind of shit be making my dick hard."

"I'm already hip," Nizzy acknowledged, picking up his new Xbox 360 controller, unpausing the 2K. "You know that nigga not going to be expecting that."

"Right," Lor'Homie thought about it for a second. His cousin was definitely on to something. "You think we can make that nigga hit Young Danny and Murdock though?"

"Hell, yeah," Nizzy picked his favorite team on the game. "That nigga a sucker for love. But honestly, I don't think we're going to have to worry about them niggas." Nizzy knew that his cousin always had a taste for blood.

"Why not? I mean, I know them niggas got their own thing over east, but them niggas still loyal to Charm—especially Murdock." Lor'Homie knew that loyal friends were just as dangerous as dedicated enemies, if not more.

"True," Nizzy admitted and thought for a moment. He knew that his cousin had a point. Young Danny and Murdock would eventually have to be dealt with whether they were directly involved in the beef or not. Just like O. That was just how things went in the streets. "A'ight, look, take Al-Qamar and 'em over east and do your thing."

"Now, you're talking my language, Cuzzo." Lor'Homie got excited.

"Listen, Cuz," Nizzy put his hand up. "I don't need you wilding out."

"I got this, Cuzzo." Lor'Homie assured, ready to quench his thirst for retribution.

"I'm serious, Cuz," Nizzy warned. "Don't go over there and make a mess. Hit them niggas and get back to the crib."

"I'm telling you, Cuzzo. I got this. I'ma pop these niggas coochie and come right back." Lor'Homie repeated confidently again. "In the meantime, you just lay low and put something together so we can snatch that bitch Ebony."

Nizzy eyed his cousin for a second and prayed that he was making the right decision. Because, the last thing he wanted to do was, wake Young Danny and Murdock up before he was ready to put them to sleep. "A'ight, Cuz, do your thing," Nizzy said, as his 2K game began. "Make sure y'all work them full faced 'Call of Duty' mask I got when y'all handle y'all business. I don't want that shit coming back to us. Not right now anyway."

"Say no more, Cuzzo." Lor'Homie stood up and gave his cousin some love before heading out the door to rally the troops.

To Be Continued...
Bodymore Murderland 3
Coming Soon

Submission Guideline

Submit the first three chapters of your completed manuscript to ldpsubmissions@gmail.com, subject line: Your book's title. The manuscript must be in a .doc file and sent as an attachment. Document should be in Times New Roman, double spaced and in size 12 font. Also, provide your synopsis and full contact information. If sending multiple submissions, they must each be in a separate email.

Have a story but no way to send it electronically? You can still submit to LDP/Ca$h Presents. Send in the first three chapters, written or typed, of your completed manuscript to:

LDP: Submissions Dept
Po Box 944
Stockbridge, Ga 30281

DO NOT send original manuscript. Must be a duplicate.

Provide your synopsis and a cover letter containing your full contact information.

Thanks for considering LDP and Ca$h Presents.

BOW DOWN TO MY GANGSTA

By **Ca$h**

TORN BETWEEN TWO

By **Coffee**

THE STREETS STAINED MY SOUL **II**

By **Marcellus Allen**

BLOOD OF A BOSS **VI**

SHADOWS OF THE GAME II

TRAP BASTARD II

By **Askari**

LOYAL TO THE GAME **IV**

By **T.J. & Jelissa**

IF LOVING YOU IS WRONG… **III**

By **Jelissa**

TRUE SAVAGE **VIII**

MIDNIGHT CARTEL IV

DOPE BOY MAGIC IV

CITY OF KINGZ III

By **Chris Green**

BLAST FOR ME **III**

A SAVAGE DOPEBOY III

CUTTHROAT MAFIA III

DUFFLE BAG CARTEL VI

HEARTLESS GOON VI

By **Ghost**

A HUSTLER'S DECEIT III

KILL ZONE **II**

BAE BELONGS TO ME III

A DOPE BOY'S QUEEN III
By **Aryanna**
COKE KINGS V
KING OF THE TRAP III
By **T.J. Edwards**
GORILLAZ IN THE BAY V
3X KRAZY III
De'Kari
THE STREETS ARE CALLING II
Duquie Wilson
KINGPIN KILLAZ IV
STREET KINGS III
PAID IN BLOOD III
CARTEL KILLAZ IV
DOPE GODS III
Hood Rich
SINS OF A HUSTLA II
ASAD
KINGZ OF THE GAME VI
Playa Ray
SLAUGHTER GANG IV
RUTHLESS HEART IV
By Willie Slaughter
FUK SHYT II
By Blakk Diamond
TRAP QUEEN
RICH $AVAGE II
By Troublesome
YAYO V
GHOST MOB II

Stilloan Robinson
CREAM III
By Yolanda Moore
SON OF A DOPE FIEND III
HEAVEN GOT A GHETTO II
By Renta
FOREVER GANGSTA II
GLOCKS ON SATIN SHEETS III
By Adrian Dulan
LOYALTY AIN'T PROMISED III
By Keith Williams
THE PRICE YOU PAY FOR LOVE III
By Destiny Skai
I'M NOTHING WITHOUT HIS LOVE II
SINS OF A THUG II
TO THE THUG I LOVED BEFORE II
By Monet Dragun
LIFE OF A SAVAGE IV
MURDA SEASON IV
GANGLAND CARTEL IV
CHI'RAQ GANGSTAS IV
KILLERS ON ELM STREET IV
JACK BOYZ N DA BRONX II
A DOPEBOY'S DREAM II
By **Romell Tukes**
QUIET MONEY IV
EXTENDED CLIP III
THUG LIFE IV
By **Trai'Quan**

THE STREETS MADE ME III

By **Larry D. Wright**

IF YOU CROSS ME ONCE II

ANGEL III

By **Anthony Fields**

FRIEND OR FOE III

By **Mimi**

SAVAGE STORMS III

By **Meesha**

BLOOD ON THE MONEY III

By **J-Blunt**

THE STREETS WILL NEVER CLOSE II

By **K'ajji**

NIGHTMARES OF A HUSTLA III

By **King Dream**

IN THE ARM OF HIS BOSS

By **Jamila**

HARD AND RUTHLESS III

MOB TOWN 251 II

By **Von Diesel**

LEVELS TO THIS SHYT II

By **Ah'Million**

MOB TIES III

By **SayNoMore**

BODYMORE MURDERLAND III

By **Delmont Player**

THE LAST OF THE OGS III

Tranay Adams

FOR THE LOVE OF A BOSS II

By **C. D. Blue**

Available Now

RESTRAINING ORDER **I & II**
By **CA$H & Coffee**
LOVE KNOWS NO BOUNDARIES **I II & III**
By **Coffee**
RAISED AS A GOON I, II, III & IV
BRED BY THE SLUMS I, II, III
BLAST FOR ME I & II
ROTTEN TO THE CORE I II III
A BRONX TALE I, II, III
DUFFLE BAG CARTEL I II III IV V
HEARTLESS GOON I II III IV V
A SAVAGE DOPEBOY I II
DRUG LORDS I II III
CUTTHROAT MAFIA I II
By **Ghost**
LAY IT DOWN **I & II**
LAST OF A DYING BREED I II
BLOOD STAINS OF A SHOTTA I & II III
By **Jamaica**
LOYAL TO THE GAME I II III
LIFE OF SIN I, II III
By **TJ & Jelissa**
BLOODY COMMAS I & II
SKI MASK CARTEL I II & III
KING OF NEW YORK I II,III IV V

RISE TO POWER I II III

COKE KINGS I II III IV

BORN HEARTLESS I II III IV

KING OF THE TRAP I II

By **T.J. Edwards**

IF LOVING HIM IS WRONG...I & II

LOVE ME EVEN WHEN IT HURTS I II III

By **Jelissa**

WHEN THE STREETS CLAP BACK I & II III

THE HEART OF A SAVAGE I II III

By **Jibril Williams**

A DISTINGUISHED THUG STOLE MY HEART I II & III

LOVE SHOULDN'T HURT I II III IV

RENEGADE BOYS I II III IV

PAID IN KARMA I II III

SAVAGE STORMS I II

By **Meesha**

A GANGSTER'S CODE I &, II III

A GANGSTER'S SYN I II III

THE SAVAGE LIFE I II III

CHAINED TO THE STREETS I II III

BLOOD ON THE MONEY I II

By J-Blunt

PUSH IT TO THE LIMIT

By **Bre' Hayes**

BLOOD OF A BOSS **I, II, III, IV, V**

SHADOWS OF THE GAME

TRAP BASTARD

By **Askari**

THE STREETS BLEED MURDER **I, II & III**

THE HEART OF A GANGSTA I II& III

By **Jerry Jackson**

CUM FOR ME I II III IV V VI VII

An **LDP Erotica Collaboration**

BRIDE OF A HUSTLA **I II & II**

THE FETTI GIRLS **I, II& III**

CORRUPTED BY A GANGSTA I, II III, IV

BLINDED BY HIS LOVE

THE PRICE YOU PAY FOR LOVE I II

DOPE GIRL MAGIC I II III

By **Destiny Skai**

WHEN A GOOD GIRL GOES BAD

By **Adrienne**

THE COST OF LOYALTY I II III

By Kweli

A GANGSTER'S REVENGE **I II III & IV**

THE BOSS MAN'S DAUGHTERS I II III IV V

A SAVAGE LOVE **I & II**

BAE BELONGS TO ME I II

A HUSTLER'S DECEIT I, II, III

WHAT BAD BITCHES DO I, II, III

SOUL OF A MONSTER I II III

KILL ZONE

A DOPE BOY'S QUEEN I II

By **Aryanna**

A KINGPIN'S AMBITON

A KINGPIN'S AMBITION **II**

I MURDER FOR THE DOUGH

By **Ambitious**

TRUE SAVAGE I II III IV V VI VII

DOPE BOY MAGIC I, II, III
MIDNIGHT CARTEL I II III
CITY OF KINGZ I II
By **Chris Green**
A DOPEBOY'S PRAYER
By **Eddie "Wolf" Lee**
THE KING CARTEL **I, II & III**
By **Frank Gresham**
THESE NIGGAS AIN'T LOYAL **I, II & III**
By **Nikki Tee**
GANGSTA SHYT **I II &III**
By **CATO**
THE ULTIMATE BETRAYAL
By **Phoenix**
BOSS'N UP **I , II & III**
By **Royal Nicole**
I LOVE YOU TO DEATH
By Destiny J
I RIDE FOR MY HITTA
I STILL RIDE FOR MY HITTA
By **Misty Holt**
LOVE & CHASIN' PAPER
By **Qay Crockett**
TO DIE IN VAIN
SINS OF A HUSTLA
By **ASAD**
BROOKLYN HUSTLAZ
By **Boogsy Morina**
BROOKLYN ON LOCK I & II
By **Sonovia**

GANGSTA CITY

By **Teddy Duke**

A DRUG KING AND HIS DIAMOND I & II III

A DOPEMAN'S RICHES

HER MAN, MINE'S TOO I, II

CASH MONEY HO'S

THE WIFEY I USED TO BE I II

By Nicole Goosby

TRAPHOUSE KING **I II & III**

KINGPIN KILLAZ I II III

STREET KINGS I II

PAID IN BLOOD **I II**

CARTEL KILLAZ I II III

DOPE GODS I II

By **Hood Rich**

LIPSTICK KILLAH **I, II, III**

CRIME OF PASSION I II & III

FRIEND OR FOE I II

By **Mimi**

STEADY MOBBN' **I, II, III**

THE STREETS STAINED MY SOUL

By **Marcellus Allen**

WHO SHOT YA **I, II, III**

SON OF A DOPE FIEND I II

HEAVEN GOT A GHETTO

Renta

GORILLAZ IN THE BAY **I II III IV**

TEARS OF A GANGSTA I II

3X KRAZY I II

DE'KARI

TRIGGADALE I II III

Elijah R. Freeman

GOD BLESS THE TRAPPERS I, II, III

THESE SCANDALOUS STREETS I, II, III

FEAR MY GANGSTA I, II, III IV, V

THESE STREETS DON'T LOVE NOBODY I, II

BURY ME A G I, II, III, IV, V

A GANGSTA'S EMPIRE I, II, III, IV

THE DOPEMAN'S BODYGAURD I II

THE REALEST KILLAZ I II III

THE LAST OF THE OGS I II

Tranay Adams

THE STREETS ARE CALLING

Duquie Wilson

MARRIED TO A BOSS... I II III

By Destiny Skai & Chris Green

KINGZ OF THE GAME I II III IV V

Playa Ray

SLAUGHTER GANG I II III

RUTHLESS HEART I II III

By Willie Slaughter

FUK SHYT

By Blakk Diamond

DON'T F#CK WITH MY HEART I II

By Linnea

ADDICTED TO THE DRAMA I II III

IN THE ARM OF HIS BOSS II

By Jamila

YAYO I II III IV

A SHOOTER'S AMBITION I II

By S. Allen
TRAP GOD I II III
RICH $AVAGE
By Troublesome
FOREVER GANGSTA
GLOCKS ON SATIN SHEETS I II
By Adrian Dulan
TOE TAGZ I II III
LEVELS TO THIS SHYT
By Ah'Million
KINGPIN DREAMS I II III
By Paper Boi Rari
CONFESSIONS OF A GANGSTA I II III
By Nicholas Lock
I'M NOTHING WITHOUT HIS LOVE
SINS OF A THUG
TO THE THUG I LOVED BEFORE
By Monet Dragun
CAUGHT UP IN THE LIFE I II III
By Robert Baptiste
NEW TO THE GAME I II III
MONEY, MURDER & MEMORIES I II III
By **Malik D. Rice**
LIFE OF A SAVAGE I II III
A GANGSTA'S QUR'AN I II III
MURDA SEASON I II III
GANGLAND CARTEL I II III
CHI'RAQ GANGSTAS I II III
KILLERS ON ELM STREET I II III

JACK BOYZ N DA BRONX

A DOPEBOY'S DREAM

By **Romell Tukes**

LOYALTY AIN'T PROMISED I II

By Keith Williams

QUIET MONEY I II III

THUG LIFE I II III

EXTENDED CLIP I II

By **Trai'Quan**

THE STREETS MADE ME I II

By **Larry D. Wright**

THE ULTIMATE SACRIFICE I, II, III, IV, V, VI

KHADIFI

IF YOU CROSS ME ONCE

ANGEL I II

By **Anthony Fields**

THE LIFE OF A HOOD STAR

By Ca$h & Rashia Wilson

THE STREETS WILL NEVER CLOSE

By K'ajji

CREAM I II

By Yolanda Moore

NIGHTMARES OF A HUSTLA I II

By King Dream

CONCRETE KILLA I II

By Kingpen

HARD AND RUTHLESS I II

MOB TOWN 251

By Von Diesel

GHOST MOB II

Stilloan Robinson

MOB TIES I II

By SayNoMore

BODYMORE MURDERLAND I II

By Delmont Player

FOR THE LOVE OF A BOSS

By C. D. Blue

<u>BOOKS BY LDP'S CEO, CA$H</u>

<u>TRUST IN NO MAN</u>

<u>TRUST IN NO MAN 2</u>

<u>TRUST IN NO MAN 3</u>

<u>BONDED BY BLOOD</u>

<u>SHORTY GOT A THUG</u>

<u>THUGS CRY</u>

<u>THUGS CRY 2</u>

<u>THUGS CRY 3</u>

<u>TRUST NO BITCH</u>

<u>TRUST NO BITCH 2</u>

<u>TRUST NO BITCH 3</u>

<u>TIL MY CASKET DROPS</u>

<u>RESTRAINING ORDER</u>

<u>RESTRAINING ORDER 2</u>

<u>IN LOVE WITH A CONVICT</u>

<u>LIFE OF A HOOD STAR</u>

CPSIA information can be obtained
at www.ICGtesting.com
Printed in the USA
LVHW082301061021
699714LV00009B/305